KEL BRUEM

Every Bite You Take

The Unusualities #2

First edition

ISBN: 979-8-9878785-1-4

Cover art by T.K. Palad

This book was professionally typeset on Reedsy.
Find out more at reedsy.com

To all the boys I tried to fix before:
Get it together

Contents

Author's Note

This book deals with alcoholism, family trauma, addiction, and how the path to recovery is never straightforward. In looking to capture the impact these issues have on the individual and their loved ones, I wanted to show the messy and complicated search for comfort and resolution. That means this book also includes what some purists would call cheating. I do not include these actions lightly, but I wanted to give space to how loving someone who is so far underwater with their addiction can drive loved ones to disappear into the fantasy of another life. Addiction's rippling effects push loved ones into unhealthy coping mechanisms until all parties are lost to one another.

But this book also deals with the power of community, found family, and true love in the face of that twisted mess. It shows the power of "glimmers," or those beautiful moments that keep us going forward when all else seems lost. It tells a story of two people choosing to fight for one another in the face of traumatic lived experiences and lifelong loneliness.

I firmly believe each reader can choose for themselves what they are able to stomach in the moment. If the above topics are not something you're up to today, I encourage you to set this story down and return another time. But I hope you'll come back when you're ready. Evelyn and Will's story is not neat and tidy, but it's true love and I promise they find their happy for now until they're both ready for their ever after.

Prologue

A boy and a girl walk into a church hallway.

They are not there for the usual reasons you might guess, although their hands are clasped tightly together, the gaze between them loaded with meaning.

"I'll be right here," she says, settling easily onto a metal folding chair opposite the open doors to the left. She pats the massive Fall Vogue in her lap and gives the boy a small smile. "I'll be face-first in this bad boy, so take your time."

The boy looks to the doors and back to the girl. He is the most nervous she's seen him, palms damp, fingers dancing in the air, eyes flitting around the hall. There is a corkboard behind the girl, sun-faded fliers for potlach, Christmas pageants, and something called simply "AA."

AA is today at noon.

The boy knows those letters. Has studied them for hours leading up to this moment—part of a promise made for a new future together.

It isn't so different from the kind of promise you would've expected from a girl and a boy in a church hallway.

But right now, it *feels* different to the boy.

"It's only an hour," the boy says to the girl. She nods. She knows.

He's saying it more for himself.

"Just an hour," she says. "And you don't have to talk if you don't want to but—" She gives him a look and they both release a nervous giggle. It feels like breathing butterflies into the air and the boy feels that lightness in his heart all over again.

He nods to her and catches the kiss she blows him, dramatically rubbing it all over his face and earning another butterfly giggle.

The boy steps into the welcoming room. It is full of light, awash with the midday sun. He thinks it looks more like a sanctuary than a multipurpose room, the peeling linoleum and cracked ceiling tiles more accepting than any prayer hall he's seen. He hasn't seen many.

There is a folding table on the far side of the room where others are gathered, clutching Styrofoam cups of coffee. Several paper plates are laid out with a hopeful display of Oreos.

The others are like him—in more ways than one—even though, lined up, no one could tell. How would anyone know that the winged gargoyle laughing at something a gnome has said shares anything? Or the satyr nodding solemnly at the man dressed in a glowing toga? But the boy knows, aside from their non-human qualities, there is a dark thread between them all.

On the other side of the room, there is a floor-to-ceiling banner with a list on it. Numbered steps to find a new self—to start a new story. The boy has read these too, and he hopes they'll be the structure he needs. He hopes he can check them off like any other to-do list.

Beneath this list, a griffin claps his hands together, bird-like head turning to survey the room as he calls out, "Okay everyone, let's get started."

There is an eerie screeching of metal chairs on the floor as the small gathering creates a circle. The boy follows suit, grateful that he is quickly incorporated and doesn't have to ask for a place with them.

"I see some new faces today," the griffin says. His golden wings reach up behind him in graceful arches, his eyes are sharp but warm. "So, I'll do the intro spiel if no one minds."

An agreeable murmur rises from the group.

"I'm Gary," he says, placing a clawed hand to his chest. It rests against his maroon sweater vest. "And I'm an alcoholic."

"Hi Gary," the room repeats back in a wash of sound.

A tingle goes down the boy's spine.

"I lead these meetings for Unusual Addicts because not even those of us with supernatural powers are free from the hold addiction has over us," he continues. "You'll notice the human 12 steps behind me. It relies heavily on the presence of a higher Power or a God."

The man in the glowing toga lets out a cheeky whistle as Gary continues.

"Obviously some of us may have trouble with that reliance given the realms we may or may not rule over," Gary gives the toga man a wink. "So instead, think about the higher Power as any picture bigger than the frame you're viewing the world through. Maybe that's religion, maybe it's community, maybe it's family."

The boy thinks about his best friend, prepping the tour boats alone for their shifts today so the boy could be here. He thinks about the text from his business partner and confidant, warming his pocket.

He thinks about the girl in the hall.

"Attending today is what we call the first step," Gary continues. "And that may be big enough for our new faces. But if you feel called to share, please know you are welcomed without judgement."

Gary gives the room a slow, glowing smile, as if it is intended for everyone personally.

"Would anyone like to start?"

The boy feels a pull in his gut.

The boy takes a deep breath.

The boy stands.

"Hi, I'm Will," he says. "And I'm an alcoholic."

As the room echoes back to him, as he begins to tell the story you will soon hear, I need you to know that this moment—this light-filled room with its battered walls and dingy floors—is not the end anyone expected.

But it is the much-needed beginning.

1

Will

New England, 50 Years ago

Made a searching and fearless moral inventory of ourselves.

I've always been like this—alone, alert, endlessly hungry.

I've tried to remember a time before, but the only things in my farthest memories are flickering shadows and muted voices. I don't know where I'm from. I don't know how I got here. Maybe it's like this for all beings born from the gods—the divine abandons us with human weaknesses, and the only way to survive is to block it all out.

It was less depressing to let my shark side take over and run the show. It was easier to pretend I didn't know loneliness, that I didn't have a human heart beating in the open ocean with no answer.

That's where the monstrousness found me, like a growing ache along my spine, pushing a liquid venom through my veins.

It was fear. Fear and shame took root one unforgettable day.

I was younger then, more easily ruled by an eager heart. I was enjoying the warm water closer to the shore in a place I have never returned to, and I heard voices—human voices—calling to one another. Curiosity got the better of me (sharks are forever nibbling at strangeness to better understand the world) and I swam closer.

The water was almost too shallow for me here and the shark in me warned about getting too far from deeper waters, whispered knowledge passed through my DNA that to touch sand was to die a slow, sun-bleached death.

From where I paced the shoreline, I could see four humans—two big, two small. They were sitting together on the beach, playing in the sand. As I watched, the two small humans added sticks and rocks to the shaped mounds of sand that the tallest human was carefully building. The other tall human, a woman I thought, with long dark curls cascading down her back, welcomed one of the small humans into her lap, wrapping her arms around them and rocking back and forth in the sun.

I wrapped my own arms around my shoulders and swayed in the water, letting my eyes drift closed as I imagined resting my head on the sun-warmed skin of someone who loved me.

I don't know how long I watched them, but eventually the two tall humans began gathering their things, gesturing to the two small humans in a way that indicated it was time to go. I waited until they were just specks in the dunes, but I imagined that they knew I was in the water. I imagined they were promising to come back to the same place tomorrow so we could see each other again.

I imagined, for the first time, that I wasn't alone anymore.

The next day I returned and so did the group of humans. *Family,* something whispered from deep within me.

They were a family.

This time, I braved even shallower water, feeling the heat from the sand below the waves warm the underside of my tail. My shark instincts were screaming but I shoved them aside in favor of finally seeing the woman's face light with joy as one of the little humans brought her a shell they found on the beach. The tallest human—a man—was beginning to get a sunburn along his shoulders as he dozed in the sun, periodically peeking with great affection at his family gathered near the water.

A voice rang out, pinging off the water and bouncing up into my heart. I realized one of the small humans was pointing directly at me and waving. I ducked beneath the water and waited. When I resurfaced, the family had moved a little further up the beach, but the little human was still peering over his shoulder periodically. He had a mop of black curls that he pushed from his face with tiny hands and a pout that I could see even from that distance. I was endeared by him immediately and I wondered if he could swim. Would he want to see the shells with creatures still inside them, tottering along the ocean bottom?

I imagined his delight as I guided him through kelp forests, pointing out wide-eyed rainbow fish and the gaping jaws of giant clams. The fictional joy was enough to decide it for me.

This time when I resurfaced, and the little human spotted me again, I waved back. He leapt in the air, his waving growing more agitated as he let out a joyous shriek.

My human—my *friend*—was excited to see me. He would be excited to come with me, too. I knew it.

I gestured for him to come into the water, waving my arms wildly and making swimming motions. He began to run straight toward me, but the tall man leapt up and intercepted him, scooping him under the arms despite his protests and depositing him further up the beach. When the tall man stopped long enough to follow my friend's frantic pointing, I ducked beneath the water.

I didn't wait for the tall man to find me, turning and swimming off for the rest of the day.

I would try to take my friend for an adventure the next day.

But I shouldn't have returned.

There are so many things I still feel in my wretched heart from my early days in the ocean, but this is the one that digs in the furthest, that refuses to relent in breaking me apart.

The third day, I returned, braving water so shallow I feared I wouldn't be able to swim away.

Someone saw me rise from the water—must've seen only a young man's face from that distance. The woman waved her arms, gesturing me inland, shouting words I didn't understand and couldn't fully hear. I waved back, my heart about to burst. They continued to call. I could see the crackling sunburn on the tall man as he stood behind everyone else—the woman who kept waving, my friend and his double, tanned and laughing in the sun.

After a few moments, my friend leapt into the waves, a circle around his waist that kept him buoyant. He paddled out to me and screamed with joy as he got closer and closer.

Worried I wouldn't be able to turn fully around to take him toward the kelp forest, I did my best to wiggle backwards out to deeper water. My friend continued swimming toward me. The shouts from the shore grew tense but didn't lose their friendly tenor.

Then, from the shore, terrified howls. My friend's face dropped in shock as he reached me. He pointed behind me, saying something in a low voice that I couldn't understand. Twisting my neck to follow his gaze, I saw my dorsal fin breaking the surface.

I tried to gesture with my hands to show the boy that there was nothing to be afraid of. The shark was me. I was the shark. No one would hurt him.

As the little boy began backpedaling in the water, the waves pushing him closer and closer to me despite his frantic efforts, I heard the screaming from the shore grow louder, shriller. The woman was halfway into the water before the tall man dove past her, swimming directly toward me with a confident stroke.

My poor human heart panicked, desperate for connection, for an end to this constant call into silence. I wasn't ready for this moment to be snatched away from me yet.

I reached out and grabbed my friend. If he could just see for himself, he would understand, he would know it was me. He thrashed against me, immediately terrified, fat tears streaming down his face. He kept screaming the same word over and over again. The tall man was nearing us, determination in every stroke.

Panic gripped me.

He had to see. He had to know. I had to *be known.*

I dove down, clutching the little boy against my chest.

I had only meant to show him the truth of who I was—a strange-shaped friend but not a monster, no one dangerous.

But I failed to understand, despite my human heart, how little air a screaming child can hold in their lungs when dragged under the water. I didn't know how weak human lungs are, especially when they are still growing. I watched the bubbles float out of his mouth, his eyes rolled back from shock, his form going limp in my arms. I tried to shake him awake, tried to prod or poke him somewhere to bring him back to alertness.

Nothing worked.

I felt the tell-tale emptiness of a dead thing in the water, and I let him go. His body floated to the surface like kelp cut loose.

I did not resurface to hear the wails of the boy's family or face the wrath of the tall man. I let fear drive my actions, let my shark brain take over and propel me away from the threat of the humans.

Some hours later—the sun had not quite settled below the curve of the sea—I was wallowing in deeper water, trying to make sense of the afternoon's events. What had killed the boy? What had compelled me to haul him underwater despite knowing instinctually that his body was not made for being so far down? It had to have been some outside force, some unknown part of my DNA that I had yet to understand.

It wasn't my fault. It couldn't have been my fault.

I would never hurt someone on purpose.

The sound of a boat engine broke my concentration. It was speeding, circling closer and closer to where I swam.

Curiosity rose in me again and I quickly pushed it down. I had caused enough damage with my curiosity.

Before I could react, something hot and sharp shot through the water, grazing my right side and drawing blood. A harpoon continued past me and into the dark of the water below. A second followed quickly, this one narrowly missing my left arm.

I was being hunted, whether because of my actions that afternoon or for some other type of trophy. The humans had come for me.

But I would not be made prey in my own waters.

I pushed against the water, shooting myself directly into the side of the boat. I rammed myself into it, feeling it tilt easily as one body hit the water. I rammed it again and again until it was light enough to be empty, and I could sense several thrashing humans around me.

Spinning in a slow circle, I took them in. There were four men I could see, the first two already with their heads above the water, limbs flailing against the open ocean's current. The other two were treading water, eyes open against the salt, faces wide with horror as they held their breath and their screams.

The tall man was one and it was his face that birthed the monstrousness within me. He looked at me as if I were the most grotesque and evil creature he had ever seen, as if I had crawled from the pits of hell and not the bottom of the sea. That look was enough to unravel any ideas I had about my divine origin.

That look cemented my future as much as it erased my past.

I was the monster he thought. I was sure of it in that moment as much as anything else.

Some wounded, irrational part of me decided in defiance that I would show him what a monster could be—what a monster could *truly* do—if he was so sure of what I was.

But before I could act on my new life's purpose, the tall man and his friend pushed up for air and I saw my opportunity for escape. The shark in me took hold, hauling me away from the storm of emotions threatening to push me over a new ledge.

I swam away as fast as my body would allow, and when I finally sensed I was free from the humans, I slowed my pace but did not stop. I would continue away from that fated shore, in search of new waters to make my home. And I would avoid humans, although the resolution broke what little was left of my human heart. I had gotten away this time, but I could not bank on luck for the future.

And I could not forgive myself for my lost friend, the image of him drifting lifeless in the water haunting me as I swam on.

I didn't *want* to hurt anyone else.

If I could not avoid humans, as it would soon become obvious I could not, then I would drive them away with my monstrous new identity.

No one swims willingly toward the creature in the water.

2

Evelyn

New York City, The Other Day

I don't usually fall in love.

I watched that shit wreck my family in a vise of responsibility and duty even as my parents disintegrated. Love had always been too tight, too close, too much.

Love was for other people.

But then I met Will Burleigh.

Holy Shit.

Something about him did it for me. That was all I'd been able to tell anyone. But the truth was, sitting there at dinner that night in New York, there was something *big* growing between us. We'd just said goodbye to our best friends on their way to Ireland after a whirlwind week of attending haute couture runway shows inspired by mermaids (that's a whole other story, Caoimhe will have to tell you). My coverage for the Boston World was sitting in my editor's inbox early, and my focus was entirely on the hot mershark sitting across from me.

We were both dressed to kill, him in a suit we'd had tailored so expertly no one serving us $100 steaks would've guessed it came secondhand—a skill I would never get tired of boasting. His long dark hair was pushed back from his face, putting the sharp angles of his cheeks on display and his soft grey eyes glittered in the candlelight.

"You look incredible," he practically purred across the table at me. His voice shot straight between my legs. I wondered if I could convince him to meet me in the bathroom.

People fucked in Michelin Star bathrooms, right?

I wore my holy grail find, the black leather mini dress from Chanel's 1992 fall/winter collection—sleeveless with bright brass buttons down one side. I paired it with red kitten heels, stockings, and my favorite Harley Davidson jacket. I'd just had my hair trimmed, cleaning up the pixie cut with the swoop of purple through it that framed my cheekbones in sharp perfection. I looked a little bit like Will's escort for the evening, a thought that warmed me up for the evening's plans.

Will finished the glass of wine he'd ordered to go with our steaks, polishing it off before he even cut into his dinner. I arched an eyebrow. He held up a finger for my patience and threw me a cheeky grin.

"Watch this," he said as the waiter circled us with a wine bottle.

"Can I get you another?" he asked, gesturing to Will's empty glass.

Will leaned back in his seat, resting his forearms gently on the table.

"No, thank you," he said. The waiter nodded and disappeared as Will turned back to me, grinning wider than before. It was almost as if he weren't the type of guy to chug cheap whiskey straight from the bottle—as if he wasn't a man running from a past I was still patiently waiting to understand.

"Careful," I said, watching the way his fingers delicately gripped the knife as he took another bite. "I might start to mix you up with a normal person."

I crossed my legs as his Adam's apple bobbed, as he closed his eyes and savored the bite. When he looked at me again, there was a low heat in his gaze.

"Only the most stable and boring for my baby," he said.

God, tell me why that turned me the fuck on?

New York City shrieked and sang through the crisp fall air as we stepped from the dim, quiet restaurant. It was like stepping out of the tomb, the transition from muffled murmurs to full-tilt city sounds.

And no other city in the world sounded like New York.

I glanced up at Will who caught my eye and smirked as he placed a hand on my lower back, guiding me out the door and into the crowded street. He never lost contact despite the press of sound and bodies around us.

Maybe it was the sudden way the city opened around us, alive with possibility and guts that only a place like New York has. Or maybe it was the high of being treated like royalty as models strutted by. Maybe it was that we'd finally slept together after weeks of promises and whispers and teasing that was enough to drive even the heartiest woman insane.

But it felt like something new was beginning, for Will and for me. For both of us together. I felt like I was stepping into my happy ending.

As Will and I continued walking, he looped his arm around my waist, hugging me into his side. I let our hips find a rhythm together, swaying with each lazy step just on the edge of the bustling sidewalk. The streetlights were a warm glow above us, like a moon come down to Earth, and the glittering windows that rose to the sky were grounded stars.

I thought about last night and felt heat creep up from my core to my cheeks in a sudden wave.

Will and I weren't shy about sex. But we were also a little fucked up about it, each in our own way. He'd asked to slow down, then I'd asked to slow down, and eventually it'd been a month before we were ready.

I know, it doesn't sound that long to you, but for me that was an *eternity* when it came to sex.

We'd been pretending to date so our best friends, Leith and Caoimhe, would follow suit. But it worked out that we dropped the "fake" from our "fake dating" routine only a week into things.

Evelyn Sharp had a *boyfriend.*

I hadn't had an actual boyfriend in years. Men were a disappointment, starting with my dad at the very beginning. He was a man who only cared about his family when it suited his fantasy of the week—or when the military benefits were worth it. Otherwise, he was selfish, hot-headed, and generally missing from my life.

Naturally, like any good girl with unstable adult figures, all the other boys I picked followed suit. I'd had enough of it to last me, so I'd filled my life with other things—casual sex, classic cocktails, and only the best in vintage couture.

But with Will, for the first time in a long time, something clicked into place. Sure, he was a hot mess, but there was a diamond in all that wreckage. And unlike all my other "I can fix him" moments, this time, the guy also wanted to fix himself.

Trust me, that makes a world of difference.

Maybe it was a mershark thing? Will was the only non-human entity I'd dated. It was possible I'd just been waiting for a formerly impossible partner to manifest in my life.

And it came with some *serious* perks. Like last night.

He looked up at me from between my thighs, eyes dark, a muscle ticking along the edge of his jaw. The callouses on the edges of his fingers tickled the inside of my thighs before teasing down to my clit. I bucked against his arms where he held me down as he circled that tender spot with less and less restraint until I was sure I was going to come with the next forceful swirl of his hand.

"You want my cocks?" he asked, voice low. He'd asked me this before—dirty talk was definitely my thing—but it'd always been teasing, promising the future, something to get my mind riled up with my body. But this time, there was something in his voice that made me sit up and get a better look at him.

"You finally gonna deliver on all your bullshit?" I asked, arching an eyebrow and grinning at him. I felt a thrill up my spine as his eyes darkened in response to my challenge. He pushed up against my legs, firmly gripping my thighs to keep me in place as he angled himself above me. The single silver chain he wore glinted in the dim light that sent orange slants across our room. I knew the way his teeth sharpened, and his pupils widened was no trick of the light. He was a predator.

My predator.

I gasped as I felt the head of his dick nudge against my entrance. His grip on my thighs kept me from opening further or greedily scooting down to meet him, knowing there was a second cock to rival the first.

I felt like I'd been empty for an eternity, clenching on air or the barely satisfying grip of his hand.

Mama needed to be dicked down and she needed it now.

"Answer the question, you greedy little—"

"YES." I couldn't keep the scream from my throat. I grabbed the back of his neck and hauled him down to my mouth, tangling our tongues in a battle for dominance. I'd let him win this time, and he must've sensed it.

"I must have something you want," he teased, pulling back as he nipped my bottom lip. He twisted his hips so that his cock pushed only a fraction further into me and I threw my head back in simultaneous frustration and delight. I was going to kill him.

Well, I was gonna fuck him and then I'd kill him.

"There's no other reason you'd be so desperate right now." Will withdrew from me, and I whimpered, thrashing under his arms on the bed.

"Not desperate," I panted, sitting up on my elbows and giving him a look. "Determined." I pulled off my top, tugging my bra with it, knowing I was

throwing my trump card on the table too fast. But I didn't give a shit. This would work because it always worked.

"Fuck, Eve," he sighed, crawling back over top of me and immediately lowering his mouth to my eager nipples. He sucked, circling his tongue in a tight loop before biting down. I saw stars before he moved to the second, kissing into my sternum as he moved his hands onto my spine—as if he were imprinting his mouth against my skin and needed the leverage.

"I love your perfect little tits," he murmured before taking my second nipple into his mouth. I swatted at the side of his head. "What? They're not huge but they're still perfect."

I was gonna kill him.

As he worked my second nipple into his teeth, I felt like I was going to explode.

"You have to fuck me, Will," I gasped out. "Right now."

"So I was right." He nuzzled my face with his nose, whispering against my lips. "I do have something you want."

"Please, please, please," I whined, lifting my hips to grind against his stiff cock. The shaft of one found my entrance while the head of the other met my clit. "Fuck, I'm gonna come."

"Good," Will said, grinding into me with renewed force. "We gotta get you ready for me."

"But—"

"I won't stop at one, Evelyn," he said, reaching down to grip his cock in one hand and using it to tease my clit before tracing down to my opening and back up. "You've been such a patient, perfect, good girl."

"You bastard." I shuddered as my trigger phrase pushed me over the edge. Again, my poor pussy clenched on air as my orgasm shuddered through me. I nearly cried from frustration.

"You deserve so much more," he whispered into my neck as the last clench of pleasure rippled out. "And I'm going to give it to you."

"Eve?"

I jolted back to reality. I hadn't realized how lost I'd been.

"Whatcha thinking about?" he asked with a sly smile that slowly grew sharp in the low light, that predatory glint once more sparking from his eyes.

"Fucking you," I answered, grinning.

He hauled me against him in the middle of the sidewalk and we both ignored the annoyed noises from passersby as we clogged traffic. I could feel him growing hard through his pants and I shifted my hips against him. He gripped me hard, bruising in a way that sent waves of pleasure up my spine.

I loved being wanted, needed, like this. I loved feeling that desperation from his every touch.

"You're going to wreck me, Evelyn Sharp," he said before slanting his mouth over mine and claiming me on the sidewalk. If I had my perfect world, I'd haul him down on top of me and we'd fuck on the sidewalk. That's how crazy this guy made me.

But I didn't think Caoimhe would love a call from jail when she and Leith had just left the country.

"Not if you wreck me first," I teased.

"Will Burleigh," a voice called from half a block away. Suddenly, Will was in front of me, pushing me behind him with a protective arm. I peeked over his shoulder to find the source of the voice.

The street around us had come to a halt, every person paused mid-step as if they'd planned the world's most boring flash mob. The air shimmered with a strange light, and I tasted salt on my tongue.

Magic.

I was only just beginning to recognize it after meeting Will and learning that my best friend Caoimhe was a leprechaun, but once it was pointed out to you it was unmistakable.

The voice belonged to the only other figure still moving—an imposing red-headed woman with dark eyes and a dangerous scar running the length of her delicate neck. She was dressed from head to toe in purple, including a dramatic velvet cape and the sickest pair of knee-high black patent boots I'd ever seen.

As much as she scared me, I was into her look.

"I see you've finally tricked some poor soul into loving you," the woman called. My chest tightened and my throat grew thick.

"We haven't got that far," Will called back, voice cracking. I cringed for both of us. Hot double-dicked sex aside, "we" were still very much a work in progress. We definitely hadn't dropped the L bomb yet.

But…

"Doesn't matter what you think," the woman strode forward, closing the distance between us with a supernatural speed. "Magic doesn't lie. Don't tell me you haven't noticed the change."

Up close I could see the unnatural shape of her pupils, slitted like a fox in the sun. Something about her made me dizzy. I couldn't look directly at her for more than a moment before she became wavy and unfocused.

Will didn't say anything, but I noticed the tick in his jaw, the way he clenched his teeth, the vein in his neck beginning to pulse. His eyes were wide, and his silence scared me more than this woman.

What difference? What change?

"You know I can't let you get away that easy," she sighed, reaching a velvet gloved hand to touch Will's cheek.

"Fuck off," I said, frustration punctuating each syllable and I swiped her hand away. "Lady, we don't know you and we don't want to. Get the hell out of here."

The woman glanced from me to her hand, arching a single eyebrow.

"Interesting," she said before turning her attention back to Will. "If I were a more gracious witch, I'd let you have your last moment together. But I'm not."

She placed her hand in the air, palm flat out between her and Will. A pulse of air, filled with a metallic smell and something else, salty and unnamed, flashed by us.

The sounds of the city clicked back on again and when I blinked the woman was gone.

"Come on," I said tugging on Will's arm. "Let's get out of here." But Will didn't budge.

He looked down at me with a strange rage across his face. His pupils were entirely dilated, and I thought immediately of his fearsome shark form. His teeth sharpened in front of me, and he bared them, leaning over me and snapping once directly in front of my face.

"You 'get out of here,' little fish," he growled. "Before I make you my next meal."

"Will, that's not funny," I snapped, stepping away.

"No?" He tilted his head to the side, his voice pitched up in mockery. "Not funny to see a little fish standing up to a shark? I should eat you and see if you kick all the way down to my stomach." He snapped again, his teeth sharper, longer—his eyes darker, meaner.

I pushed him, putting distance between us and for a moment, I thought he might come after me. But he stayed put, staring at me with his head turned to the side, as if he'd never seen me before and was trying to figure out what to do with me.

"Hey, miss," a guy in a Mets bomber jacket and red beanie stopped his brisk walk and gestured toward Will. "This guy bothering you?"

"Yeah, lady," Will echoed, mocking the stranger. "Are you bothered? Or do you like it?"

"Easy," the man said, squaring his shoulders so he was between the two of us. "It doesn't have to be like that."

"Or what?" Will turned his full predator gaze on the stranger, tilting his head slowly to the side. My instincts kicked in and I shoved the stranger out of the way just in time for Will to lunge forward. We tangled in a mess of limbs and teeth, landing hard on the concrete.

Shouts rang out around us, and I felt something hot running down the side of my arm. Enough fights at recess had taught me that meant I was bleeding, but I didn't pause to inspect the injury, focusing instead on Will's gnashing teeth just inches from my face.

I didn't want to hurt him, but he was acting crazy—like he didn't even know who I was. What the fuck was with all the "little fish" sadist bullshit? That woman had done something to him, I knew it. This was not the Will I'd fallen for.

This was not the man he'd worked so hard to become.

I flailed an arm around and smacked Will directly in the nose. Just as suddenly as the attack had started, it was over. Will's face grew blank, and he stood up, untangling himself from me with all the gentleness of someone who has fallen into a pile of garbage. Then, without another word, he turned and ran, sprinting off down a side alley and disappearing into the growing dark.

Warm hands helped me up and several voices at once asked if I was okay, did I know that guy, did I need the cops. I shook them all off, only one thing on my mind as I took off down the same alley.

Will was going to get hurt. And I had to find him before that happened.

3

Evelyn

With every beat of my heel against the pavement, moments with Will flashed through my mind.

His drunken sharp smile in the stairwell the first night we met.

Our hands clasped in a firm shake as we agreed to fake our way through pushing our best friends together.

The night it stopped being fake.

"Will!" I called out, peering into the whispering shadows of the city. I pushed back against the frantic helplessness of trying to find one man in a city of eight million people.

Of trying to chase down my heart in such a sleepless place. "Will, come back!"

More steps, more flashes.

Watching him dump his cabinet stash of corner store whiskey down the sink drain, the smell sharp enough to peel the paint off the walls, the feeling between us strong enough to drown out everything else.

The shake in his fingers those first few days as he reached for me.

The stark contrast of this rapid timeline we were on—from drunk on the stairs to turning down a second glass of wine at dinner in just a few weeks—twisted my heart in my chest.

I couldn't let him be swallowed by yet another type of monstrousness. Not after I'd seen who he was—who he *wanted* to be.

My voice felt feeble, swallowed quickly by a growing breeze and cars streaming past. Ahead, a flash of familiar dark hair, of a well-tailored suit jacket. I sprinted, wheezing and knock-kneed from running in heels but I caught the man's shoulder before he could cross the street. The stranger brushed me off, face knit in confused irritation. I apologized, defeat threatening to clench my heart until I couldn't breathe.

I was never going to find him. Not like this.

I pulled my phone out and tapped out a full frantic text message to Caoimhe, then deleted it. Leith would want to know but there wasn't anything they could do from thousands of miles away in Ireland. My finger hovered over Patrick's number. Caoimhe had given me the vampire's information for "emergencies."

"This is a different world we're in now," she said, squeezing my hand. "Who knows what can happen? I'll feel better knowing you can reach out if you have to."

I tapped the call button. The phone rang twice before a drawling bass voice answered.

"Will is gone," I gasped out into the phone. A stitch was building in my side and my ankles were screaming.

"Who is this?"

"Goddamn it, Patrick," I sighed and leaned against a building, trying to catch my breath, trying not to freak out.

"Ah, Evelyn. How are you this evening?"

"Shitty. My boyfriend turned into a crazy shark man and took off. We're in New York and now I can't find him."

"He is a mershark, they will sometimes shift. I thought Caoimhe would've—"

"*I know,*" I snarled. Apparently even supernatural men needed to overexplain everything to me. "There was a strange woman. She did something to him."

"Describe her." There was a rustling of what sounded like sheets and the sudden loud click of a light switch.

"Were you fucking asleep?" I asked, incredulous. "You're a vampire and it's 11:30 at night. Isn't this your primetime hour?"

"The hours I keep are not pertinent to this conversation," he huffed.

"'Kay, well, you're telling me about it later then," I demanded.

"The strange woman, Evelyn," Patrick prompted.

"Evil Little Mermaid vibes," I said. "All purple Party City outfit, box dyed red hair, weird scar on her throat that she definitely could've covered with a little—"

"Mirra."

"At what?"

"No," Patrick sighed into the phone. "The woman's name is Mirra. She's a sea witch of ancient power and origin. She hasn't made an appearance on land in a century, and the last person to see her in open water fifty years ago was—"

"Will," I finished. "How is that possible?"

"Well, merfolk don't age the same as—"

"*Patrick,*" I hissed into the phone. "I know. If you don't start talking to me as an equal, I'm going to mail garlic to your basement."

"There's no need for threats," Patrick sniffed.

We both waited in silence on the phone. After a few seconds I caved. I needed to find Will and being right wasn't worth losing the precious seconds we had.

"I'm sorry," I said. I started to walk again, wishing my direction had any purpose. Will could be anywhere—almost literally if he'd hopped a train or a bus in the time since I'd lost him. "I really need your help, and I'm running out of time. I need to find Will. Do you have any idea what I should do? Is there some connection here in New York you could contact?"

"There is," Patrick said, and hope flared to life in my chest. "Find the City Hall subway station. I'll give Billy a call."

"Hold on," I said, lowering the phone and stepping into a bodega. The man behind the counter nodded in greeting, leaning on the counter as I approached.

"How ya doing?"

"Stressed, baby." I batted my eyes and let my shoulders drop. "Do you know where City Hall station is?"

The man shook his head. "It's closed," he said. I noticed a gold cross nestled in the chest hair poking from beneath his maroon button up. The hair across his head was thinning and the lines around his eyes and mouth told the story of many nights spent smoking and laughing.

"For good?" I asked.

"There's the museum, they'll let you see it, but you can't catch the train from it. Where you trying to go, gorgeous?"

"To meet a friend." I threw him a wink and popped my leg as I caught him looking me up and down.

"Have him meet you here, I'll keep an eye on you." He gave me a look like I imagined a protective uncle might—I'd never had one so I couldn't be sure. Either way, I didn't think, given his holy necklace, that he'd make a good friend for a vampire. And I trusted Patrick not to throw me out as bait for anyone dangerous.

"You'll scare him off," I said. "He won't want any competition."

The guy laughed and smacked the counter. "You sure you wanna be running around with a guy like that?"

"Who said anything about running?" I waggled my fingers at him and thanked him as I stepped back onto the street, lifting the phone back to my mouth.

"What was all that?" Patrick asked.

"City Hall station doesn't exist anymore," I said. "Pick another spot."

"It can't be, I was just there the other—"

"Decade?" I finished for him. I was getting impatient. "There's an entire city, Patrick, pick another spot."

"I suppose the Metropolitan Museum of Art will do, although it will be quite a trek for Billy. He isn't as young as he used to be—"

"Great, the Met, I'm headed there now." I hung up, unable to stomach Patrick's babbling any further.

I flagged a cab and hopped in. As we pulled away from the curb, I tried not to think about all the ways Will could've gotten himself into trouble in the time we'd been apart. I remembered what he told me the night we decided to try being together for real.

"I did horrible things before," he said, his hair falling into his eyes as he sat heavily on the edge of the bed. "Things I can never make right no matter how hard I try. There is so much blood on my hands and it will never come clean."

"Would you do it again? Given the chance?" I asked, sitting down next to him. The cheap mattress dipped, slinging us against each other, knee to knee, thigh to thigh. I steadied myself with a hand out against the mattress, the other reaching for Will's hand.

"I don't know, Eve," he said, tears making his throat thick. "I lose control of myself when I'm—" He stopped himself. He squeezed my hand but didn't look up. "When I'm like how I used to be."

I didn't know it then, but he was talking about his mershark form. He was a true predator in that shape, stunningly lethal in the water with a thick grey tail and pupilless black eyes. He'd shown himself to me the same night Leith showed himself to Caoimhe, transforming in the frigid water of the Boston Harbor.

But I hadn't been afraid. I realized while I treaded water against the waves that there wasn't anything Will could show me that could unsettle me. I *always* expected to be unsettled. We'd never put roots down anywhere growing up, following my dad's military career wherever it took us. And when both of my parents were home at the same time, there was still uncertainty on the horizon—would they be screaming at each other when I walked through the door from school, weary from yet another day as the new kid? Or would they be making out in the kitchen, oblivious to my existence?

So, when my fake-soon-to-be-real boyfriend turned into a half-human half-shark hybrid, glinting silver skin under the moonlight, I could finally take pride in how hard I was to surprise.

The cab pulled up outside the Met and I handed the driver his fare.

"The museum is closed this late," he said. "You sure?"

I nodded. "I'm meeting someone, I'll be fine." I thanked him and stepped out of the cab, but he rolled the window down, calling out to me again.

"Why don't you wait here until your friend shows up? I'll turn the fare off. It's what's right."

I flashed him a confident smile and nodded. "My friend is shy," I said. "And I've got a gun in my purse. I'll be alright. But thank you." I handed him another ten for his kindness and threw him a wave as I stepped away from the cab.

I did not have a gun in my purse, but I did have a vampire on the way and that was practically the same thing.

I didn't have to wait long on the steps of the Met, but it felt like an eternity. Shadows stretched long from the edge of the forest-like park surrounding me on all sides. Muffled shouts rang out from several blocks away, sometimes growing closer before vanishing altogether. Somewhere a siren wailed. Every person walking by—steady or unsteady—could be either my salvation or my undoing, and it made my palms sweat to make eye contact. Every time a passerby glanced up at me on the steps a little too long, I regretted my perch out in the open. But then I'd glance again at the shadows surrounding the museum and decide I'd take my chances where I could see any would-be attackers.

Just as I was wondering if I should've taken the cab driver up on his offer, a strikingly handsome man with white-blonde hair spiked up at all angles and a sweeping black trench coat started up the stairs.

"Evelyn," he said in greeting, a thick British accent lilting his words.

"You don't look that old," I said.

"A common truth for my kind," he said. Up close I could see the unnatural pallor of his waxy skin. Beneath his open trench he wore a blue silk shirt that clung almost perfectly to his figure. Several pairs of mismatched silver earrings hung from his ears.

He smiled, and I could see both his fangs flash for a moment. "Let's not dally."

I nodded, following the sweep of Billy's coat as it dramatically fluttered down the stairs of the Met.

"You'll need to tell me everything that's happened so far," he said, brisk steps clacking out into the night. I noticed he was wearing a sleek pair of black and red Ferragamo loafers and my respect for him rose significantly.

"Not much," I said, half-jogging to keep pace. "We finished dinner, stepped out onto the street, a strange woman did some voodoo on Will, and he turned land-shark feral before he ran off."

"Your friend—"

"Boyfriend."

"A shame," Billy tutted. "I only come across a woman of your taste every decade or so."

"Is that a double entendre?" I grinned.

"It could be." He grinned back and I didn't mistake the dark flash in his gaze. "But, your boyfriend?"

"Will. Will Burleigh," I said, immediately wondering if vampires had the same Fae rules that Caoimhe had briefed me on. Too late now.

"He's a mershark, yes?"

I nodded as we crossed an empty street, trying to push down the eerie feeling that settled on my shoulders. New York at night was one thing. An *empty* New York felt wrong. The shadows were too long, and I couldn't be sure if I imagined them curling and snaking around the edges of my vision. A pair of glinting eyes peered out of a window as we walked past, and I could feel them on the back of my neck.

"He's most likely been reverted," Billy said, glancing over his shoulder before placing a protective hand against the small of my back. It was comforting, so I let him leave it there. "He'll be seeking water so he can change back to his full form as soon as possible. He'll want to feed."

"If he hasn't already," I sighed, remembering his gnashing teeth only inches from my face. I shook my head, reminding myself again that *that* was not my Will. That was not the person he was becoming, the person he was proud of himself for. That was an old version—a person who we could both leave behind soon enough.

I hoped.

"When you say reverting…?" I let my question trail off.

"The Sea Witch has cursed him to forget," Billy said. "Whether that's his true heart, or anything in his present life I can't be sure. But he has clearly forgotten the love of his life and that will mean a reversion to the creature he was before you changed him."

I stopped dead, suddenly feeling as if the sidewalk was moving and the buildings above me were leaning in too close.

"I'm not—I didn't…" I gasped out, a hand to my chest. My breath was coming hard and fast growing more ragged by the second. Love of his life? Changed him? That was all too, big too fast, too much.

"Oh, dear." Billy paused his march just long enough to place a hand on my shoulder and tilt my chin so that I had nowhere else to look but his eyes. They were deep red, like a Hollywood carpet walk, but the longer I looked, the deeper they became, swirling with golden flecks and deep brown striations.

Before I realized what had happened, I found my breath again and Billy was releasing me, holding me steady with the one hand still on my shoulder.

"Thank you," I said. "Is that a vampire trick or...?"

He shook his head. "Good old-fashioned breathing techniques," he said.

I nodded, feeling embarrassment flush through me. Will was in danger, and I was freaking out over a stranger labeling us before I felt ready. Get it the fuck together, Evelyn. You're better than this.

"You're alright?" Billy asked, brows creasing in worry.

I looked away. "Which direction?"

"Toward the Hudson," Billy said, turning to face me in a whirl of coat, ceasing the march but maintaining the urgency as he leaned down to me. "It will be faster if we fly."

The tightness in my chest threatened to regrip my lungs.

"How long to walk?" I gasped out, swatting at the fluttering folds of his coat. I took a step back and immediately regretted it. There were phantom eyes in every window, prickling the hair on the back of my neck.

"For a human?" He squinted at me. "Thirty minutes?"

"Is that an assessment or an answer?"

"I offered a solution," he said, holding his hands up in apology.

I thought of Will, slipping into the dark rapid river and disappearing forever. And that was the *good* outcome. I took a deep, shuddering breath, forcing my shoulders down from my ears.

"You have to promise not to drop me on a rock somewhere over Central Park to get easier access to my insides."

"As I am not a seagull," he said, holding his hand out. "And you are not a clam, that is an easy enough promise to keep."

Part of me didn't care if I'd offended him. Patrick could lecture me on vampire etiquette later. If that was even a thing. Part of me wanted to punch Will in the dick for hanging a cloud of anxiety over my first hangout with a real-life New York City vampire.

Part of me couldn't breathe and didn't want to.

I took Billy's hand and before any second thoughts could take hold, we were airborne.

The air was so cold it sliced against my face and legs. I wished I'd chosen a warmer ensemble for dinner—is there an equivalent to "bring a jacket just in case" but for losing your mershark boyfriend? Is there a wrap that will keep away the chill of seeing recognition vanish from eyes you've stared at long enough to know their every speckle?

In the movies, vampires are always flying over cities with their beloved and the scene is gentle, glittering, and temperate. The girl's hair blows around her face in perfect glamor and the flush in her cheeks is only that of true love.

In reality, flying over a city is a five minute ride with a stunt devil who is actively trying to keep you from being slammed into this skyscraper or that one. The clutch of their arms on your waist is bruising because they don't want to drop you, and the only thing you can see is bats chasing the bugs that are now plastered all over your teeth.

When we landed, Billy set me down as gently as he could given that I was clawing my way out of his arms to vomit up moths or crickets or whatever other nighttime creepy crawly I'd swallowed.

When I recovered, I stood on shaky legs and looked at where we'd landed. A well-maintained path ran the edge of the inky water beside us. A chill breeze whipped across the river, rustling the trees that dotted the landscaping behind us. I walked to the railing meant to keep joggers, drunks, and curious teens from tumbling down into the current. I tried to see if there was a gap in the fencing somewhere—anything that would make it easy for Will to slip into the water as he shifted. But there was no point of access that I could see from any angle.

"Now what?" I nodded to Billy, trying to hold in how hard I was shivering.

Billy shrugged.

And that was all it took to light my fuse.

"The fuck you mean?" I mimicked his shrug. "You drag me through every mosquito in the city cause you're so sure this is where Will has gone and now you all of a sudden don't know anything?"

I moved so now I was directly in front of the vampire. "You think you're funny, buddy?" I growled at him, putting on my best sneer. "You think this is all a fun little prank? 'See what the stupid little human is up to, drag her through some aerial tricks, maybe eat her later I dunno.'"

Billy didn't even flinch, his startling red eyes fixed on mine. Did his pupils widen a little or did I imagine it? I held my face as still as I could, refusing to break eye contact.

"You are," he said, flashing his fangs at me intentionally. "Very funny."

Then, several things happened at once.

I pulled my arm back to swing.

Billy's face flickered to something ancient and dangerous.

A guttural roar sounded from behind us.

We both whirled around to see Will charging at us full-force. His clothes were torn and covered in blood. His eyes were pitch black and his mouth hung open at a strange angle, full of extra rows of razor-like teeth.

Before I could breathe his name, he sprinted past us and vaulted himself over the railing. I caught the twisting shift of his tail growing in the air before he landed with a massive explosion of water.

I ran so fast that my hands caught the icy railing straight on, sending a painful spasm into my bones. I screamed Will's name out into the night, the air slicing every letter to shreds before it could so much as nudge the water's edge. But I kept screaming. I didn't know what else to do.

Then, almost out of my line of sight, a familiar head bobbed above the water before sinking back down.

He didn't even glance at me.

4

Evelyn

Boston, 2 months ago

"Leith, walk her home," Will said. We'd just shared a round of beers to celebrate Caoimhe's client's success before the focus shifted quickly to solving Mister Flipper's PR crisis. Caoimhe wanted to go home to write out the plan while it was fresh and Will had keenly spotted an opportunity for getting the two alone.

He was alarmingly good at this matchmaker business.

He was also alarmingly close to me, knees pressed against mine, hand wandering to my thigh under the table. His fingers pressed gently along the inner edge of my leg and it took all of my control not to immediately spread myself open at their request. Will was leaned in to me and I could feel his eyes on my face, burning into my skin while I watched Caoimhe and Leith maybe a *little* too closely.

"No," they said in unison, panic making their voices spike.

"I'll be fine," Caoimhe said, her face threatening to settle into the kind of closed off that not even a pole vaulter could get past. I had to act fast. But before I could open my mouth, Leith solved the problem for me.

"I don't mind," Leith said and they locked eyes again. It was enough to make me want to smack them both. How could they *not* see the way they were looking at each other?

"It's not far," Caoimhe said. She was trying to convince us she didn't need an escort but I recognized the concession in her voice—*Yes, bestie, it's just a quick walk with a very sexy man just give it a go.*

"It would make me feel better," I said, reaching across the table to grab her hand. It was an unfair advantage to pull the "just two girls in this dangerous world" card, but I could feel guilty later—maybe at their marriage reception.

"Alright," she said, giving me a soft look before turning to Leith. "Thank you."

I waited for the old wood door to creak shut behind them, before pumping a fist in the air.

"They are *so* gonna make out later," I said, clinking my mostly empty beer against Will's definitely empty bottle. "Good thinking on getting Leith to walk her home."

Will bowed dramatically from his seat, throwing his arms wide and gesturing to an imaginary audience. "Yes, yes, I am a genius," he said and I swatted his arm, laughing. I couldn't help but notice that the place where his hand had been on my leg now suddenly felt cold. With Leith and Caoimhe gone we didn't have to pretend to be obsessed with each other, so obviously he'd stopped touching me.

But still.

"Should we get another round?" I asked. But Will was already up at the bar flagging down the bartender. When he returned, we clinked a crisp cold cheers and I winced after my first sip, watching Will continue to chug until most of the bottle was gone.

"You good?" I arched my eyebrows at him, remembering all-too-clearly the smell and weight of him, too drunk to get up the stairs without two people shoving him. "I can't carry you on my own, I am but a delicate flower." I batted my eyelashes in what I hoped was a joking, coquettish way so that my real question was softened.

Will let out a massive belch and someone behind us yelled, "nice!"

"Yeah, I'm good," he said. "Just thirsty." He dropped his hand back to my leg and fixed those fierce grey eyes on me. I was simultaneously relieved and alarmed. Was he touching me now because he was getting drunk?

"Just thirsty," I repeated, peeling his hand off my leg, my body cooling from its earlier fever.

He looked dramatically from his abandoned hand to me and back.

"Do I offend?" he asked, placing a hand delicately to his chest.

"There's no one here to pretend for," I said, aware of how icy my voice had become.

Will leaned forward, pulling my gaze back to his. There was a faint line in his forehead and his eyes had softened. He braced one arm along the back of my chair, the other across the table so that I was angled directly in his sights.

"What if that doesn't matter to me?" His voice was a soft purr, his breath a hoppy whisper along my neck. I shivered, not unpleasantly.

"Then you're drunk already," I answered. But already the ice was warming. I was usually much better at playing hard to get.

"Ah," he said, leaning back into his chair and taking his warmth with him. "I see."

I arched my eyebrows again and locked eyes with him, taking a sip of beer but never breaking eye contact. I waited for him to continue his thought, refusing to prompt him for more. He could play Mr. Cryptic if he wanted but that was the one game I wouldn't entertain.

He chugged the last of his beer and pushed the empty bottle across the table. He gestured to it with an open palm.

"I am not drunk off two beers," he said. "It takes a lot more than that."

"I could've guessed," I shot back.

"But something is clearly bothering you," he continued as if I hadn't said anything. "And I think it's in our best interest as…plotting partners…" he glanced up at me through a swoop of dark hair and I tried not to let the fluttering in my stomach get to me. "We should be straight with each other. So if you have an issue, say it."

"I don't have an issue," I said, looking away and fiddling with the label on my beer.

"Bullshit," he hissed. Warm, soft fingers gently slid along my neck, his thumb caressing the edge of my turned chin. Despite myself, I leaned into the touch, finding my face turned yet again back to his stormy gaze. "Talk to me, Eve."

"It's not my business," I said, nuzzling into his hand in hopes that we could change the subject.

"It could be."

He was looking at me with a new intensity—something darker, stronger, than before. I couldn't look away.

"You drink a lot," I said finally. I figured if I phrased it as an observation rather than an irritation it wasn't crossing any lines. Not that it mattered—he'd practically kicked open any gates he might have had in that moment. "Again, not that it's my place to comment on it."

"Ah, but here we are, commenting," he said. His thumb continued to trace a deliciously lazy route along my skin. I was going to start purring. This was getting dangerous. I grabbed his hand and put it down onto the table, but immediately found my fingers woven through his.

Was I doing this? Was he doing this? What was happening?

"Look," he said, putting his other hand on top of mine, wrapping me in the comfort of his callouses. "I didn't get to be a successful businessman by not communicating expectations with my partner. And since this is strictly a mutually beneficial venture until you fall in love with me, then we obviously need to set some expectations for our parts in this."

"I am not going to fall in love with you!" I sputtered.

The Evelyn doth protest too much.

I shoved the thought so far out of my mind all it would ever know for the rest of its life was the vast reaches of space.

Will simply shrugged and threw me a wink, tracing the back of my hand with his. It sent shivers down to my very core, and I tried to discreetly squeeze my thighs together.

"Fine," I said. "If we're going to be successful in getting Caoimhe and Leith together, then we both have to be focused. And that means sober."

A flash of fear crossed his face so quickly I thought I imagined it.

"Why?" he asked. "Aren't we supposed to look like we're having the time of our lives?"

"Caoimhe knows I never sleep with sloppy drunks," I said. Which was true and mostly the result of a one-night-stand with a smoking hot bassist who had absolutely destroyed my favorite suede jacket. "It'll blow our cover if you're drunk every time we're together."

"I can be sober," he said, but his eyes were flicking around the bar.

"Like I haven't heard that line before," I snapped.

"Fine," he said, standing up suddenly and hauling me up with him. "I'll prove it."

I followed him out into the late sunset, the soft pink light giving Will a hazy glow as we quick-stepped across the crooked cobblestones.

Our hands stayed clasped the entire way.

I reluctantly let go when we reached his front door and fumbled around for his keys.

But I hesitated before following him inside.

"What does your apartment have to do with you being sober?" It wasn't fear, but nerves that tickled down my spine.

"You'll see," he said, sliding his hand into mine again and pulling me gently across the threshold. I let him, the familiar thrill of going to a guy's place for the first time mixed with the anxiety of not knowing what this was or what we were doing.

For someone who claimed we were "plotting partners," Will was doing his damndest to blur some lines.

I followed him up the familiar stairs to the landing he shared with Caoimhe. We both glanced quickly at her door before looking back to each other, erupting into whispered giggles before Will unlocked his own door and pulled me in after him.

His apartment was standard bachelor bullshit—plenty of boxes not yet unpacked, a leather couch across from an obnoxiously large TV, not a single piece of art on the bare walls. Will clicked on the light in his kitchen and began pulling multiple bottles of whiskey from the cabinets. I recognized the bottle from the night we pushed him up the stairs. After the first six I expected it to stop but he just kept going.

"Holy shit," I said, watching in horror as the counter quickly filled with bottles. They glinted a dull reddish brown in the fluorescent kitchen light. "You're a fucking alcoholic."

Will flipped on the tap and wrenched off the top of the first bottle, immediately turning it upside down into the sink.

"It's not what you think," he said, his voice sad above the rush of water.

"Really? Cause it sure looks like what I think."

He grabbed another two bottles and twisted them open, setting them upside down in the sink next to the other. The smell in the air was so strong it turned my stomach.

"These are for just in case—"

"You need to blow up a bank?" I cut him off. "Or kill every sewer rat in the city?"

He braced himself against the counter, shoulders pushed up to his ears, head staring down at the cheap linoleum.

"In case I can't stand it anymore."

"Can't stand what?" I hadn't moved from the doorway since Will had started dumping his supply. I took a few steps forward, closing the distance between us until I was standing next to him. I placed a hand on his arm and watched his shoulders slowly relax.

"I don't think I can tell you yet," he said. He took my hand with both of his and lifted it to his lips, kissing the tips of my fingers. "But I promise when I'm ready, when you're ready, I will."

This was getting *way* past "plotting partners."

"Will," I said, voice caught in my throat. "You don't have to do this. If I'd known—"

"No," he said, mouth still grazing across my fingers. His lips were soft and it was killing me that my hands were all he was kissing. "I do. Because when I'm with you, I can." He looked up at me, grey eyes fierce but clear, the storm clouds parted just for me and the view was spectacular. "I don't know what it is about you, Evelyn, but you make me want to be better. Like I haven't been in a long time."

My heart pounded in my chest, threatening to break free of my ribs and float across the space between us to ease the needy look on his face.

"Do you think all this will work?" I asked, gesturing dumbly to the upturned bottles.

"Probably not," he said. "But I'm willing to try. And if this fails, I'll try something else. And then something else. I'll keep trying, Evelyn."

I'd seen grand gestures before—roses, champagne, chocolates tied in bows. I knew false promises from a mile away. And I'd learned to guard myself against falling for anything that resembled a trap—anything that would be good one day then back to trouble the next.

So even though there were a hundred red flags waving in the direction of Will, I let myself be pulled down his path.

"Well, I guess that works," I said dumbly. I tugged my hand down from his mouth and gave in to the other one that itched to touch him, letting my fingers slide up along the base of his scalp and into his hair. It was soft and clean, and now he was so close to me there was only one impulse left to crush. But first:

"Thank you," I said. "For being willing to try."

"For you, anything," he said. And then I kissed him.

Maybe it was because I wasn't immune to all the touching and flirting with a hot guy even if it was meant to be pretend. Maybe it was because no one had ever told me, even if they failed, that they'd never stop trying to please me. Maybe it was because I was starting to genuinely like Will Burleigh, covered in flags as he was.

Whatever it was, our first kiss sent fireworks shooting through my brain and tingling weakness shuddering through my limbs. The soft press of his lips against mine, the urgent way he gripped my hips like I might escape if he let go—it was like thunder in my chest when the storm was right above me.

Kissing Will was unlike kissing anyone else.

And I knew then I'd follow him into whatever mess he was hiding from me, even if it took us the rest of forever to untangle it.

5

Will

New England, 50 years ago

I lost more and more deep water to an influx of fishermen, their boats getting larger and faster every year. There were few places for me to hide, fewer ways for me to avoid them.

Despite the memory of that boy's lifeless body floating above me, haunting my every moment and motivating my isolation, humans continued to reach me. Didn't they know what a terror I was? Didn't they know how much pain I could bring them?

I tried to hold true to my promise to be monstrous, but the humans were dauntless. No amount of dorsal fin display or shadowy ankle-snatching was enough to scare anyone off entirely. They always came back—sometimes with more people to try and catch a glimpse of the monster.

And still, my lonely human heart beat through the water. Some days I wished I could tear it out of my chest and throw it onto the shore where it might finally find peace.

Maybe some creatures were not meant to unite. Humans want to stay still, huddled together, safe in a pack. Sharks cannot stop moving or they will die. These two instincts were at war in my soul, pushing me first toward a coastline, then hauling me back out to deep water—my own personal hellish tidal pattern.

Somehow, one day, I was miraculously alone, and I let myself float along the crest of the waves, enjoying the sun on my skin. I let the call of seabirds wash over me, a sweet meaningless noise much like the liquid whisper of the water, wave crashing onto wave before melting back into itself.

Suddenly, voices. Human voices.

Panic gripped my chest, instincts pulling me down below the water before my human heart could reach out. I don't know how long it had been since the boy—time had little meaning in the ocean. But the memory flashed across my mind as the shadowed hull of a small boat floated above me. I turned to swim away but movement in the water caught my attention. A silver flash, like a minnow or a sardine. Hunger lanced through me, and I turned toward it as it flashed again.

No fish had four limbs and long red hair. It was a human woman, plunged into the water from the side of the boat. As she pushed herself back up to the surface, I saw the flash of silver again—some kind of decoration on her leg.

I was mesmerized by it, my vision narrowing to just the flash in the water as her legs treaded water above me. Before I knew what was happening, her ankle was within my reach and my hands were moving through the water toward it. I had to inspect the flash, had to know what twinkling creature could captivate me so entirely. My teeth ached to connect with the light, to understand it as only my bones could.

And then the woman kicked me.

Not on purpose. Not in fear. Just a swing of her leg to continue swimming as humans do. But she connected directly with my face. There was a scream from above and a thrashing in the water as I swam away while the woman tried to scramble back onto the boat. I watched from a good distance, trying to see if the boat would move, if it was successfully startled enough to continue away from my part of the ocean. But it stayed, and after some time, more humans leapt into the water.

A ripple through the water from beneath me pulled my attention away. Another merperson swam opposite me, flipping onto her back a moment to wave and smile before continuing on her way, the sun glinting off her sea glass scales.

For once, my human heart and shark instinct beat together.

I'd never met any of my mersiblings despite knowing I couldn't possibly be the only one in the ocean. The world was too big, the water too deep, to be entirely alone. This woman wasn't the first I'd seen, but something pulled me toward her. Forgetting the humans, the boat, the silver flash, I followed.

I was able to catch up just enough to keep sight of her tail in the water, the darkness of distance partially obscuring her. We swam like that for some time, never closing the gap as hard as I pushed myself. Finally, she stopped, hovering in the water near the opening of a cave along the ocean floor. I overshot her, still going at my max speed to try and catch up and had to circle back around to her.

When I reached her, she was grinning, teeth sharp and feral, eyes wide in the murky depths. Her pupils were strange—slitted, not made for a life in the water. Her entire body was covered in the same opaque glossy scales, transitioning her human half into her fish half seamlessly. The slits of her gills along her neck were translucent when they gasped open for more water, as were the webs between her fingers. A single cord around her neck held a shark's tooth, large and bone white. I shivered. Ropes of brilliant red hair floated around her face, her features soft and rounded like the cheeks of a guppy.

I cocked my head to the side, curious about my new sister. She gestured for me to swim closer, rising to meet me. She placed her webbed hands on either side of my face and pressed her forehead to mine.

"Hello, brother," said a voice in my mind, cool, soft, sweet. I should've been afraid of this new enchantment, but instead I found myself immediately soothed by her voice.

"Hello," I replied back, surprised at how I sounded within my-self—deep, resonate, adult.

"I have been looking for you."

"Why?"

"You are as curious about the humans as I am."

I didn't stop to wonder how I could be found in an entire ocean. There was something about the mermaid, her chilly forehead crisp against my brow, that told me she was not all that she seemed. The water pulsed around her with some unknown force.

"I shouldn't be curious." The image of the boy rose to the front of my mind, and I felt the sudden swish of the mermaid's tail through the water. She pulled away for a moment, flashed her teeth at me, a strange light in her eyes.

"Show me the rest." So I let the memory of that day wash over me, including the tall man who hunted me later.

"You lost." She continued in my mind. *"You could've defeated those men and yet you swam away in fear."*

"I didn't want to hurt anyone."

"You gave up your territory for creatures you could devour in moments," she growled. A chill spread through my veins, as if the ice in her scales was pushing into my body. *"I can make it so you are never afraid again, so you rule the seas like the kings you are descended from."*

"Will I hurt them?" My human heart was crying out against this

mermaid, pleading with me to leave, to never look back, to stay as far away from her as I could. But the ocean was shrinking. She would find me the same way all the humans continued to do so.

I was tired of being a hunted thing.

I thought about the boat, filled with humans who had screamed in fear of me just moments ago. Humans that would never reach out and connect with me like this mermaid was. If I couldn't befriend them, then it was best to no longer fear them.

If I was to be alone for the rest of my life, I wanted to at least not feel like this anymore.

"You might," the mermaid said. *"But all the greatest rulers cause small harm for a greater good. The ocean needs its king, sweet shark. Let me take away your fear."*

"Why would you help me?" My human heart filled with suspicion. I wanted to trust someone who was clearly of my own kind when the humans on land had done nothing but scream and shame me. But still. Something was wrong. I could feel it.

"I have spent too many hours afraid like I see you are now," she said. *"Our kind should not fear but be feared. This is our world the humans are invading."*

"They can't all be bad."

"I didn't say they were."

I pulled away and considered the mermaid for a moment, her glossy eyes, translucent gills. The cave behind her grew darker and darker the longer we tread water there, pushing the salty waves through our lungs.

"What will you do?"

"It will feel good, sweet king."

The shark's tooth around her neck swayed with the push of the water stirred by the slow kicking of our tails.

"You must be tired," her voice lulled me. *"Swimming constantly back*

and forth, always afraid. Wouldn't you like a rest?"

I nodded, something hot and tight filling my chest.

"I am your sister. My name is Mirra. Let me help you."

"Where are the others?"

"You can meet them later." There was an edge of impatience in her voice, but it was quickly replaced with more dulcet tones. *"They will be so proud of your fearlessness once we are through."*

I was tired. I wanted to not be alone. My sister could help me.

"Tell me what to do."

"Take my hand," she said, extending the webbed claws.

I took it, clasping it tight.

Mirra's face split into a predatory grin and a soft green glow lit up from within her gut. The light split out through her sea glass scales, illuminating the cave behind her. Too late, I noticed the skeletons lining the cave floor. They stared up at me with wide, dead eyes as bottom-dwellers skittered between their many rows of teeth. Ribbons of flesh that once cut through the water with expert grace danced in the current, shredded and munched.

Sharks.

I tried to pull away, to free myself from the mermaid's grasp, but something more than her claws held me in place. As I watched in horror, her eerie green light grew brighter and brighter, pulsing out around us and wrapping itself around our hands.

"The deal is made, little king," her voice cackled inside my head, all promise of softness evaporated. *"I will take your fear as promised, because you don't deserve it. You don't realize the power of your softness."*

Her free hand struck out, grabbing my chin and squeezing until I had no choice but to open my mouth to avoid the pressure. Like a crab with a fish, her talons darted into my mouth and pulled. Bright white pain flashed behind my eyes, and I tasted blood in the water.

She released me, and the last thing I remember clearly is my tooth in her hand, held aloft to the filtered sunlight. Her face contorted into a vengeful glee, and I only had a moment to wonder how I had wronged my supposed sister before a supernatural darkness clouded my vision.

* * *

The next years came in flashes. I remember mostly insatiable hunger, flesh in the water, cries from the shore. Every memory I have is like that woman's silver flash in the water—a quick glimpse of something I don't quite understand but am desperate to study closer.

* * *

The sea was alive around me, life shimmering in every push of the water against my body.

But I wasn't interested in plankton.

Hunger heightened my senses, making every flash of light, every shadow, every movement a possible next meal.

There. Flailing in the water—an unnatural pushing and flapping ignited my curiosity. I cut through the water like an arrow through the air, zeroing in on the motion. My form was made for this, my powerful tail propelling me forward at an almost unnatural speed, my humanoid arms flat against my side, ready to reach forward and drag my prey in for an exploratory bite.

When I reached the creature in the water, my heart slowed, and I loosened my arms to create some drag as I began to circle.

The creature was a human—a young male wearing the weird cloth over his genitals that humans had decided would protect them in the water. His sandy brown hair swayed in the water, matching the motion of his arms as he pushed back up toward the surface.

I let him see me, circling around close enough to signal to his prey instinct that he was now in danger. The fear in his eyes quickened my pulse, sent a wave of pleasure across my brain that kicked my tail into gear. This was my ocean he had entered. I was the king of these waters, fearless and unconquerable.

Before I could savor it much longer, my instincts took over.

I grabbed him and held on as he flailed against me. The water filled with bubbles as he screamed with no sound, releasing the last of the oxygen that would've buoyed him to the surface if I let go. Before he was finished thrashing, I leaned down, unhooked my jaw revealing all three rows of teeth, and bit down.

Blood filled the water, the smell of it driving me into a frenzy. I let my thoughts recede, let the monster in me rear forward and take over. I thrashed and tore and whipped my meal through the water until he was little more than limbs and flesh floating in front of me. I swam back and forth through the carnage, coming away with a different bite each time as if I were plucking hors d'oeuvres from a tray.

Sated, I swam away toward deeper water, leaving the rest to float to the bottom for the shelled creatures who hungered there.

6

Evelyn

New York City, Present Day

"Are you going to be like this much longer?" Billy asked, staring at me over the diner mugs between us, contents long since grown cold. "I've got a whole thing about sunrises."

I shook my head, realizing I'd been staring out the window in silence. *"Only the most stable and boring for my baby."*

Yeah, fucking right.

"You can go," I said, instinctually sipping the coffee and wincing at the cold bitter taste.

"I never leave a damsel in distress."

I rolled my eyes so hard they nearly took flight.

"Look, he'll come back," Billy said, reaching across the table. He took my hand, and I wriggled it away. I was in what Caoimhe called "petulant princessland" and I didn't give a shit.

"He won't," I said, sounding incredibly well-adjusted and not at all despondent. I am very much the queen of adapting to shit situations. And this was the shittiest of shit, so naturally I had it handled.

"How long have you been together?" Billy tried for my hand again and this time I let him. His hands weren't cold, but they weren't the warm comfort I was hoping for either.

"Officially? Two months," I said.

"Are you serious?"

"Don't start."

"All this over a three week relationship? Not to be trite, but there are other fish in the sea, love."

Without thinking I flipped our hands over so that the back of his slammed onto the flimsy table. Dishes rattled and I was pleased to see him wince.

"Don't," I said, pointing at him with my now free hand. "Start."

"Alright," he said, and settled back into the booth, draping his long arms along the back so that his shoulders shrugged forward. His silk shirt gaped open, and he looked up at me from under the shock of his hair. "I'll go with you."

I arched my eyebrows. "I'm going home," I said.

"Exactly." He winked at me, and I picked up a fork. He dropped his hands out of sight and then it was his turn to roll his eyes.

"You are clearly not in a state to be traveling alone," he said. "I'll accompany you back to your people. That way you get where you're going, and I rest easy at sunrise knowing you didn't get mugged because you were too busy crying over a fling."

"My flight is at noon," I said, annoyance slamming in to smother my grief. "And I'm not leaving until I find Will."

"He's not in New York anymore," Billy said, the edges of his voice softening.

"You don't know that."

"I do, love, I promise you I do."

"Then where is he, great and all-knowing Billy?" I snapped, crossing my arms and leaning back in my seat.

"Patrick and the others will know how to find him—better than we do," he said. "You have to get back to Boston and you shouldn't do it alone."

He was referring to the Boston Unusualities Society, or the BUS, was the group of supernatural and magical beings in Boston that Patrick belonged to. They'd formed after the unfortunate death of Caoimhe's dad and had been working to recruit and support other magical beings in hiding across the city. So far, I'd only met Pete and talked with Patrick, but I hadn't seen where they met or been introduced to the others. As a human, the rules were strict about letting me waltz in.

But Caoimhe liked and trusted the BUS. They'd helped her reunite with Leith after all that chaos on the boardwalk when he'd transformed into his mershark form in front of a pier full of carnival goers. And they'd made it so Leith could pass through the city unnoticed until the fervor died down—there were still #IAmAMermaid posts going around twitter.

The BUS was my best bet at helping Will.

"If you can't handle sunrise, how are you going to do midday?" I narrowed my eyes.

"We'll leave tonight," he said. That meant I'd get home way later than I'd planned for.

"I don't have the cash to just change my flight like that," I said. "And besides, I didn't ask for your help. It's fine. I got it."

"Have you ever flown private?" He waggled his eyebrows at me.

Shit. Now he had my attention. I was nothing if not a slut for luxury.

"You don't live this long and continue to fly commercial, love," he said, catching the shift in my demeanor and leaning forward across the table with a hungry grin. "I can arrange for my pilot to be ready as soon as the sun goes down. We'll be to Boston before Patrick's next nap."

"Okay," I relented. "But only because I have a solemn vow to never pass up an opportunity to live like a Kardashian."

"Stick around, love, I can make that happen."

I felt my cheeks burn and immediately felt guilty.

"I have to get back," I said, standing from the table.

"I can drop you off," Billy offered. I shook my head violently before his offer was fully formed.

"I'll walk," I said, reaching into my pocket and pulling up the contact screen on my phone. "Put your number in here so I won't ignore you when you call me later."

"I love American women," Billy said as he tapped his number in. "You're never shy about getting what you want."

There was a glint in his eye and a hungry bite of his fang as he handed me back my phone. And I definitely didn't feel a heat in my gut at the attention because that *would* be betrayal.

"I'll see you tonight," I said, throwing a wave over my shoulder as I pocketed my phone. I left with all the cool, collected grace of an unruffled monarch, stepping out into a city coming to life. I played this role all the way back to my hotel, where I slid out of my jacket and dress, stopping only a second to peel off my tights before stepping into the immediately hot shower.

"I love you, brand new pipes," I cooed as the steam billowed around me. The water was deliciously warm, sliding down my tired muscles. I flinched and looked down to see red swirling around the drain. Right. I'd cut myself on something when I'd stopped Will from—

"Not Will," I whispered to myself as I checked my arm. It was a shallow cut and it seemed like the blood in the water was mostly leftover that had dried on my skin.

"You're going to wreck me, Evelyn Sharp."

"Not if you wreck me first."

My practiced façade melted away in the shower, leaving behind my trembling heart and exhausted body.

How had we gone from totally gushing over each other to tussling on the sidewalk in such a few short minutes? A quick mental inventory of ex-boyfriends told me this wasn't a new dynamic for me—totally in lust, fucking on every piece of furniture and park bench in sight, obsessed with each other, then suddenly screaming at each other, or throwing things in the street. But it usually took longer. And there were red flags I breezed by that the inevitable was coming.

I never took red flags as warnings. I preferred to let them guide my path.

But with Will it had been different. And I'm not talking about any of the magic stuff that happened last month with my best friend secretly being a leprechaun and Will and Leith being mersharks with two dicks (which apparently is just a thing? A glorious, wonderful, overstuffed thing but that got left out of the fairytales for *sure*).

With Will, something was different. He didn't tell me one thing then do another like everyone else. He said he'd do something and then he did. Not perfectly and not immediately, but he delivered on his promises.

It's probably some armchair psychology bullshit, but my mom used to say "this time we'll stay, this is home, baby" and then soon enough we were packing everything back into the same boxes we'd set out in our new recycling bins. Dad would say "we won't fight like that anymore, honey," and then an hour later he'd be in yet another screaming match with mom in the kitchen.

No one had *ever* backed up their words with action.

Except Will.

He was a smart-mouthed recovering alcoholic with a whole compli-cated backstory, but he was the most stable guy I'd ever dated. And I could see that stability in him, running through his storm like a comforting undercurrent for us both.

I stepped out of the shower, wiping at my face where I'd started to cry.

This was so stupid.

Will was out there somewhere, and I *would* find him. I didn't need to be wallowing already.

I slipped under the covers in the fluffy hotel bathrobe, enjoying the cool sheets on my warm skin. The duvet settled over me with a soothing weight and I could hear the soft clinking and rattling of the housekeeping carts in the hall. I closed my eyes and rolled over, hoping that sleep would settle into my chest and give me a breather from all this "When Will My Husband Return From the Sea" bullshit. But I already knew it wouldn't be that easy.

"Alright, fine," I sighed, rolling back over and loosening the tie on my robe. I closed my eyes and focused on my memory of the other night.

"I won't stop at one, Evelyn," he said.

My hands slid down over my thighs and back up, circling my bare pussy. The sheets tickled there, and I twisted under them, enjoying the sensation.

"You've been such a patient, perfect, good girl."

I ran one hand back up my body, reaching up to twist my own nipple hard enough to send a shock through my spine. The sensation sent happy endorphins slamming over my sad little brain and my other hand abandoned my vagina, quickly twisting the other nipple.

"You deserve so much more, and I'm going to give it to you."

I could practically hear him in my ear, his breath hot on my neck, the weight of him over me. I refused to open my eyes, one hand pushing down between my legs and circling my clit as the other continued to work my nipple.

"If you're faking me out right now," I gasped, grinding against the teasing tip of his first cock.

"You'll what?" He thrust once into my eager, wet soaking pussy, still only

halfway into a space that was achingly empty. "I'm not scared of you."

Without warning, I shoved myself up and pushed against him, taking his surprise as opportunity to mount him fully on top. As he slid into me to the base, I could feel his other cock erect, prodding at my ass. The sensation was new, and I was surprised to feel a thrill along the base of my spine.

"Only stupid men don't fear women," I said, leaning down so that our noses touched as I rode him, careful not to bump against his second cock too hard.

Will slid both hands up into my hair and tugged, sending sparks straight to my core. But then he paused, cupping my face gently. "This is okay?" he asked. "It's not too much?" I stopped, stunned by the tender turn of his mouth, the concern in his eyes.

"It's amazing," I said, kissing him once. When I pulled back, I tilted my chin at him in a challenge. "But I thought you were going to give me so much more?"

I had to push myself up on one hand to get better access to my fingers as I rode three of them, desperate to fill myself like Will had filled me.

"Only if you're ready," he said, something intense and unnamed glowing in his face.

"I'm fucking ready," I said, pushing back up and bouncing a few times on his first cock and this time purposefully angling my ass against his second cock. "Give me your cocks, Will."

He flipped us back over, careful to never break connection. He slipped a hand behind my back and pushed, arching me up toward him. He reached down and slid a finger along the place where we met, hot and wet. He pressed in alongside his cock and I gasped, startled at the stretch but not uncomfortable.

"More," I gasped as he pushed his finger in further, nudging a second against the entrance.

"So greedy," he growled, voice low with a fresh need I'd never heard before. "You're gonna take everything I give you, aren't you?"

His voice was making me clench against him, twisting again against his teasing hands.

"Both," I groaned. "Please, both."

I would've split myself open in that moment if it meant I got to feel him fill me completely. I didn't give a shit.

A third finger broached my opening and I had to breathe a moment to accommodate it, but I stretched again.

I reached one hand up to Will's face, tracing his jaw and running my hand through his hair. My other hand found his asshole, teasing the tip of a finger into it.

His face snapped and there was the predator again, eyes dark, jaw set, shoulders trembling with restraint. I pushed in a little further and this time, he pulled his fingers away from where he'd been stretching me, grabbing both my hands and slamming them above my head. Before I could react, he gripped my wrists in one hand, firmly but not uncomfortably.

"Such a hungry girl," he said. I could've moved my hands if I wanted, but I chose to stay. I was surrendering myself entirely to the man I had provoked. Every part of me was on fire with need and I ground against the cock inside me in response.

"Such a greedy little cunt, it's so hungry for more. I should make you wait. Just as punishment for pushing me."

He rose over me, the muscles in his chest flexing with the angle. I took in the view, let his words wash over me.

"But now I'm hungry too," he said, and he reached back down with his free hand. I felt the head of his second cock nudge my entrance. "And you don't want a hungry shark in the water with you."

He waited there, finding my eyes. I nodded, giving him my best sly smile.

"You better fill up, then," I said, grinning.

He pushed into me against his first cock, and I gasped, shocked at the sudden stretch, stars dancing in my vision. I breathed for a few moments, shifted my hips, then nodded. He pushed in further and I could feel sweat sliding down my back. I was the fullest I had ever been in my entire life and by the time he slid the second cock home I was nervous that if he moved, I would explode.

"Okay?" he asked, bracing himself on either side of me and pushing my sweaty hair from my face. My hands were free now and I wrapped myself entirely around him.

"Perfect," I said, and then I was immediately lost to the sensation of all of him thrusting within me. He moved slow, every piece of him hitting every piece of me and the pressure that built was different this time—intentional, overwhelming, complete.

"Eve, I can't—" Sweat slid down his face, his jaw clenched, brow furrowed. "You feel too good."

I was thrusting against myself, slamming my fingers in and hooking them hard, desperate for release. Nothing could compare to that night. Nothing would ever compare again.

"Do it," I said, kissing the side of his mouth. "Fucking do it."

He picked up his pace and a blissful blackness slid over the two of us. I was entirely lost to the heat building in my core with a rapid intensity that I knew was going to break me when it let loose.

I was going to die like this and I didn't give a fuck.

Both cocks suddenly flared within me, spreading to cover even more of that perfect spot sending sparks into my vision. I came with a scream just as Will groaned into my ear, thrusting in a final time and holding it there as my pussy clenched along both his cocks.

I twisted my hand so that my thumb could find my clit and as I hooked my fingers and thrusted, I flicked my clit. I came with a cry, feeling the pulse of my pussy against my hand as a fresh wave of sobs threatened to crawl up from my chest. I swallowed hard to keep them at bay, focusing instead on the physical relaxation that flowed through my entire body.

"I'll keep trying," I whispered to the empty hotel room, echoing the same promise Will had made to me that day in his kitchen. "No matter what." I laid down, letting darkness fall over me.

55

7

Evelyn

New York City, Present Day

The tarmac was wet from that afternoon's rain, the smell of engine grease and gasoline cutting through the promise of fresh air. A soft wind blew, ruffling the dramatic duster I'd chosen for the occasion, paired with knee-high Steve Madden boots and a Chanel scarf I'd jacked from the sample closet at work. I clicked across the cement, dragging my bag—our bags. I'd had to repack Will's suitcase and lug it out of the hotel with me. He would owe me one later.

Whenever that was.

I pushed the unsettling thought away, trying not to chill myself further.

Come back, I thought as loudly as I could, hoping there was some yet unknown magic pushing my thoughts out to Will, wherever he was, however deep he was buried beneath himself.

Billy was waiting, hands in his pockets, Ray Bans reflecting the tarmac lights. His usual coat hung down to just above the Gucci loafers he was wearing for the flight.

"I should've guessed you're not a light packer," he smirked.

I let Will's suitcase slam into his shin as I handed mine off to the attendant.

"I have to be prepared for every occasion," I said, batting my eyes at him and taking too much glee in the way the muscle in his jaw twitched. "Press junkets, networking dinners, boyfriends getting cursed. You never know what New York is gonna throw at ya."

Billy handed off the offending suitcase and offered me his hand to board the thin stairs leading up to the single door. I took it, ignoring the way my breath caught in my chest, and boarded the jet.

Inside, four luxuriously plush seats faced each other in what could've otherwise been a conversation nook if it weren't on a plane. Behind that, a love seat stretched across from a small flatscreen TV. At the back of the plane were two more plush seats matching those up front. I chose the first seat facing the cockpit. I took a moment to run my hands across the soft leather as I settled in. If I wasn't convinced Billy was watching my every move, I would've shoved my face into the back of the chair, just for a smell of the real thing.

"We're preparing to taxi, Mr. Barlow," the attendant said. He was tall, thickly built but not stocky, with well-maintained salt and pepper hair. The wrinkles around his eyes and mouth said he laughed a lot, but his tone said it wasn't something he did on the job. His uniform was less formal than I'd expected, a simple button-up with a branded logo in the corner and a pair of slacks.

"Thank you, Charlie," Billy said, taking the seat across from me. He relaxed into it as if it was made for him, as if he did this all the time. Which he probably did, I realized. "Will you bring a champagne for the lady?" Billy arched his blonde eyebrows at me, asking for confirmation.

"I'd love that," I said to Charlie, giving him my most charming please-get-me-schnockered-smile. "Thank you, Charlie."

Charlie quirked a half smile at me and nodded, disappearing behind a curtain at the front of the plane.

"So?" Billy gestured with his long arms.

I shrugged, refusing to give him the swooning poor-kid act.

"It's alright," I said.

He laughed, flashing his fangs in the low artificial light. Over his shoulder, the last dregs of the storm were giving way to a peculiar twilight, all deep purples and blues.

"You sound disappointed."

"The Kardashians give you custom slippers when you board," I said, accepting the glass of champagne that my best friend Charlie had just appeared with.

I caught Billy's eye over the rim of the glass before I took a first glorious bubbly sip. I wasn't imagining the simmer in his gaze.

The plane began to move, gliding into position.

"So," Billy leaned back, bringing one foot up to rest easily on his trousered knee. I refused to let my gaze drop down. "Tell me how you and Will met."

"So you can make fun of me more? I don't think so."

"There might be some useful information in the story," he said. "Something we can use to find him or jog him back to himself."

I arched an eyebrow at him and sipped my champagne, avoiding his steady gaze.

I really didn't want to talk about Will right then. The night before had left me lonely, aching, and foggy.

But if it would help bring him home…

"My best friend and I found him drunk on the street and had to push him up the stairs to get him home," I said, smiling despite myself. It sounded bad on paper, but the memory inspired joyous bubbles in my chest that had nothing to do with the drink in my hand. "I touched his butt and that was that."

"I don't think so."

"Oh, were you there? I've heard vampires can be lurkers."

"More than you know, love."

I rolled my eyes. We sat in silence for a moment as the engines rumbled around us. I closed my eyes as the momentum of takeoff pushed me against the back of my seat, as the sensation of being airborne gripped my heels.

"You're not telling me everything," Billy said once we'd leveled out. Charlie swooped by and replaced my glass with a crisp fresh one, filled to the brim. "You've officially been together three weeks and you're willing to throw yourself into the Hudson for him because he's got a great ass?"

I shrugged. "You've obviously never seen his ass."

"I don't like being lied to," he growled.

"And I don't like being pushed," I snapped back. Years of being the new kid on the playground had hardened my boundaries and my ability to defend them. Incredibly, I got picked on because I was new *and* had a binder full of vampire drawings while knee-deep in my Anne Rice phase. Little me was losing her mind that I was having a standoff with a real vampire and not sucking his face the first chance I was given—and it was clear I'd been given a few chances already.

"Evelyn," he said, as if my name was the frustrating part of this conversation.

"Billy," I mimicked, downing another half a glass of champagne.

"When did you know you loved him?"

I stared into my glass, refusing to look up. There was that L word everyone kept throwing at me. How was it so obvious to everyone except me?

"I didn't say I did."

"Now I know you're lying to me," Billy said with a harsh laugh. "And probably to yourself."

I thought about that night, sitting on Will's bed while he told me how much he had to atone for.

The plane lights made the champagne look two-dimensional, like something meant for display. I glanced around the plane again, my eyes snagging on small imperfections—a streak on a window, a scuff on the ceiling, a loose thread in a seat. When I finally looked back to Billy, he felt startling real, all sharp angles and penetrating eyes in a space that begged for ignorance. "He told me he'd done…that he'd messed up earlier in his life and he carried that guilt. He wanted to do better so he could be the type of person who could be with me."

"A project," Billy scoffed.

Before I could think, champagne flew through the air, splattering across Billy's chest and seat. The glass trembled in my hand and rather than smashing it into his teeth, I forced my hands to let it go. It dropped with a dull thud to the carpeted floor before rolling out of sight.

I swear steam was rolling off his shoulders, evaporating the sticky alcohol off his designer jacket.

Slowly, like a cat stalking a mouse, Billy unbuckled his seat belt and stood, coming to brace his arms on either side of my seat. He leaned in until our faces were barely inches apart. Neither of us broke eye contact. Neither of us blinked. Neither of us breathed.

"I'm going to let that go, because you're clearly under duress," he breathed. "But believe me when I tell you that my dry cleaning bill would bankrupt your meager earnings."

I was going to fall into those eyes, chasing the gold through the red, swallowed entirely.

"You had to stand up to tell me that?" *Goddamn it, I looked at his mouth.* And he definitely saw me do it.

His mouth tilted at the corner and I let him lean another inch closer.

"You like riling up men who could kill you," he said, voice rough with restraint.

"I'm a woman on the edge, obviously." I could barely keep my own voice level. He was so close I couldn't clench my legs together without him noticing.

Don't cheat on your boyfriend.

But he's gone. He left like everyone else.

He may never come back—so what am I holding out for?

The thoughts lanced through me, one right after the other, the last one sharp enough to cause a physical wince. Billy immediately leaned back, letting one hand linger on the edge of my seat as he peered down at me with concern.

"I'm sorry, love, I thought we were—"

"It's not you," I said, rubbing a hand over where the pain had already disappeared in my heart. "And whatever you thought we were, we were *not.*"

Billy strode to the front of the plane, disappearing behind the divider curtain for a moment. Charlie stepped out a moment later with a bottle of cleaning spray and a cloth. In a few swift movements the seat was cleaned, the glass was cleared, and I was left with my embarrassment as he disappeared behind the curtain again.

"We'll be landing soon," Billy said, sticking his head out of the curtain like a roguish magician. "Would you like a descent cocktail?"

"No roofies, please." I let my hands drop into my lap, inspecting my damaged manicure with distaste. I was going to need acrylics that could hold up to street fighting apparently. I didn't know how I was going to explain that to Marie at my next appointment.

"You're no fun." Billy feigned a pout as he strode back to me, coat swishing despite the short distance. I wondered if he'd had it enchanted for dramatic effect. In his hands were two impossibly decadent cocktails in tall glasses. Skewers stacked with fruit stuck out of each next to a petite pink umbrella.

"There's no way you made these," I said, accepting mine with a smile that surprised even me.

"You've read all the books," Billy said, sipping delicately from the twisty straw. "I am…how did the fellow put it…impossibly fast."

The drink was sweet and sharp, the perfect mixture of liquor and fresh fruit. I wanted to dive straight in and go for a swim. I sucked down one long gulp and let it hit my system before taking another. Could I marry a drink?

"If you did a speed run as the bartender, then why do you look surprised at the dragon fruit?" I laughed despite myself, already feeling lighter after my dark moment. Billy had pulled the speckled slice of exotic fruit from his skewer and was sniffing it with a crinkled nose. He tentatively took a bite off the edge before chewing thoughtfully.

"Charlie, you're a genius!" he shouted, breaking his own farce before I could catch him in it. "What dragon makes fruit? We must get one."

The tell-tale drop of the plane had me pounding the last of my drink out of habit before I realized that Charlie would most likely let us keep drinking through landing the way he had through takeoff. I buckled myself anyway and let my eyes drift shut. I could feel Billy's gaze on me, but I ignored him. Let him look all he wanted.

He wouldn't be getting that close to me again.

* * *

Caoimhe: Did you guys make it back okay?

The text stared up at me as streetlights flashed through the windows of Billy's private car. If I didn't answer, Caoimhe would call. She would worry. If I texted and lied, she'd know. If I texted and told her the truth, she would call.

She was halfway across the world from us, making amends with her grandmother, introducing her mershark boyfriend to the entire leprechaun clan, healing with her mom. This was not the time to bother her with my mess. And I'd technically already landed hours later than I was supposed to.

I typed out a response, erased it, typed again, erased it. I set the phone down in my lap and stared out the window like the familiar streets would tell me what to do.

"Penny for your thoughts?" Billy didn't turn to me, equally entranced with the view out the window.

"I'm not that cheap," I said automatically.

"I would heap diamonds on your lap in exchange for your insights, but you would accuse me of coming on too strong."

His face made me look back out the window—too honest for such a statement.

"You have a weird way of joking around," I said to the chilled glass.

"I could say the same of your ability to take a compliment."

"You'll want to turn here," I said to the driver, a man whose face I still had not glimpsed in the thirty minutes we'd been in the car and who had not said a single word in that time. Automatically, he followed my instructions, turning into the alley behind my building. There was only one entrance in the back that led to a labyrinth of stairs and identical landings, compared to the modern front exterior with it's all glass staircase that put my every footstep on display.

"Stop here, please," I said, and the car slammed to a halt. "Your driver's—"

"Obedient," Billy finished for me in a way that ended the conversation. "Let me help you with your—"

"I got it," I said, waving off his help. The trunk was popped as I rounded the back of the car and hauled both suitcases out. The wheels rattled against the pavement, thudding to a stop as I fumbled for my keys. I could still feel Billy's eyes on me, heat rushing down my spine at the thought. Could vampires read thoughts? The lore was hazy on that one—some, not all. Was he one of them?

I frantically tried to think of anything but how close his face had been to mine on the plane but the harder I tried to push it from my mind, the more it resurfaced.

My keys jangled in front of my face. I heaved a sigh and took them from Billy's outstretched hand.

"You set this up?" I asked, arching an eyebrow at the easy way he leaned himself against the doorframe with one arm, the other slouched in his pocket.

"You dropped them while you were trying not to think about kissing me."

So he can read minds.

"I try not to," he said, giving me a shy smile. "I think it's rude. But your mind, Evelyn, is often so guarded that I can't get in—unless it's something you can't stop yourself from wanting so bad you're practically screaming."

I blushed.

I hadn't blushed in *years*. I either went for the flirtatious offer before it could make me doubt myself or I ignored it. Blushing was for wishy-washy bitches who got caught slipping up.

"You need to leave," I said, voice not even remotely demanding.

"I do," he agreed. But we both stood there.

I unlocked the back entrance, holding the door open with my hip while I shoved the suitcases through.

"I could—"

"No," I snapped. "You could leave."

"I could."

Still, we both stood there. If I could get myself across my own threshold, I could close the door in his smug, handsome face and finally go home.

Alone.

It only took the first step to find my momentum and then I was in the dank, silent maintenance hallway for the building.

"Thanks for the ride," I said, then swung the door shut behind me refusing to wait for a response.

8

Will

New England, 50 Years Ago

*A*dmitted *to God, to ourselves, and to another human being the exact nature of our wrongs.*

I wish I could tell you the exact nature of my wrongs. They are nothing more than a gut feeling and a few flashes in the water—earrings dislodged, scales left behind, a charm bracelet trailing on a stiff wrist. I could get out from under the weight of them if I could remember their faces.

* * *

Before my crimes were heavy, they were delicious. Fish are stupid. They run from instinct, expertly zig-zagging because that's what the fish that survived before them did. There is no emotion, no grace, no drama. I chase because they run. It is as it has always been.

But every human I destroyed in the water was vengeance for my former terrified self. It was how I felt able to put a hand through the past to comfort the little shark who just didn't want to be alone and was hunted for it.

Now who was the prey?

Now who was the monster?

I did not have that thought until it was too late.

* * *

It was late, the water black beneath a moonless sky. I cut through it aimlessly, swimming to feel it across my fin, against my skin. Swimming to live and nothing more.

I could feel the slow drift of forms beneath me, fish hovering low in the water or along the ocean floor as they slept. For once, the ocean felt quiet.

For once, I did not fear being alone.

Then, sea-glass in the water, tearing up out of the depths at an impossible pace. My sister rose up before me, eyes aflame, body alight with that terrible green glow. She looked possessed in the dark water, the only light for hundreds of miles.

But I did not fear her any more than I feared the dozing fish beneath us.

She gripped my wrist in her talons, clamping down as she hauled me to her, thudding our foreheads together in the same position we had spoken in the last time.

"You have betrayed me, brother."

"How?" All I had done was take my throne like she instructed. All I had done was fearlessly devour whatever I pleased, ruling the water with an admirable ruthlessness.

The chord around her neck bore many more teeth this time, and I squinted to see if I could find mine among them.

"You got greedy," her voice inside my mind this time was a venomous hiss. There was no sympathy or comfort here, no soothing wave of words over my panicked brain. *"You ate what didn't belong to you."*

"This is my ocean," I said. *"I eat whatever I please."*

"You have gone too far," she snapped. *"You have destroyed the object of my soul's desire and I will make you pay for it."*

"It is possible, but I do not remember it," I said. *"There have been too many fine meals since our last meeting."*

Before I could defend myself, my sister drew blood, raking her talons across my forearm in three even slashes. I watched as she sucked the blood from the water as if she were inhaling a fine mist. Her eyes glowed brighter, and she bared her teeth. The water around us began to pulse with her strange light. She had a grip on me and again I could not swim away, trapped in the whirlpool that grew around us.

"I curse you, brother. I curse your arrogance and your indifference. I curse you to carry the pain of every kill, the remorse of every family you destroyed, and the guilt to know what you've done until the day you find true forgiveness among the humans."

The whirlpool grew tighter and faster, whipping around me in a frenzy and pulling me free of my enraged sibling. I was lost to the pace of it, spinning and spinning until in a daze I lost consciousness.

When I came to, the sun was high in the sky. I'd been floating above the waves for some time, based on the dryness in my mouth, the cracks in my lips, the ache of my skin. As I flexed my arms and tested my tail, a fresh ache screamed in my chest. It was a sharp and heavy pain, as hooks hung on my heart, dangling at the end of an anchor.

I ducked under the waves, seeking solace, but the water echoed disembodied screams all around me.

I tried to plug my ears. I tried to block it out. But the longer I stayed in the water, the clearer the horrors became.

A woman's voice cut across the others, thick with agony and choked with tears.

"All that washed up was his left arm," she said. "They had to cut his finger off to return his wedding band because the flesh was so waterlogged. I can't believe we lost him like this. What could possibly do such a thing?"

I knew immediately without any further details, my gut twisting in recognition, that this was the wife of a fisherman I had eaten one early morning. I was enraged at the encroaching boats on my territory and initially thought to scare them off. But one curious bite ignited a frenzy and I'd devoured all of him save his left arm.

I shook my head and took off, trying to outpace the voice. Instead, as that voice grew quieter, another took its place, as if the waves were bringing me new sobs with every push of the current.

"I should've gone with her." A man this time. "All she wanted to do this weekend was swim in the ocean, finally. She waited her whole life, and I couldn't be assed. I didn't want to leave my beer unfinished, so she went alone. And now…" a rattling crash as if something heavy was broken. "Now she's never coming back."

This one was a young woman, alone in the water, legs kicking lazily above me as she floated in the sun. I hadn't even been hungry.

I took off in a different direction but still the waves insisted. Still my heart hung in heavy pain.

It was silent for just a moment, finally. I nearly threw up from the sudden, jarring, all-encompassing silence. And then.

"Where's Daddy?"

I sped up to the surface, not giving a damn who did or didn't see me. There was a beach to my right, a good distance away even with my natural speed. I headed straight for it, keeping my head above the waves.

After some time, the water became too shallow for me to continue swimming. I ground against the sand, hauling myself forward fistful by fistful of sand until I could feel the sun on my exposed flank. I looked back to see my tail so far from the water that the tide barely lapped against it as it began to go out.

The sun beat down. Birds circled overhead. The sand was scorching.

I laid my head down, closed my eyes, and thought of the days before I met the mersibling who ruined my life.

I could never return to that moment. So I would return to whatever seafoam I was born of, giving my body over to the hungry gulls above.

9

Evelyn

"I really don't think it's a good idea," Caoimhe's voice echoed off my bathroom walls. I stuck my tongue out at my phone while I finished applying my foundation. "You're a wreck. You really think you're gonna be up for dealing with your coworkers?"

I never responded to C's text the night before, so exactly as predicted, she called the next morning. I caved immediately when she asked if everything was okay, catching her up as succinctly as I could while stretching in my all-too-empty bed.

"My coworkers are the ones who have to deal with me, C, don't forget that." I dusted blush over my cheeks before deciding against a contour. The last few days had hollowed my face enough. Was Lost Mershark Boyfriend a new look?

"Fair," Caoimhe laughed into the phone. "But I'm worried about you. You do this, where something bad happens and you just go back to work like it didn't."

I shrugged, opening and closing several eyeshadow palettes indecisively. "Nothing wrong with maintaining structure in the face of total chaos," I said. "I went to school every day regardless of whether or not I'd go home to the same house I left from."

"Just because something *has* worked for you doesn't mean it's the only way," Caoimhe continued. "You have to learn to take care of yourself."

"How's the boundary-setting going with your mom?" I snapped, irritated that I suddenly hated every eyeshadow I owned.

I could hear C roll her eyes through the phone. She let the silence stretch between us and I caved first.

"Fine," I said, picking up the neutral palette I'd set down four times already and haphazardly rubbing it onto my lids with my fingertip. "I'll take a half-day."

"Thank you," Caoimhe said with a small sigh. "Really, Eve, thank you. I hate that I'm not there."

"I miss you too," I said, blowing a kiss to the phone before applying my favorite dupe for Liv Tyler's lipstick in The Lord of the Rings. "But focus on what you're there for. I'm a big tough girl, I can handle things on my own."

I had purposefully left out all mention of my latest helper, Billy. I was trying to avoid even thinking about him.

"I know you can," C said. "But that doesn't mean you should. Please accept Patrick's help and whoever else from the BUS is available."

"Oh, Patrick has already helped enough," I muttered.

"What was that? You sound far away."

I picked my phone up off the counter and clicked off the bathroom light.

"I gotta head into work, C. I promise to text you later," I said.

"Only a half day. Don't burn yourself out."

I rolled my eyes but smiled. Caoimhe really loved me, even if her way of showing it was to be a little overprotective. She'd tried to bully me out of dating Will when we weren't actually dating because she was worried he'd eat me.

The jokes write themselves.

"Only a half day, I promise." We said our goodbyes, promised again to text, and hung up. I took a deep breath before strutting down the glass-encased stairwell that led to the building's front door. If I had to be on display every morning, I'd decided I would make it my own personal pump-up moment. By the time I stepped out onto the street and headed toward work, I could feel my former swagger aligning in my gut.

The office was full of the usual harried conversations and phone calls that made up the background of a morning at a busy newspaper office. The afternoon would be silent, with each and every photographer and reporter out on assignment and the design team hard at work now they could focus.

"Sharp." Harvey Pottsman thought he was old school despite this being his first job out of grad school. He only referred to us by last name, still made us pitch in a round robin, and chewed on a toothpick as if it were a fat stogie.

"Pottsman," I responded, reaching my desk and immediately finding nowhere to set anything down. It was covered in red roses, arrangements crammed into several heavy glass vases that threatened to snap the cheap particle board in half.

"Those came for you," he said. "Your new boyfriend?"

I reached for the card, ignoring the question.

"For your thoughts," it read. *"Because diamonds would break your cheap desk."*

I ripped the card in half and dropped it in the bin under my desk.

"Uh oh," Harvey mocked. "Ex-boyfriend then."

"Did you need something?"

"Damn, Sharp, I thought a week watching skinny people walk around would put you in a better mood," he said, holding his hands up.

I picked my bag back up and threw it over my shoulder, heading for one of the empty rotation desks the freelancers sometimes used. Harvey followed.

"So, when are you sending your coverage?"

"Excuse me?" I sent the draft before Will and I went to dinner in New York, making sure there would be no confusion about missing deadlines.

"Your article about the mermaid clothes," he said. "I don't have it."

"You wouldn't have it," I said, trying not to slam my laptop on the empty desk. "Because Carrie has it for edits."

"Why don't I have it?"

"Harvey, I love our little chats, but I don't have time to explain to you how to do your job today." I sat down, opened my laptop and began furiously clicking at my backed-up inbox. The idiot continued to hover. I heard him breathe a few times as if steadying himself. I refused to look up.

"You know, that's not—"

I slammed the laptop shut and he flinched, cutting off his own thought.

"I'm taking a mental health day," I said, shoving everything back into my bag with more rage than I'd unpacked it.

"For what?" he asked.

"That question is fucking illegal," I hissed, leaning into him and relishing how he shrunk back. "But if you must know, my boyfriend threw himself into the Hudson two nights ago and they haven't found him—his body."

I stormed out, leaving Harvey stunned in silence behind me.

I'd deal with all that later.

In the elevator, I sent Caoimhe a simple text.

Me: You were right.

It barely took a minute for her to respond.

Caoimhe: Proud of you. Enjoy shopping for me.

But I wasn't going to indulge in my normal mental health day routine—shopping, perfect French fries, a vampire movie with a glass of wine. No, I was going to take my frustrations out another way.

* * *

"Oh, I didn't know we picked up street fighting as a hobby." Marie clicked her teeth at me as I set my fingers on the padded tabletop riser.

I winced. "Are they that bad?"

Marie was almost sixty, thin as a rail, dressed head-to-toe in black and was never without orange-red lipstick. She was the product of a certain era of East Coast beauty schools which meant my nails could only be what she called "normal" colors unless it was Halloween or a special occasion. If I asked for anything different—green, blue, neon—she would blow a bubble out of her ever-present gum and roll her eyes before telling me I'd never beat her husband count with nails like that. The current number to beat was five.

She was also the only person I took advice from.

I looked down at my hands. The fish scales she'd meticulously sketched across my ring fingernail for the mermaid show were practically scratched off and several of my other nails were chipped or broken from wrestling with not-my-Will on the sidewalk.

Marie sat down and went to work, quickly dissolving my destroyed manicure and whipping out her tray of "respectable" nail colors.

"If I don't ask for anything weird, can we do coffin for the shape?" I put on an exaggerated pout and batted my eyes. "Pweeese?"

In response, she whacked the back of my hand with her file.

"I'm not giving you anything long if you're gonna be scrappin'," she said.

"I promise, it's not on my regular schedule—"

Marie flipped my hands over, gently tapping where my nails had dug into my palms leaving small, scabbed crescents. I must've clenched them at some point—flying with Billy? Screaming at Will? How had this become my life?

"Come back without these, I'll let you have orange coffins," she said, smacking her gum and flipping my hands back over.

"Deal," I said. But the excitement I should've felt was engulfed by the memories of the last few days.

"You okay?" Marie asked, pencil eyebrows knit together in worry. "Is this about that new piece of trouble you've been chasing?"

That's what men were to Marie—pieces of trouble. She didn't think they deserved the recognition of being the entire problem, but they usually slotted into a larger issue you may or may not already have.

I shook my head then stopped. "Kind of?"

She clicked her teeth again.

"What did I tell you?"

"Black nail polish is for teenage goths?"

She smacked me with the nail file again and I giggled, the gloom lifting temporarily.

Marie fiddled expertly with my cuticles before whipping out a bright red polish. I shook my head again and pointed to the maroon nestled in the back of the tray. She rolled her eyes but made the swap.

"Chase goals, Gucci, and gold. Never guys."

"The three Gs," I nodded solemnly.

"Tell me 'bout 'em," she said, focusing in on my nails.

She meant my Gs—my goals at work or for myself, my latest fashion scores, and how I was saving for my future.

I sighed.

"Well, I did just fly out to cover an exclusive show in New York," I said. Marie stopped what she was doing and clapped, a grin splitting her face. She had unnaturally white, square teeth and I could see the gum clenched between them. I beamed back.

"That's my fucking girl," she said.

"And if Carrie likes my coverage, I can ask her about Paris."

Marie put a perfectly manicured hand over her heart, closing her eyes and sighing dramatically. We'd been discussing my chances at covering Paris Fashion Week—the only fashion event in the only city in the world I'd dreamed of since I was a little girl. When Carrie had announced The World would be sending a reporting team this year, I had obsessed over how to ensure I was on it. Obviously, I'd immediately told Marie.

"You're gonna do it, girl," she said. "It's gonna be your year, I can feel it."

I let the praise simmer. In Marie's salon, surrounded by beauty advertisements from the 80s, inhaling chemicals that would destroy my sense of smell before I was fifty, I could believe her. Will would come back, I'd go to Paris, and the next year would be mine.

"Thanks, Marie," I said, letting go of a heavy breath. "You have no idea how much I needed to hear that."

After my appointment, I was feeling optimistic and motivated. First step in claiming the year Marie foresaw? Finding Will.

I dialed Patrick without thinking that it was broad daylight and he'd be dead asleep. When he didn't answer, I headed straight for Caoimhe's building where I knew the Boston Unusualities Society met.

If I couldn't find the whole crew, I knew Pete, the (literal) troll that owned the building, would be there at least.

I needed to know how to find Will. I needed to know what Billy's fucking deal was.

I needed to not be alone.

A few quick stops on the T and I was clicking across the dangerously charming cobblestones that lined Caoimhe's street. It was romantic as hell so of course she'd chosen to live there, but it was hell on my precious shoe collection. I'd snapped off a heel more times than I could count going to her place.

And to Will's.

Shit.

I stopped with my hand on the double front door of the building. Will lived across the hall from Caoimhe, both on the third floor. In the hazy chaos of my morning, I hadn't considered that going to the BUS building meant also going to their building and facing Will's empty apartment.

A totally irrational thought took hold and I let it, hope hauling me forward by my heart. I sprinted up the stairs, wheezing as I reached the top but refusing to stop until my hand was pounding on his front door.

What if he had come home?

"Will," I called in-between gasps, slamming the heel of my hand against the door. "Will, goddamn it, open up." I switched back to a fist and pounded repeatedly. I stopped for a moment to press my ear against the door. Was I imagining the sound of shuffling?

"You motherfucker!" I kicked the door and shook the handle. Why hadn't I made him give me a key? "I know you're in there, open the fuck up!"

I dropped my bag and kicked off my heels, stepping a few paces back and gearing up to slam the door with my body when a familiar voice rose up from the floor below.

"Miss Sharp," Pete drawled. "May I help you?"

"I need in to Will's apartment," I leaned over the railing, looking down at the troll's bulbous features. "Please. It's an emergency."

"Is he not at home?"

"He might be, I don't know, but I have to know he's—"

"Miss Sharp, I cannot allow access to a tenant's apartment without express permissions."

"I have it."

"You do not." Pete was coming up the stairs now, his flat, bare feet scraping callouses across the wood. I tried not to stare too long at his long cracked nails growing from toes so hairy you could braid them. I didn't need to be judging.

He *was* literally a troll.

His usually manic brown hair had been slicked back into a low ponytail. With his hairy mole and yellowed eyes, the effect was more sex offender than founding father.

"Pete, something has happened to Will. He's been cursed and he's not himself," I said. "I lost him in New York, and he could be here. Please let me in."

"This is most serious, Miss Sharp," he said, hands remaining clasped behind his back. "We will need to—"

"Pete, if you don't let me in, I will let myself in." I pinched between my eyes where a headache was growing. Some feral, rabid part of me was going to start chewing on the doorframe if I couldn't get into that apartment. It was taking all my focus and energy to reign that part in.

"I cannot allow that, Miss Sharp," he said, pulling a flip phone from the clip on his belt. He held the first key down for a moment before raising it to his ear.

My jaw dropped. I was witnessing the only person to still use speed dial in this century.

"Hello Miss…" he glanced at me and coughed, clearing his throat. "Hi, Kelly."

My eyes popped wide to match my dropped jaw. No fucking way.

"I'm with Miss Sharp. She says that Mr. Burleigh has gone missing." There was a shriek on the other end and Pete clapped the phone shut before it could echo further.

"She should be here in a few moments," he said. "In the meantime, do please join me downstairs for a cup of tea while we wait."

I watched him go down the stairs before glancing back to Will's door. Now would be the perfect time to kick it in. I crept forward, pressing my ear against the door a second time. Silence on the other side.

If Will *was* home, he didn't want to see me right then. But he probably wasn't. And I wasn't sure which hurt more.

Besides, Pete had Kelly Nerida, the siren owner of Mister Flipper, on speed dial. *And* he referred to her with her first name—he didn't call *anyone* by their first name. That juicy bit of gossip could keep me busy while I figured out how to solve my Schrödinger Mershark problem.

"Could we have a beer instead?" I called, trailing behind him into the depths of the building.

10

Will

New England, 50 Years Ago

"'Sha doing, buddy?"

The slurred voice startled me awake. I couldn't move my head without feeling like my brain was slamming into my skull. My limbs were heavy and my skin pulled taut as if it had been crisped over coals.

When I was able to finally look at the person interrupting my death, I couldn't focus well enough to notice any recognizable features. It was nighttime, however, and they were definitely not afraid of me.

"Alright? You out here all nekkid." The unfocused form swayed dangerously to one side before they swung an arm to find their balance. They crouched down and I smelled something chemical and foul in the air as they spoke close to my face. "Come to Uncle Joe. We'll getcha right."

Uncle Joe patted my back roughly and the singing pain of my sunburnt skin was enough to wake me up the rest of the way. I sat up, the world spinning dangerously off kilter. As I waited for it to settle, I noticed my body felt lighter. Something was different.

My stomach dropped down to unfathomable new depths as my eyes finally focused on my lower half.

Where there had once been the strong, sleek shape of a shark's tail and dorsal fin, there now lay two pale skinny human legs. I tapped one and nearly screamed in shock as the touch fired up into my brain.

Those were mine.

I had legs.

How did I have legs?

I pressed the heels of my palm into my eyes and tried to think. I tried to call up the shark part of myself but found only the barest whisper.

Survive, it said.

I had tried to kill myself to avoid living with the pain of a human heart, and the shark within me refused, instead transforming me entirely so I could adapt to this new world I had dragged myself into.

And the greatest joke of all was that my heart still hung heavy with those piercing hooks. The waves crashed against the beach, threatening the faintest of screams with each dissolution.

"Ey," the form who had spoken to me early called again. This time, when I turned to look, I saw the clear silhouette of a human man in rags waving to me. He held a glass bottle with some kind of liquid in it and he gestured toward the fire behind him. "Get right."

Unsure what to do with my new legs, I tried to mimic the man's movements—upright on two legs, arms at my side. But I immediately fell flat. My limbs were pins and needles from however long I had slept and my skin screamed with every movement.

"'s'wrong wit you?"

I shook my head.

"Ya stupid?" The man came and crouched directly in front of me, spewing more of his foul breath into my face. Up close I could see the glazed look in his blue eyes, the dark shadows on his cheeks, the dirt and facial hair pocked across his face. His teeth were yellow, and it was clear he was missing a few.

I thought of my mersibling and realized that was one thing me and this fellow had in common—missing teeth. Maybe there was more common ground.

"Stupid," I echoed back to him, testing out my new voice. I had less teeth than I was used to, and the word didn't quite shape well. But the man nodded solemnly.

"I thought ya might be, stayin out here like ya did." He took a long swig off the bottle and then gestured to the fire a second time. "Come on. Getcha right."

I shook my head again. I couldn't stand or move without my body protesting. Maybe there was still a chance I could die if I stayed where I was.

"Alright, stupid," he said. He leaned down without warning and scooped me up in his arms. He carried me across the sand in a zig-zagging dance, humming something to himself breathlessly as he did so. But his heroism was short-lived. He caught his toes in the sand and stumbled, sending me flying forward through the air.

I landed heavy on my side, dangerously close to the fire, slamming the front of my head against a piece of driftwood. Pain lanced across my vision, white hot and then gone. The world had not stopped tilting and something warm and wet trickled down over my eye. I reached up, my hand coming away covered in blood.

"Whoopsy daisy oopsy loopsy," the man sang, stumbling up to the fire and dusting the sand off his face. It sparked in the fire behind him as he turned to inspect me. "Yeralright," he said in one long word I didn't understand. He pulled off the first layer of his clothes and handed it to me, gesturing to the wound on my head.

I held it there and accepted the bottle he handed to me. He gestured for me to drink from it, so I did. The liquid was bitter and burned so intensely I immediately spit it back out. The man snatched the bottle back from me, muttering something about waste.

"Kinda man can't hold his shwiskey?"

"Stupid," I said, which earned a guffaw. The man took a swig, then handed me back the bottle. This time I forced myself to swallow.

A heady warmth spread through my chest immediately, momentarily easing the ache in my heart. Without waiting, I drank deep a second time, relishing how the burn seemed to disintegrate the anchors I'd been trying to escape. I didn't need to die—I just needed an endless supply of schwiskey.

"Told ya," the man said. "Uncle Joe getcha right." He smiled at me, his few teeth glowing in the firelight.

A wind whispered by us and I shivered. I looked down at my new form again, confused. Was I cold? Why didn't I have any blubber?

"Ah yeah," he said. "Put that on." He gestured to the cloth I held to my face. It was covered in blood when I pulled it away. When I reached up to feel my forehead, I found a gash across my eyebrow, wincing immediately at the touch. But there was no blood trickling down my face so I attempted to shrug into the clothing.

It was made of some scratchy thick material that further irritated my burned skin. I tried to fit my head through the big hole and my arms through the little one, but apparently that was wrong. The man—Uncle Joe, as he had referred to himself repeatedly now—howled with laughter and nearly rolled into the fire.

"You are stupid," he said, as if someone had lied to him otherwise. "Don't even know how to put on a sweater. I should let you freeze."

"Stupid," I said. "Sweater."

"The little hole for your little noggin," he said, pointing to each part of the sweater. "The long holes for your arms. The big hole for your big ass—" He stopped dead and squinted at a part of me that made me cross my legs and twist away.

"Well, I'll be damned," he said. "God seen fit to bless you better than the rest of us." He put a solemn hand over his heart before pulling a sack from behind the driftwood where he was perched. He rummaged around for a while before producing more clothes.

"Your legs through each hole on those," he said. "Gotta protect that blessing, Stupid."

11

Will

New England, 50 Years Ago

The only thing that held the pain at bay was the liquor Uncle Joe gave me. So I didn't stop drinking.

I learned more words while sleeping on the beach—some from Joe, some from the families that passed by.

Cold.

Hungry.

More.

Mine.

Gone.

Empty.

Gross.

Scary.

Low-life.

Vagrant.

Each time I formed my new mouth around the sounds, adding to my vocabulary.

Uncle Joe thought this was hilarious, cackling into a dry hacking cough every time. He was nice so long as he had a shwiskey bottle in his hand. I found out quickly the punishment for not keeping him in a steady supply. Getting kicked while I was sleeping because he was in a foul mood felt somehow worse than dodging harpoons in the water.

I started wandering through town while Uncle Joe slept during the day. The pavement was harsh on my bare feet, the heaviness returning two-fold to my heart. It seemed the longer I kept it numb, the sharper the sensation when it returned. And still the guilt weighed on my shoulders. Constant, ever-present, unforgiving. Without shwiskey to alleviate my symptoms, the curse made me want to lay back down on the sand and wait for the seagulls to pluck my flesh apart. There was no other way out from under this.

At least there were no mournful voices on land.

I got good at stealing. Who wouldn't in my lack-of-shoes?

At first, I was invisible. Incredibly, it wasn't *my* shame or guilt that made the people in the store avoid looking at me for too long. Their eyes slid right off me so they could stay comfortable in their own lives.

I wouldn't get why until much later.

So I took advantage, swiping shwiskey bottles here and there, then not so here-and-there. After I drunkenly tried to walk out with a crate under my arm, the store owner chased me out with a gun.

Things got harder after that. There was less shwiskey. Joe got meaner. I started begging, which my newfound invisibility totally blocked. If no one would stop and listen, stop and look, then no one would put anything in my outstretched hands.

I missed the quiet of the ocean, the simplicity of the water through my gills. The air here smelled like so many things all at once *and* it carried sound. It was too full. And still my heart hung heavy, dropping further and further down into my body some days I could barely feel it beating.

One night, I found myself in an alley in town. There was no shwiskey again and Joe had started throwing huge chunks of driftwood across the beach while screaming. I didn't need any more scars on my face so I ran, not stopping until I could no longer hear him.

I leaned against the brick wall, catching my breath. It was a muggy summer night and I desperately wanted to plunge into the cool water to wash the sweat and dirt from my new skin. I hated how dirty this form was. It needed so much cleaning—shaving, washing, scrubbing, trimming.

Noise and light streamed from a sudden open door, and I ducked down, throwing my arms over my eyes. I couldn't do it. Not tonight.

"Hey," a gruff voice called. "You. You the bum's kid?"

I waited, ducked under my own arms. Sometimes if I stood still enough people would remember I was invisible.

"Come on, kid," the voice continued, closer this time. "Don't be like that."

I pulled myself in tighter, tried to make myself smaller. Some hidden piece of me, smothered by too much shwiskey, tried to gnash its teeth but it didn't have the energy.

"God, look at ya," the voice sighed, and the gruffness smoothed. "No one's kid should live like this."

I glanced up, peering one eye up at the source of the voice. The man was tall, broad-shouldered, black shirt rolled up to reveal muscular forearms with the type of artwork I'd seen sailors display at sea. The alley light shone off his bald head, and he reached up to stroke the bushy read beard that stuck out in all directions from his chin as he considered me with dark, pinpoint eyes.

"Not a kid," I said.

He nodded sympathetically. "Sure," he said. I don't think he believed me.

"Not Joe's kid," I said. I wasn't anyone's kid. And if it involved getting kicked and thrown around all the time, I figured that was better for it. Sucked to be anyone's kid if that was the truth.

"Right," the man said. He nodded thoughtfully for a moment. "What's your name? Will you work?"

I tried to think if I'd ever been called anything other than brother or Stupid. There wasn't a need for names in the water. But humans had them—especially humans who wanted to be safe and normal and accepted. I'd have to figure it out later. Right now, I needed help.

"Will work," I said, although I wasn't sure what I was agreeing to.

"Alright, Will," the man said. "My barback bailed and the nets got hauled in this afternoon, the place is packed. I need help. I can't pay you, but I'll give you a meal and a drink and you can sleep in the office once the place empties out."

I didn't know what most of the words he said meant but I heard "drink" and "sleep" and I stood up, nodding emphatically.

"Work," I said. "Will work. Will work." This man would have shwiskey. And it was a bonus that maybe I wouldn't be sleeping next to a volatile Uncle Joe on the sand.

Inside, a low ceiling hung over the heads of ruddy-faced fishermen, some stripped down to thin tank tops against the heat. Sweat shone on every set of cheeks, teeth flashed in laughter and in rage. Looking out over the crowd, I remembered watching a pod of dolphins hunt and I felt a shiver go down my spine.

I was not the predator here. I was not the king.

"Alright, Will," the man said. He pointed to an empty bin just in front of us beneath the bar. "We're outta ice. Start there." He pointed to a large bucket just to the left of the bin and gestured toward the end of the bar where it opened onto a room that was a hot-white pit of heat and noise. "The machine is in the kitchen. Keep your head down and stay out of the way. The cooks won't bother you. Come back and fill the bin."

I nodded, heading off dutifully to follow the alien instructions.

I made it maybe three steps into the kitchen before a huge sweaty man in a stained apron blocked my path. "Get the *fuck* out," he bellowed.

Before he could swat me with the spatula in his hand, the bald man appeared over my shoulder. I don't know how he got there so fast. Maybe he'd followed me.

"He's working for the night, Carl," the bald man bellowed back, something strange pulling at the vowels in his words. They got longer, like they were being pulled down by something heavy and his mouth needed a break.

"No," Carl leveled the spatula at the bald man. "Arnie, we are *not* taking in strays. Not tonight."

"Didn't see you complaining when I brought in Bonnie," Arnie said.

A tension shot between the two men, and I fought the urge to duck.

"Fine," Carl said. "But he's not serving food smelling like that. We won't get business again."

"Like he smells any worse than that bullshit you serve." Arnie gave me a shove. "Ice machine is that way, kid."

I made it to the machine in a few steps and shoved open the sliding door. I bent down to receive the waft of chilly air that brushed my face. This was not the same ice I knew, and yet it had to be. I reached out to see if it felt the same when a shout from the kitchen made me flinch. Remembering where I was, I shoved the bucket into the machine, coming away with a heavy haul of ice.

The metal handle of the bucket, now weighed down with several pounds of ice, cut into my bare hands. I had to waddle to get it through the kitchen, under Carl's watchful gaze, and back behind the bar. When I finally made it to the empty bin where my journey had started, Arnie was already in action, pouring shots, filling beers four at a time, and sliding glasses across the bar with expert precision.

"'Bout time!" He called but he threw me a wink. A few people leaning on the bar arched their eyebrows at me before snickering. "I thought Carl cut you up into hamburger meat."

"Is that what you're serving in this joint?" a voice called from the crowd.

"I plead the fifth, man, I know one of you is married to the health inspector's sister."

A roar of laughter washed over the bar, like waves crashing against a beach. The sound buoyed me for a moment as I dumped the bucket into the bin. My whole body was shaking from a type of exertion I'd never had to do in this form. Is this how weak I would be until I returned to the ocean?

"You brought in another stray?" A man directly in front of Arnie asked. His eyes were glassy, and he didn't seem to be looking at anyone in particular. Arnie set a beer down in front of him with a particularly loud *thunk*.

"How'd ya know?"

"I can smell him," the man said, mouth turning down.

"Nah, Lenny, that's your own ass," Arnie shot back and another wave of laughter erupted.

"Mea culpa," the man said, taking a huge swig off his beer. "Buy the guy a shot, on me. Call it a welcome."

"You heard the man, kid," Arnie said. "What's your poison?"

I stared blankly.

"Come on, kid, whatcha want to drink? Lenny's buying."

"Shwiskey," I said, a grin splitting my face in half. My heart thudded in my chest, rising from the depths at the promise of relief.

Lenny laughed. "A man after my own heart," he said. He nodded and Arnie poured the amber liquid into a glass a little taller than my own thumb. I downed it immediately, letting the burn incinerate the first arms of guilt that held me down.

"You take that like a pro," Arnie said, something strange flitting across his face before the smile returned. "I'm running out of glasses, go grab the clean rack from the kitchen."

The rest of the night was a blur. I filled the ice bin, brought clean dishes, took dirty ones. I restocked the beer cooler twice then stomped on the cardboard crates and threw them in the massive metal container in the alley that I'd been crouched next to only a few hours prior.

Finally, the bar began to clear out. Arnie stood behind the bar talking quietly with a customer. I was standing still for the first time in hours, my limbs shaky from the running and the shwiskey that customers kept buying me as The New Kid. Arnie waved at me and called across the bar.

"Carl, make the kid something to eat."

"No," Carl called back from behind the swinging door.

Arnie excused himself from the customer and cleared the distance to the kitchen at a startling speed.

Before anyone could blink, Carl came flying out of the kitchen, landing with a thud that shook every glass behind the bar.

Arnie stood in the kitchen doorway, muscles taught, face crimson, a vein bulging in his neck.

"The fuck did I tell you?" Arnie said through gritted teeth.

"I'm not feeding a street bum cause you got a conscience," Carl said with a surprising amount of pride for someone who was struggling to get up off the floor. "He can't stay here, he's disgusting."

"You got two options," Arnie said, stalking to Carl with a slow, meaningful pace I recognized. He was homing in on his prey. "You can make the kid a meal, or I can kick your ass." He stopped in front of Carl, lifting one foot and settling it between his legs.

"Seeing how you can't even get your fat ass off the ground, it would be the easiest ass whooping of my life," Arnie said. Carl yelled in pain but I couldn't see what was happening. "You're the disgusting one, Carl." He let Carl out from under his foot and the cook finally scrambled to his feet. His shoulders were folded in, his head hung low.

"Go make the kid a fucking burger," Arnie said, moving aside so Carl could return to the kitchen.

"Come on," Arnie said. "Let me show you the office."

On the opposite side of the bar from the kitchen, a crooked door hung low on the wood-paneled wall. Inside, a single table that looked like it'd been pulled in from the bar, was covered in stacks of dusty paper. There was nothing on the walls and only a bare lightbulb on the ceiling.

"It's not much, but it's indoors," Arnie said. He pointed in the corner to a neatly rolled blanket and a small square pillow.

I turned to Arnie and my shwiskey-floating heart immediately made me think of the families I'd watched on the shore. When one of them did something good, the others would wrap their arms around them and everyone would be happy.

I wrapped my arms around Arnie who stiffened the minute I touched him. He smelled like sweat and beer. After a moment, he patted my shoulder solidly and pried me off him.

My first hug.

"Go eat," he said. "You can work tomorrow if you want."

12

Evelyn

Boston, Present Day

I want you to imagine a troll's apartment. No. More than that. Okay, also more than that. Like *really* dig into what you think the filthy, dank, hoarder hole probably looks like. Got it? Good. That was not Pete's apartment.

Everything was the pristine white and chrome of a modern luxury hotel. Despite the basement location, natural light filtered in from renovated skylights, bouncing off thoughtfully placed mirrors. The soft smell of cinnamon wafted through the air as I took in the mid-century modern furniture, the marble countertops, the Smeg appliances.

"Holy shit," I breathed as I walked in.

"I'm afraid I don't keep beer on hand, but I could open a bottle of red if you'd prefer?" The troll held a delicate green bottle over his forearm so I could inspect the label like we were someplace with a Michelin star and not a basement unit. I nodded, dumbstruck. He gave an agreeable grunt and set about opening the bottle. He produced a delicately intricate glass contraption designed to look like two dragons in flight over a mirrored lake. As he poured the wine into it, the dragon mouths filled with the red liquid before swirling out in a spiral to fill the lake.

"Holy shit," I repeated.

"Elven make." Pete gave me a smug grin. "After you've used their aerators, all other wine will unfortunately taste like dirt. I apologize for the future impact on your palette."

I was too dumbfounded to check his self-satisfaction, so I let him pour me a glass from the aerator—Pembroke, stemless—which he did by placing the glass under a cleverly hidden tap to empty the lake portion of the aerator slowly.

"No colored liquids in the living room, right?" I said with half my usual sass. I was intimidated to drink anything *anywhere* in his apartment.

"Please, make yourself comfortable." Pete gestured to the low sofa nestled into a uniquely shaped but stylish shag rug. I nodded, suddenly feeling gouache with my shoes still on. But it would be awkward to walk back to the door with my wine in hand to take them off, so I kept moving forward.

"Pete...I...*wow.*" I took a sip of the wine, continuing to look around. The wine *was* perfection, transporting me to a vineyard somewhere in California where the sun's slanted rays bounced off dark wood trellises and aged oak barrels stood tall against the late summer sky. "I had no idea you were so..." I used my free arm to gesture stupidly around the room.

Pete, to his credit, simply nodded and sipped his own glass.

"My people are often assumed to be of a certain ilk," he said. "But we appreciate what others don't—the natural wonder of light that has traveled hundreds of miles to fill a cavern underground or a sunrise sparking against all parts of a bridge."

"Pete, you're a poet." I was shocked. Pete was the landlord. Pete was the troll. Now Kelly's name on speed dial was starting to make sense.

My compliment sent a flush through his sagging cheeks, and I couldn't help myself—I was a little charmed by it.

"I try to ensure beauty does not go unnoticed," he said, staring pointedly into his wine glass.

"Beauty like a certain tour company manager?"

"My relationship with Miss Nerida—"

"Kelly," I corrected.

"—Kelly," he gave me a look over his wine glass. "It is purely platonic."

"Sure," I said. I set my glass down on a royal purple geode coaster and crossed my legs. "But you want more."

"I want only what Kelly offers," he said, staring down into his drink.

"There's no secrets in that wine glass, Pete," I said. He glanced up at me, eyes wide, the blush growing deeper. "Nothing that isn't obvious from your face, anyway."

He cleared his throat and looked away again, something suddenly fascinating in the art to his right. I gave the tasteful landscape a quick glance before settling back on the troll. He needed a pedicure—the poor technician would need an electric sander to get any real work done—and a haircut. A facial, a trim, and some clothes with clean, simple lines. I refrained from holding my hands up in a fake frame like they always did prior to 90's movie makeover montages.

"Does she know how you feel?" I asked after a few moments.

"No," Pete sighed. "And it would sever our current friendship so I would rather you and I keep this superfluous emotion between us."

"Love is not superfluous, Pete," I said, sitting up straighter. I seemed to be talking about this a lot lately. Old Evelyn was screaming at me to stop being such a sap, especially given that the man currently holding my heart in his scarred hands was still *maybe* avoiding me. Or he was still *maybe* lost in the ocean and would *maybe* never come back.

I shook my head, trying to clear it.

Pete considered me for a moment. "May I inquire after Mr. Burleigh?"

I sighed. "You may. We were in New York," I said, continuing to tell Pete about the last few days. When I finished, he stood, walking to the sofa. He placed one thick hand on my shoulder. It was damp through my shirt and I had to consciously hold in a shudder.

"We will return your love to you," he said. "But it may take all of us. Hold strong."

My love. How many times would others say it to me before I accepted it? If even a troll noticed, then maybe it was time to be honest with myself.

Maybe I was in love.

Or I would be if he came back.

Wordlessly, Pete strode away into the back room and clicked the door behind him. I was left alone in his pristine living room with nowhere to put the weight in my chest. I picked my wine back up and sipped again. As much as I ached to drown in alcohol, the wine wouldn't let me, washing over my senses with every taste.

I let my eyes wander back to the landscape I'd noticed earlier. It was a pastoral country scene, the kind Thomas Kincaid loved with a covered wooden bridge and deep red fall foliage. But the longer I looked, the more I forgot the bridge and the trees. It was the space beneath all that the artist had chosen to focus on, swirling in layers of shadow and light to pull the viewer into a captivating hidden landscape that seemed to continue deeper than was physically possible given the two-dimensional medium. Was I imagining things or could I feel the draft of stepping into a cave? Could I hear the drip of water against stone someplace behind me?

Knocks on the door broke my trance and I stood, somewhat dizzy from having stared so hard.

The knocks continued until I crossed the apartment and opened the door. Kelly Nerida's frantic face met me.

The Latina siren was about my height with a soft round face framed by luxurious black curls. She wore her usual Mister Flipper uniform—jeans that fit her perfectly (so jealous) and a red polo with the company's logo stitched over her heart.

"Eve!" She wrapped me into a tight hug, throwing me off balance physically and emotionally. I had been under the impression Kelly didn't like me from the get-go, and she hadn't exactly been supportive of my relationship with Will. Will and Leith told me she didn't like *any* humans and I shouldn't take it personally—so naturally I immediately decided it was something I'd done. "I'm so sorry. We'll find him, it'll be okay." She gave me one last hearty squeeze before letting me go.

"What happened?" Her dark brown eyes searched mine and I wasn't sure I had it in me to repeat the story yet again.

"Miss Sharp, why don't you wait to explain to Kelly what has happened when we are with the rest of the Society?" Pete's voice came from the far end of the apartment. He was clicking the door shut behind him again, two thick leatherbound books under his arm. I noticed he had slipped into an expensive pair of loafers not unlike what Billy preferred and again I had a flash of his future self.

Oh yeah, we're doing a makeover montage.

"Does the BUS know?" I asked.

"I spoke with Miss Honorjaw," Pete said, shepherding me and Kelly out the front door. "She is calling an emergency meeting. The others should arrive shortly minus our vampiric members."

"Are you part of it now?" I asked Kelly who nodded.

"I joined while you were gone," she said. "Blood oath and all."

I had no idea if she was serious.

Pete led us just past his front door, the laundry machines humming behind us. He held up what looked like a couple of twigs tangled with a pocket-sized harp. He flicked the harp a few times, plucking out a few tinny notes, and I gasped as the brick wall in front of us rearranged itself into an archway. Stunned, I followed Pete and Kelly down the narrow, pitch-black stairwell until suddenly, we were stepping into a cavernous room filled with lanterns. Plush fabric hung from the ceiling and a delicately embroidered tapestry covered the back wall. A large round table made from deep magenta wood was in the center of the room.

I followed Kelly to the table and took the seat next to her. I noticed intricate carvings along the arms of the chairs and a small puff of dust rose from the cushion as I sat. Pete settled himself a few seats away to the right of the head of the table. He had barely flipped open the first leather book before the door screeched again and a spiky-haired woman wearing a tattered Metallica shirt and leather pants strutted through. Her keen, wide eyes took in me and Kelly before she visibly sniffed the air.

"Are we allowing humans?" she asked, joining us at the table.

"Under emergency circumstances," Pete said without looking up. "Miss Sharp is human, yes, but she also was the last to see the missing mershark."

"You're the feisty one's girlfriend," she said, angling that penetrating gaze at me. "Nice."

"Thanks?"

"What Roxy means," Kelly said, giving the woman a meaningful stare. "Is welcome and we hope we can help."

"No, I mean what I said."

"She's coming off a hunt," a voice called from the open doorway. It belonged to a squat bearded woman carrying a massive box of fresh pastries. The smell made my stomach flip and my mouth water simultaneously. Had I eaten? It didn't matter, I was going to. "Roxy can be a little meaner than usual if she didn't catch anything."

I tried not to think too hard about what or who Roxy might be hunting.

"I'm Wilhamena," the bearded woman said, giving me a genuine smile that crinkled her bright blue eyes. She had a darling smattering of freckles across her nose and cheeks, and her deep red beard and hair were braided to match, small gold hoops accenting the intricate work. "It's nice to finally meet you, Caoimhe and Leith have told us so much."

"All painfully true," I said, immediately snatching a steaming scone from the box she opened. I recognized the logo on the flap, and I remembered Caoimhe whispering to me one night that the Savvy Squirrel was run by a dwarf woman.

"Confectionary perfection as always, Miss Honorjaw," Pete drawled, delicately choosing a bear claw from the box. I tried not to look too closely at his yellowed nails.

"Are we expecting the shimmery thing?" Kelly asked before biting into a picture perfect donut, complete with pink frosting and rainbow sprinkles.

Roxy shook her head. "They're manifesting this week."

"Right, so it's just us gals and Pete then," Wilhamena sat on the other side of Roxy and next to Pete. I noticed the head of the table stayed empty. I wondered if that was where Patrick sat—or Caoimhe? It struck me how little I knew about my best friend's new involvement with the BUS.

"This meeting of the BUS is called to order," Pete said, flipping open the second leather book and scratching a note quickly onto the page. "It will begin with Miss Sharp relaying the circumstances of the disappearance of Mr. Burleigh to the Society."

Kelly reached over and took my hand. I was surprised at her gentleness but grateful all the same. I took a deep breath and began the story from the beginning.

13

Will

New England, 45 years ago

We admitted we were powerless over alcohol — that our lives had become unmanageable.

"Get fucked," I yelled across the bar, letting a wicked smile split my face as I slid the brown glass bottle down to the regular who was flipping me shit.

I turned to the next fisherman, still dripping water around him from the rainstorm raging outside. The bar was packed, just like it had been that first night five years ago and so many other times after. The only difference was Arnie had taken over the grill, kicking Carl out halfway through my time at Bears & Growlers.

Carl never did warm up to me. Arnie made that his problem instead of mine.

I'd graduated from sleeping in the office to staying with Arnie and his three huskies. It was a hairy, loud mess of a trailer but I had my own room with a door that closed and a window I could open on clear days. My tumultuous time with Uncle Joe was a nasty memory—a nightmare proved real only by the healed scar across my eyebrow.

I avoided the beach as if I were made of lead.

Which I still felt like I was.

Thankfully, there was always schwiskey.

And there was nothing like working in a bar to keep you in a steady supply of the only thing that kept the anchors from pulling down your heart.

"What're ya having, bud?" I asked the fisherman. He grunted out his order and I filled it quickly, hollering through the kitchen door for a basket of fries and a BLT. Arnie saluted to let me know he'd heard without breaking his expert dance of flipping burgers, dropping chicken tenders, salting fries.

Most days were like this, me and Arnie in sync in Bears & Growlers, not thinking about much else but filling glasses and wiping spills. I started each day with a swig of whiskey, following up the start of my shift with another. Then ended with a few more drinks to help lull me into sleep. It was almost a dosage, how I drank. And I was never sloppy. It was only enough to quell the constant ache in my heart.

But still, some early mornings, after the bar was closed and Arnie had drifted off with a husky under each arm, I'd watch the sunrise over the water just a stone's throw from the trailer. And I'd remember the power of my body cutting through the water, the thrill of the ocean reaching out around me. And just as intimately, I'd remember the taste of human flesh between my rows of teeth, and I'd have to find a toilet or trashcan or empty box to vomit into.

I hadn't shifted back since Uncle Joe found me on the beach. I couldn't. I was too terrified of what I'd see and hear in the water. That first memory haunted me still, waking me from a dead sleep in a cold sweat.

"They had to cut his finger off to return his wedding band because the flesh was so waterlogged."

Nothing more schwiskey couldn't fix. An extra swig or two on rough mornings and I was out the door, ready for the day.

It wasn't perfect. But it was fine. And I was grateful for every day I stayed out of the water and kept moving forward from my past.

I should've known it wouldn't last.

It was a rare slow night at Bears & Growlers. I was taking notes on inventory, getting ready to order stock when the door swung open. It slammed dramatically against the wall, screaming on its hinges, flooding the dim seating areas with the type of sunlight that made you feel guilty for being in a place like this so early.

"Alright, Clint Eastwood," I hollered, waving a hand at the silhouette in the door frame. Arnie had rented a bunch of movies with men shooting each other and slamming through swinging doors. I didn't understand what everyone was stressed about or why they were always sweating through their threats, but since I lived and worked with Arnie, he got to pick the movies we watched. He loved them—called Clint the last "true man" in Hollywood.

"Close the door, would ya?" I called, setting the clipboard down. The figure was backlit, so I couldn't see who they were. I assumed it was another regular, in a foul mood from a poor morning haul, and I busied myself with glassware until they arrived at the counter. Mean customers still made me nervous, like my ribs remembered Uncle Joe's temper more than my brain did, and I knew I wouldn't be able to return to the pending stock order until the person was served and no longer my problem.

"So, this is where you've been," a familiar voice had me whipping around to face my mersister. She was in her human form, sea glass scales replaced with porcelain skin, a shock of red hair twisting out from under the bucket hat crammed down low across her forehead.

She was dressed like I had been at first—borrowed clothes of all sizes and for all types of weather. There was the bottom of an evening gown poking out from under her rainbow wool sweater and she wore one sandal and one running shoe, neither with socks.

Despite how ridiculous she looked, there was no mistaking her wild eyes and sharp teeth, the hungry way she stared me down.

"Mirra," I said. The caged animal in my gut began to quiver.

She leaned across the bar, digging sharp nails into the wood as if she would shred it to shavings with one well-placed talon.

"Aye, brother," she hissed. "Did you think you could hide from me?"

I shook my head, frozen to the spot.

"Your actions will always catch up with you," she said, setting herself with a wet thump onto the barstool. "You cannot outrun your curse."

My breath came in ragged heaves. My heart pounded in my ears. Every instinctual piece of me was screaming at me to run out of the bar and never come back. If I kept running, she would never catch me.

"I will always find you," she said, as if reading my mind. She pulled a chain from around her neck covered in more than sharks' teeth now. But as if drawn to a bright light in the dark, I found my own tooth immediately. "We are connected."

My thoughts raced, tripping over each other to come up with the best exit strategy. There was the back alley where Arnie found me five years ago. Maybe she wouldn't be so persistent as to check *every* trash bin. But no, this was a sea witch with a vendetta. I couldn't make it that obvious.

I could leap over the bar and blow past her until I was sprinting down the street. If I kept going long enough, I'd make the next town before her and then—no. Not that either.

I could go back to the beach. If she followed, I'd trick her into meeting Uncle Joe and then maybe she'd never come back on land again.

"Hey," Arnie stood in the doorway to the kitchen holding a pair of tongs like a weapon. "Ya good, kid?"

I forced myself to take a breath and nodded.

"I'm sorry, I didn't mean to distract you," Mirra smiled sweetly at Arnie, all trace of menace gone. "I just wanted to visit with my brother a little while I was in town."

"You have a sister?" Arnie's face stayed the same and he never took his eyes off her. He was waiting for me to tell him I'd never seen her before, to throw her out, that this bitch was crazy.

He was waiting for me to ask for help.

But I couldn't drag Arnie into my curse. Not after everything he'd done for me.

"Yup," I swallowed around the dry lump in my throat. "This is Mirra."

Arnie turned to me, finally, and studied my face for a long time. I held it as naturally as I could until he finally said, "Alright, take a break and have a visit. It's slow enough in here, I'll be fine."

Mirra shrieked in glee and clapped her hands together. I grabbed a bottle of whiskey off the shelf and two highball glasses, pouring liberally into each.

"What is this?" she sniffed it and winced.

"Schwiskey," I said, savoring the burn of it down my throat. I imagined it was scouring my soul clean of all the things that Mirra's curse still held me responsible for. I imagined the heat blooming in my chest was freedom. When I opened my eyes, Mirra was watching me carefully. "What do you want?"

"I can't check up on my brother?"

"Not after cursing me to feel like hell all the time."

"Is that how it feels?" she cocked her head to the side, sending a fresh cascade of red hair tumbling down her shoulder. She pouted her lips out in mockery. "You poor thing."

I looked away from her, feeling the anchor weights return three-fold.

Of course she was right. I had done unforgiveable things and my curse simply ensured I felt the weight of them. I had no right to complain.

"Why haven't you returned to the water?" she asked, tracing one sharp claw along the edge of the highball glass. She still hadn't taken a sip. I refilled my own glass.

"You know why," I said.

"You barely discovered what the curse would do before you tried to beach yourself," she hissed. "I wouldn't have wasted such an intricate spell if I knew it would be that easy to hold you accountable."

We sat in silence for a moment as I polished off my second glass. This was more than my usual dosage for the hour, but I was far off from being drunk.

"Which was it?" she asked, a soft purr back in her voice.

I stared at her blankly.

"Which memory hit you first?"

"You're sick," I whispered.

"Tell me and I'll go away."

"Hey, kid," Arnie called through the window, motioning to an order I hadn't put in.

I motioned to Mirra to wait and quickstepped to the plate. Arnie grabbed the edge before I could take it.

"You good?" His eyes were crinkled in worry, the curve of his mouth pulled down. I didn't deserve his softness.

"Fucking dandy," I snapped, pulling the plate from his grip. "Where the fuck does this go?"

"Up your ass, then," Arnie rolled his eyes and threw a hand in the air, turning away from the window.

I scanned the restaurant, seeing only one other table occupied by a few surly looking fishermen. I dropped the plate between them, muttered something about it being on the house, and returned to my spot across from Mirra.

"You've made a friend," Mirra said, her multifaceted gaze trained on Arnie in the kitchen.

"No," I shook my head. I suddenly didn't want her to know if I had friends or a place to stay or a favorite of Arnie's huskies who sometimes woke me up in the mornings for a run through town when everyone else was still sleeping.

"He cares for you," she said, not looking away. "But he doesn't know."

"He's just a human," I said. "Just a stupid human."

Her gaze flicked back to me, and I was frozen again. There was the rage I remembered from our last meeting.

"Ah," she said, cocking an eyebrow. "So you *do* know they can be good. And you like this one." She pushed herself up from the barstool on unsteady legs. I remembered how strange it felt the first time I walked and wondered if this was her first attempt on land. "It seems your curse is already teaching you some things."

"It has."

"Are you sorry?" She was leaning across the bar now, claws leaving divots in the wood. Fear pulled all my bones into its loathsome grip, refusing me any movement. If she crossed the feeble wood barrier between us, I wouldn't have the guts to run.

"Yes," I breathed. *Stay on that side. Please stay on that side.* But despite the way Mirra turned and cocked her head at me, those swirling eyes threatening to pull me under if I looked too long, she stayed silent a moment. If she could hear my thoughts like in the water, she gave no indication.

"Would you know what you took from others if I took his life?"

"Yes."

She cocked her head the other way and grinned, her signature luminescence sparking out between her teeth. "We could make that deal."

"What?"

"An eye for an eye, a soul for a soul," she said. "A heartbreak for a heartbreak."

"I've had enough of making deals with you," I said, eyes trained on the scrabbling of her claws on the bar.

"Everything is a deal, brother," she said. "Trade one inhale for one exhale. Trade your steps for what you leave behind. You can't avoid making deals because you're scared."

"Trade a tooth for a mistake," I mumbled, glancing again to see that Arnie was still blessedly working in the kitchen, humming to himself.

"I could give you happiness," she said.

"Like you gave me freedom?"

"You warped my gift," she snapped and her claws crunched into the wood. She pulled herself up onto the bar so that her head hung ludicrously into the walkway where I worked. She looked up at me, swirling eyes maddening through streaks of red, stringy hair. "Don't you want to be happy?"

"I am," I said, feeling the lie fall flat.

Mirra tutted at me, shaking her head rhythmically from side to side.

"This is happiness?" she asked. I recognized the cloying sweetness that infused her words. "Miserable, drunk, watching the tide leave you behind each day?"

"You don't know anything about my life here," I said. "And if you want to make me happy, lift the curse." I jutted my chin up in a challenge and crossed my arms.

"That's what I'm offering," she said and the hairs on the back of my neck rose, tickling my senses like the current used to when a larger predator was swimming toward me.

"Explain," I said, holding my posture.

"You took my human," she said, and I didn't miss the venom in her voice. "Give me yours. I'll lift the curse."

"You could do that?"

"Of course," she scoffed. She pushed up on her forearms, lifting her head to look at me and kicking her awkward feet up behind her. She looked like one of those dancers who stood on tables in very high heels and very little clothing that Arnie sometimes watched in movies.

"If it's that easy, prove it."

She rolled her eyes. "Do I look like some stupid titan?" she hissed. "Make the deal and then I'll set you free."

Something nagged at the back of my mind and it was more than the guilt over how readily I would hand Arnie over for my own gain. Arnie had been the only human to believe I was more than some undesirable, that I deserved kindness and a warm place to sleep. Arnie stood up for me, housed me, clothed me, employed me.

Was there still so much shark in me that I would betray my human side for yet another of Mirra's twisted deals?

My human heart screamed from under the anchor weights. I downed another glass of whiskey. The heat bloomed, the pain left, but so did the clarity of my vision. This was more than I usually drank in a day already and we still had the dinner shift.

"You're not telling me something."

"What would I hide from you?"

I laughed, pouring another whiskey.

"How about 'I'm gonna fucking yank your tooth out now?' or, I dunno, 'taking away all your fear is gonna make you a psychopath?' Any of those would've been helpful." I slammed the bottle on the bar hard enough to jar the regular at the far end who was dozing into his beer.

Mirra slid back, resettling on her seat.

"Would those details have changed your mind?"

"I don't know, because I didn't have them," I said. "Can't choose an octopus' eighth leg if the first seven are choking you, ya know? No point in weighing hypothetical options—you never gave me the chance."

"Would it change your mind now?"

"What do you mean?" A chill crept up my spine. My feet felt fused with the floor and my shins ached from the way I arched my body to pull away from Mirra.

"I'll tell you this time," she said. "The details."

"Then tell me." There again, the nagging. I was forgetting something. Something important.

"I will devour your human the way you devoured mine," she said, flashing me those glowing teeth. "And then I shall undo the curse. You will be free to return to the ocean whenever you please."

"Without any more visions or voices?"

"Only those that you bring upon yourself."

The whole thing was trickery, I was sure.

But.

You could go home. The shark part of me was thrashing against my controls, desperate to make the decision for me. Cut free. Go forward. Never stop moving. I closed my eyes and tried to steady myself, the sound of the ocean in my ears almost as clear as if I were already diving down into its depths.

When I opened them again, multiple new patrons had shuffled in and were waving at me gruffly. I downed the latest whiskey I'd poured myself and began to take orders. But I was drunk. I dropped beers, mixed up which fisherman got which liquor over ice, and Arnie returned a ticket that looked like a toddler had doodled on it.

"Get a grip, man," he growled through the window, concern still etched across his face.

He didn't deserve my betrayal. He was a good man.

Home, my shark whispered.

As the bar grew more and more crowded, Mirra stayed exactly in place, her eyes never leaving me. A new guilt crawled onto my shoulders and threatened to pull me under—one that had nothing to do with my curse or the mersibling seated at my bar. No, this guilt was my own. I deserved the weight of it pressing against me as I continued to grapple with the opportunity presented.

For the first time in years, I let myself remember what it felt like to be enveloped by the ocean, to cut through the water. I remembered the sun filtering through, sparkling off coral and the glinting scales of fish. I remembered the joy of swimming from place to place, beholden to no one and nothing. I remembered, most of all, with a deep, aching pain in my chest, how it felt to be *light* again.

I downed another whiskey and started delivering food, focusing twice as hard on putting one foot in front of the other.

Free, my shark whispered. My knee hit the back of a chair and the entire tray flew across the room, landing in an explosion of burgers and angry yells.

I muttered apologies as I scrambled between the stomping boots of drunk and irritated customers. I tried to gather as many plates as I could, stacking them only for them to slide off each other again in a maddening cycle. A shadow loomed over me, and the familiar bulky presence of Arnie made me feel smaller than ever before.

"Go home," he said. His voice was not sharp, but it was not the kindness I was used to. He was clearly upset but when I glanced up to meet his eyes, all I found there was concern.

Yet another wave of guilt slammed across me and I wasn't sure I could keep my head above water anymore. I desperately wished to just be able to tread water for a moment without the fear of drowning in all this shame. Would it never stop?

All Arnie had ever done was help me and now, not only was I contemplating handing him over as Mirra's next meal, but I was fucking up his restaurant in the process.

I stood, trying to make sense of the world as it tilted one way and then the other. Arnie reached out to steady me. I swatted at his hand, knowing I would miss.

"Sober up," he said. "Come back tomorrow. We'll talk then."

Humiliated, smothered in shame, and drunker than I'd ever been on the beach, I stumbled out of the bar without another glance back.

I didn't make it far before Mirra found me. She produced the rest of the shwiskey bottle I'd been drinking from under her sweater. I lunged for it but she jerked it out of my reach, causing me to topple over at her feet. My chin cracked painfully against the cement and something warm and wet trickled down my neck.

"Everything is a trade, brother," she said, snarling down at me.

"Anything," I heaved. The weight in my heart was threatening to pull me under. The schwiskey solution was no longer efficient. My dosage was off. I had to keep trying or I'd never be free of this heaviness. "Please, before I'm pulled to hell."

"Dramatic," she teased. She popped the cork off the bottle and held it out to me. Again, when I reached, she pulled it away. She wagged her finger at me. "Sister knows best," she said. "Let me."

Cowed, I opened my mouth and waited. Mirra poured a cruel amount of whiskey into my mouth, carelessly sloshing it across my nostrils so I choked on the burning liquid. It spewed out across my chest and the ground around me. It was all I could smell, the fumes turning my stomach.

And still, my human heart was sinking.

Mirra braced one hand on my shoulder to steady herself as she leaned down to my ear.

"Let me have him," she whispered. "And you can end this."

No, this is wrong. Something is—

"Yes," I said. My thoughts were garbled and my world was spinning. I couldn't keep Mirra's face in focus but I was sure she was smiling because everything was glowing that soft light from the depths that spelled trouble. "Yes, make me free."

Her mouth moved but I could no longer hear her. Her unsteady footsteps thudded in front of my face and then away. The last thing I remember was a familiar yell from inside the bar.

14

Evelyn

Boston, Present Day

If I had to sit at this table for one more second, I was going to lose my *goddamn mind.*

"I'm telling you, there are too many unknowns," Wilhamena said from across the table, head in her hands as she massaged her temples.

"I'm telling you, there is no other way," Roxy snapped.

"As much as I love being treated like an amateur," Kelly said, voice dripping with sarcasm. "Shouldn't my opinion weigh a little more here? Since it's *my* song?"

"If you'd used it more than once we wouldn't have to tip toe." Roxy ran a clawed hand through her ragged hair for the thousandth time. "But you're right. Wilhamena, we need to trust her."

"If it goes wrong…"

"It won't."

After I explained to the emergency BUS assembly what happened to Will, Kelly immediately offered to use her siren song to lure him back to Boston. The two had a connection she could call on—I tried not to let that piece of new information make me jealous—and she was convinced it would be both the safest and simplest way to get Will home. The problem was there was no guarantee that the only creature Kelly would lure into the harbor was Will—and who knew what other monsters lurked in the depths of the ocean?

The alternative was to literally scour the ocean for him, a thought that made me want to crawl even deeper underground than we already were.

Pete pointed out the danger in luring a bloodthirsty mershark to land and Wilhamena was convinced Kelly would have the entire city stumbling over themselves to find her instead of just Will.

The conversation started logically and tapered off into exhausted snipping when no one could agree.

And here we were—several hours later, strapped to this table, the sugar from Wilhamena's perfect donuts making me crash.

"Why don't we take a break? I could use a coffee."

"Marvelous idea, love," a familiar voice called from the back of the cavernous room. I whipped my head around to see Billy strutting toward the table with a smirk. Another man, lanky and worn-thru followed behind him.

"Oh god, we sat here arguing so long the vamps had time to wake up," Wilhamena rubbed her hands across her face, gently twisting one of the braids in her beard. I assumed then that the second man was Patrick. He rounded to the head of the table, and I could see in the dim light that he had a long face and nearly black eyes. Thin wispy black hair wafted off his head at the slightest breeze and despite not a single wrinkle on his face, he had the appearance of someone of a supernatural age.

"How is the emergency meeting?" he asked, and I had to squint to reconcile a voice I'd heard over the phone with a moving face.

"We can't agree on a course of action," Wilhamena said.

"That's because there's only one course of action," Roxy countered. "And these two are being tightasses about it." She jerked a thumb at a scowling Wilhamena. Pete looked unfazed.

I felt eyes on me and I did my best not to let them draw my attention away from the crew gathered around the table. I knew it wasn't a ghost or any other entity. Not in this room.

"Oh, good we've reached name calling," Wilhamena scooted back from her seat, thumping a hand decisively on the table. "It's absolutely break time. Come on. We're all going to the Savvy Squirrel. Coffee's on me."

I started to fall in step behind Kelly but Billy caught me, looping his arm through mine and forcing the two of us to climb the stairs together.

"What are you still doing here?" I whispered while actively fighting the urge to lean my head on his shoulder. He was perfectly dressed in a chocolate brown corduroy suit and he'd swapped his usual dangling silver for simple gold studs that winked out from under the white-blonde hair he was wearing soft and loose for the day. He looked like a different person but his effect on me was the same—forbidden and intense.

"I was catching up with Patrick and lost track of time," he said. "That'll happen when it's been sixty years since you've seen each other. I figured one more day wouldn't hurt."

"I don't need checking on," I hissed. If I could reach inside myself and physically hold my stomach to keep it from fluttering I would. "And don't send shit to my office again."

"Too much?" He was grinning down at me, one fang fiendishly on display. Some exhausted, sad, lonely part of me wanted to buy into his flirtation. Some part of me wanted to say, "fuck all this, let's party" and just enjoy the attentions of the handsome, fashionable vampire my inner teen was humping her pillows over.

"Way too much," I said. "What were you even trying to do?"

"The lady was not wooed." He legit looked a little confused, like he expected all women to throw their panties over extravagant floral gestures.

"The lady was love bombed." I pulled my arm free of his at the top of the stairs earning a quirked eyebrow from Kelly. The others were filing out the door and I practically kicked Billy in the ass to get him in front of me.

"You good?" Kelly asked, following me out onto the sidewalk. The sun had dipped low below the horizon and the streetlights were only just beginning to flicker on. I matched her pace, letting Billy get a few paces ahead of us with the rest of the group.

"I'm a heinous bitch and a shitty girlfriend," I sighed. "But yeah, I'm good."

"This is a lot to take on for someone you barely know," Kelly said. "No one would blame you if—"

"You would." I should've known better than to accept such warm comfort from someone who had never liked me.

"Evelyn, I'm sorry." I stopped dead at her words. She was standing stone still on the sidewalk, hands clasped in front of her. She looked at me with such sincerity I wanted to burst into flames. "I haven't been the nicest to you and it was misdirected. I wanted to protect Will but it was from things that already happened to him. If you knew…" She looked away, heaved shuddering breath. "If you knew what he'd been through."

"He was supposed to tell me," I said. "Before all this."

"He doesn't know how to hold all the parts of himself together," she said. "I don't want—" She turned back to me, brown eyes alight. "I don't want you to have to hold him when he can't hold himself."

"I'm more than up to the—" Heat razed through me and my vision began to blur.

"It's not about whether you're capable," she cut me off, holding her hands out for peace. "You're *more* than capable, Evelyn, we all know that. How many other humans don't even blink when their best friend turns into a leprechaun in front of them? You're so capable it would be easy for Will to not do the work for himself. And if he doesn't do it for himself then it will never end."

My rage died like a fire smothered with a metal lid.

"What will never end?"

"I don't think Will has been cursed," she said, choosing her words slowly. "I think his curse has been reignited."

I didn't fully understand what she was saying. A million questions slammed through me at once, all while the world began to tilt dangerously to the side. Was Will cursed? What did that mean?

Suddenly, my hand was slamming against the light pole and my feet were no longer firmly beneath me. A high-pitched whine rang through my ears and, no matter how I squinted or blinked, nothing would focus. Muffled voices sounded all around me and a pair of sturdy hands gripped my shoulders, hauling me against a hard, corduroy covered body.

More muffled voices followed me down into a blackness I couldn't claw my way out of.

* * *

I woke up in my own bed, sitting straight up with a screaming gasp like I'd just had a vivid nightmare. I reached around the bed, frantically patting myself and my satin sheets, finding my phone and checking the screen. It was 11 pm and I had 17 missed texts from Caoimhe.

I clicked on the bedside light as my stomach gurgled ravenously.

Glancing around, I froze.

I lived in a studio—a space I usually described as a "petite open concept." This meant I could see clearly that my TV was on, the flickering blue light dancing off a very perplexed Billy. He was slouched across my couch like he lived here, the suit jacket discarded, the pinstripe shirt beneath it rolled to the elbows in that perfect sexy way men were always doing. He was balancing a plate of Chinese food on his lap, expertly picking up floppy tofu in a brown sauce with chopsticks.

"What fresh hell?" I asked, my throat hoarse.

"The lady arises!" He didn't so much as drop a grain of rice as he stood and guided me toward the kitchen.

I looked around as he pelted me with questions about the latest round of contestants on *Kissing Strangers to Get Married*—Caoimhe's favorite—and shoveled food onto a plate. The pile of junk mail that usually eclipsed my dining table from view had been meticulously stacked and sorted into various piles. The boxes of books and back-issues of Vogue I kept meaning to organize had been tastefully arranged on the fully assembled bookshelf in the corner I kept meaning to take from the box. It took until my first mouthful of orange chicken to recognize that even my TV and couch were in different places than when I left for work that morning.

"Did you rearrange my furniture?" I asked, in a daze. I still wasn't even sure how I'd gotten home. The last thing I remembered was standing on the street talking with Kelly and—

"Oh my god my boyfriend is cursed," I choked out around the chicken, depositing it all half-chewed back onto the plate. Just like a dainty bitch.

"Hey now, love," Billy handed me a glass of water I hadn't seen him fill. "We all have our bad runs—"

"No, literally." I looked up at Billy sure that my face was stretched and pained. "Will is cursed and *has been* cursed. It never lifted, it just reverted somehow, and I didn't even fucking notice. Of course I didn't notice."

I threw my hands in the air and began pacing the length of my apartment.

"I always do this. I'm too busy chasing the high of a new thing I don't stop and pay attention to the context or the history and then I'm knee-deep in trouble." I wasn't talking to Billy so much as the words were just pouring out and I couldn't stop them, the sleep deprivation and stress of the last few days breaking down my walls. "Of course I don't care about red flags, I think they're only warnings if you're a judgmental pussy but—"

"Evelyn—"

"Naturally chasing down every flag in the human world wasn't enough I had to go and find magic ones."

"It isn't—"

"If I could stop being so *stupid* for five minutes then I would've seen what was happening to Will and I wouldn't have let it get this bad. If I could've just—"

"You couldn't—"

"This is my fault!" I was practically screaming now, hot tears sliding down my cheeks. "It's always my fault when shit goes sideways like this. I should've known it would—"

A hard chest met mine as a firm hand gripped the back of my neck, stopping me in my tracks before a searing kiss landed on my lips. My brain shut off, replaced by blissful buzzing silence. I surrendered to it instinctually, closing my eyes and letting my shoulders drop.

"That's enough," Billy said against my mouth.

I opened my eyes, confusion and satisfaction at war in my chest. I blinked a few times, bringing Billy's scarlet eyes into focus. They were softer around the edges than I'd noticed before and he kept glancing back down to my mouth. I resisted the urge to lick my lips, placing a hand against his ridiculously chiseled chest with the intention of pushing away. Instead, my fingers skated across his pecks and up around his shoulders.

"What the fuck was that?" I whispered.

"Doesn't matter," Billy said, still closer than he should be. "It worked."

"Of course, it worked," I said, the rapid-fire train of self-loathing kicking back to life in my brain. "I've always wanted to make out with a vampire so naturally it just takes my boyfriend being lost at sea for me to spread my—"

Another searing kiss. This one sent heat straight through my core. I swear to god my toes curled. The silence in my brain returned and this time, I wasn't going to let it go so easily.

This was a game I'd played before—sex as an escape from myself. It never ended well.

But nothing was going well currently so what did the ending matter?

Come back.

Maybe he'll come back.

Maybe he'll never come back.

Please come back.

I had to make the whirling thoughts stop.

I pressed myself against Billy, answering his kiss with a soft parting of my lips. He swept his tongue in questioningly and a small moan escaped me. His response was immediate, digging one hand into my hip and digging the other up into my hair along the deliciously sensitive back of my scalp. I could feel the hardness of him against me and it sent sparks shooting through me, pooling heat between my legs. He started to pull away and I nipped at his bottom lip in response, reaching up to pull him back down to me again and starting the kiss anew.

"Is this okay?" he gasped out, running a hand down the length of my spine and resting just above my ass.

"Shut up," I said, equally breathless. I kissed him again like his mouth had the answers I needed—like devouring him would fix everything else. But it wasn't enough. I ground myself against his cock in those perfect corduroy trousers, feeling how wet I was through my pajamas. Betrayal and guilt crept up on me as I pulled away just long enough to grab the vampire by his shirt collar and haul him to the couch. His eyes were dark, heady, focused. There was no conflict in him as I pulled him down on top of me, immediately comforted by the weight of him.

I lifted my hips, grinding against him, chasing the build in my gut. I was going to come from dry-humping this man and I didn't give a shit. Anything for those happy little sex endorphins.

Billy reached down between us and cupped my pussy with a firmness I hadn't expected. I gasped and stilled, eyes wide, body frozen for a moment.

"Here's the deal, love," he said, voice raspy with need. "You need a release and I'm too entranced to turn you away."

A shiver ran through me. Entranced? Fucking Brits.

"But I can't let you regret me," he said, pressing against my pussy with just the heel of his hand. More, God, I needed more.

"I won't," I gasped out, grinding slowly against his hand. He pushed aside the leg of my shorts and slid his hand up, finding me wet and ready.

He buried his face into my neck and groaned.

"No panties, fucking hell," he murmured. "You're going to destroy me."

"Good," I said, angling my head so I could swirl my tongue inside his ear and then up along the point of it. He shuddered against me and I felt his teeth scrape against my shoulder.

He found my clit then and everything else faded away against the white hot heat of that pleasurable pinpoint. He circled it quickly, building the pressure against my spine before flicking down expertly.

I cried out, clenching against a painful emptiness.

"There's a girl," he said, slipping a finger inside of me and crooking it against the perfect spot inside of me.

"More," I said. "More, please."

"Anything for you, love," he said and slid in a second finger. It still wasn't enough.

"All of it," I said. I gripped his shoulders roughly and gave him a shove so that we made eye contact. The desire written on every part of his face nearly made me stop but I shoved it aside, cramming it into the bottom of the barrel with my guilt and fear and worry. This was not that kind of moment.

"If you aren't going to fuck me you better give me something to ride," I demanded. "Nightstand, second drawer."

Before I could blink, he returned with my vibrator. I sat up, shimmying out of my shorts and pointed to the couch. "Lay down," I snapped. My orgasm was shimmering just on the edge of my vision, taunting me in the face of all the other things I was running from. Incredibly, I swear Billy's cock got harder at my command. I would've filed that away for later but there would be no later. This was just one more intimate thing I'd know about a man who would be a stranger again in no time.

I straddled him, lifting myself just enough to give space for Billy to slide the hand holding the vibrator between us. The tell-tale hum cut the sound of our gasping breaths and I closed my eyes as he ran the head of it through my wet folds, teasing at my opening. I rolled my hips against it, bracing myself against his chest. When the vibrating head of the toy finally slipped into me, I threw my head back and let a scream rip from my throat.

I clenched the front of Billy's shirt, rumpling it in my sweating fists. "Harder."

I commanded. Billy obeyed.

If there were going to be another time, I would've been thrilled at the opportunity to have such a hold over an immortal being with the ability to kill me in seconds.

But there would be no other times.

Billy thrust the toy into me harder, slamming against my walls and sending sparks into my vision. I rode each thrust like I was greeting an oncoming wave and still, in the back of my spine, there was an emptiness. I rode faster, chasing my orgasm harder, but it eluded me, slipping away every time I got close.

Before I could issue another command, Billy removed the toy and slammed what felt like four fingers into me at an angle, crooking them all together in a hooked motion that threatened to pull me forward by the pussy. He slid his thumb up against my clit with borderline painful force and circled it like he was trying to erase me off his hand even while he was inside of me.

My orgasm came all at once, slamming down on me like a sudden thunderstorm. But there too were all the things I'd been running from—grief, fear, rage, and desperation. They released out of me with the same choked cry that greeted the shuddering, clenching wave of my orgasm and threatened to break me down into sobs.

Instead, I cocked back and punched Billy in the face.

Something feral flashed in his eyes and his fangs flashed forward for a split second before he reached his free hand up and traced it lightly down the side of my face.

"Good girl," he whispered. "Get it all out."

"Fuck you," I groaned, slumping forward and burying my face into his shoulder.

Billy carefully released his grip on my pussy and readjusted on the couch so that he could cradle me against him, wrapping me up in his arms and pressing my face to the hollow of his neck. I felt cocooned, safe, comfortable. Entirely blissed out on my orgasm, I let my eyes slide shut again and I chased the darkness behind them, running again from my emotions but this time into sleep.

15

Will

New England, 45 years ago

Lights flashed in long arcs, cutting through the darkness that lay over the beach like a blanket. Urgent voices called out to one another and somewhere, not too far, dogs barked and strained against their handlers.

I stood at the edge of the tide, my toes barely in the water.

I had been tricked again.

Mirra took Arnie, leaving a nightmarish scene in the kitchen of Bears & Growlers before disappearing into the night. With no one else to pin the blame on but the "weird kid that used to live on the beach," the town sent the local sheriff's office after me.

Only now, staring down the possibility of sinking to the bottom of the ocean, weighed down by the echoes of my past and my tortured human heart, did I realize what my gut had been trying to tell me.

The *only* way out of my curse was to find forgiveness among the humans.

No one would forgive me for destroying Arnie, least of all myself. And now I had to start all over again.

The thought hit me like a distracted sunfish, throwing me off kilter with its weight. Where would I go? What would I find there? What could possibly be next?

The urgent voices were closer now. And I had only two options: rot in a human prison, forgotten and never forgiven. Or step into the ocean again and seek out a new shore.

As a beam of light landed on me, spraying out across the dark water that now lapped up against my knees as I waded forward, I hoped that my next chance wouldn't be wasted like this one.

＊ ＊ ＊

Boston, 20 years ago

Time passed like it always does—too quickly to be remembered. Soon enough I was back among the humans, this time in a much larger place. The air was thick with smog and the humidity smeared it against my skin as I moved through cobblestone streets to the bar where I was working this time.

Arnie set me up with more than just a job for the time being. So long as there were drunks in a human city, there would be a need for someone to pour the liquor. And I could do that.

I don't want to tell you what it was like in the ocean, suffering Mirra's curse as I tried to find a place to crawl ashore. It took everything in me to keep swimming forward, to make it further away from the town where Arnie was murdered. I had no idea how long the Sheriff would look for me—or how far that search would take him.

When I finally couldn't take it anymore, I followed the sounds and smells of a busy harbor. It took some doing, this time, to find clothes and a job. A few lucky trash bins landed me enough to appear dirty but not untrustworthy and quickly I was slinging beers at a divey fisherman's bar.

The crowd was rowdier than they'd been in the last town—more tattooed, more ragged, more worn down. They swore every other word and threw punches before bothering to speak. But for some reason they liked me—maybe because I kept my mouth shut and kept the drinks coming. Eventually they started slipping me extra muffins from their wives or a few cigarettes.

Smoking was a problem and a solution. Inhaling chemicals did nothing for the shark part of me, but my heavy human heart loved it. It temporarily boosted me, giving me a moment to breathe while I sucked down a stimulant that carried me through the rest of the day. And the burn of it in my human form slowly deadened some of my shark senses, making the clamor and overwhelm of the city easier to tolerate.

But my stability was short lived like it always is. It only took one fisherman asking why I didn't look any older while the rest of them got gray hairs and I never went back for another shift.

Luckily, Boston is not short on places to drink.

The years went on like this—work a bar for a while, make human friends, leave before they notice too much. I felt like I was and wasn't getting any closer to the forgiveness I needed to break my curse. I kept bumping against the roadblock of time. Making friends takes so fucking long. And it's so much work.

Especially when you're guilt-ridden and terrified of anyone knowing who you really are. I couldn't escape the ghost of Arnie in every place I worked. Every kitchen held his cheerful echo, every beer tap rang with his laughter, ricocheting through me and nestling in the open wound of my conscience.

That's when I met Kelly. She didn't break my curse—the being a siren thing makes her a bad candidate—but she saved me in other ways.

It was a typical meet-cute—she was fending off a would-be Romeo at the bar and I swooped in pretending to be her hubby. One sloppy fake kiss to scare off Romeo and we knew we weren't meant to be. Or, in Kelly's words, "You're not hot enough to be that lazy with your tongue."

But we stayed in each other's orbits for a few weeks before she finally leveled an accusatory finger at me over the bar one slow happy hour. When she tells this story, she likes to remind everyone it was the mid-90s, which always makes my skin crawl when I realize how long I spent slipping between bars alone.

"You can tell me," she said that afternoon, leaning over the counter conspiratorially. "And I'll tell you."

"Tell me what?" I tried to play dumb.

"What you are."

"I thought the tough exterior and melty insides would give it away," I said with a wink. "I'm the bartender with a heart of gold." I'd recently discovered Harrison Ford's character in Star Wars, and I'd decided I wanted to be Han Solo instead of Clint Eastwood. I'd started winking more and practicing my one-liners in the walk-in freezer.

She scoffed and rolled her eyes.

"Fine," she said. "I'll go first since you're being difficult."

"I don't accept love declarations on the clock," I said.

"You think I'd sign up for that lazy kissing again? Please," she said. But she straightened herself, checking over both shoulders before whispering. "I'm not human."

I tried to maintain a blank face but I'm sure my eyes gave me away.

"I don't know what you mean," I said.

She rolled her eyes again. "You're really bad at playing dumb," she said.

I shrugged and walked over to greet a rough-looking guy who'd just walked in and sat at the far end of the bar.

"Fine," Kelly said, loud enough that the guy and I both snapped our heads in her direction. "I'll prove it."

She opened her mouth and released a song so achingly beautiful time itself stopped to listen. When she finished, I shook my head to clear it, barely registering that I'd been staring in a daze. The guy had crossed the bar to Kelly. He was on his knees next to her, practically crawling up her leg to be closer to her. He was muttering something in Spanish before he cleared his throat.

"If you don't marry me, I'll die," he said.

"Alright, buddy," I said, waving at him to back up. But Kelly held her hand out for me to wait. She leaned down to him and hummed something into his ear. He folded in on himself, whimpering on the floor. She stepped over him on her way to the door, throwing me the middle finger on her way out.

"Hey, you can't just leave horny guys on my floor!" I yelled after her. "What am I supposed to do with him?"

I looked down at the stranger who still hadn't ordered a drink. And that's when it hit me, a memory of a song across the water from my life before.

Kelly was a siren.

* * *

We didn't immediately decide to go into business together. We didn't even immediately become best friends. Like I said, I was still too gun shy after what happened to Arnie. But I did tell Kelly the truth—some of it. I said I was a mershark, that I was taking a break from the ocean for a while for personal reasons, and no, I didn't want to talk about it. Yes, it was weird.

Her questions never relented but they also weren't invasive, peppered in among other moments together so that I felt her curiosity was genuine with no ulterior motives.

Meanwhile, I perfected my Han Solo personality and was charming my way through cash tips at classier establishments. Turns out human women really liked my wink and one-liner routine.

"It's because you're hot," Kelly told me one night over French fries and a six pack at her apartment. "It's not because you're charming."

"Am I not hot enough to be lazy or too hot to be charming?" I asked, gesturing with a fry. "Because now you're going back on your own words."

She waved a hand through the air, dismissing the question.

"How long do you think you can get by on that?"

"On hotness? Probably forever."

"On bartending."

"Do you have another suggestion?" I arched my eyebrows. The money I made each night shaking martinis for women in tight dresses got me into my first real apartment—a tiny little shit hole, but *my* shithole.

"There's a tour boat company getting foreclosed on down by the aquarium," she said. "How hilarious would it be if we took it over? A couple of sea-folk taking the humans for a ride across the water."

I frowned. I didn't like the idea of being that close to the ocean. I'd found a good rhythm in my life and bartending kept me close to my schwiskey dosages. Switching jobs meant I'd have to budget for it and the idea of having to calculate how much money I was drinking made my stomach flip.

"You don't look sold," she said, returning the frown. "Come on, don't you want to get out from behind the bar and see a little more of the human experience? That's why you're here, right?"

"Not really," I muttered, cracking open another beer. This was one of Kelly's typical questioning routines—suggesting my reason for being among the humans and waiting for me to agree. So far, she had offered up sociological study, morbid curiosity, and a very complex backstory implying I was on a quest from God.

She snapped her fingers in frustration. "I spent three days coming up with that one."

"Really?" I squinted at her. "You're losing your edge."

"What do I have to do to convince you?"

"Pick a different business."

Kelly sighed and took my hand in hers across the table. "Please, Will? You're the only one I trust enough to do this with. And I can't keep serving families pancakes or I'm going to let a scream loose at work."

"Juicy," I teased.

"If that's how you describe forty people with bleeding ears, sure." She squeezed my hand. "If you won't do it for yourself, will you do it for me?"

She knew I would.

And I did.

16

Evelyn

Boston, Present Day

I watched Roxy skitter across the Mister Flipper boat as we crested another swell. She couldn't seem to find her sea legs and was particularly overwhelmed by all the smells coming off the water.

"Sit the fuck down," Kelly snapped for the fifth time.

"Werewolves aren't meant to be this far off land," Roxy snapped back, clinging onto a support pole with her legs twisted under her at a strange angle.

"You could've stayed behind," Wilhamena chimed in from where she sat next to me. She had tied her beard and hair into yet another set of stylish braids, these much more adept at keeping her from getting tangled in the wind. Her turquoise parka was pulled up to her chin and her hands were crammed in her pockets.

I sipped the coffee she'd brought, staring out at the horizon line from behind my Ray Bans. I'd called out of work again, prompting a text from my editor, Carrie.

Carrie: Sorry to bother you. Can't find mer-fashion write-up. Can you email again?

Me: Dealing with crisis. Will check when I'm home. Expect it tonight. Sorry for the confusion.

I was positive I'd sent my article in before Will and I went to dinner that night in New York. I'd wanted no distractions. But the days were so hazy now, blurred together in a long string of confusion and frustration, I couldn't be sure anymore. I really should've gone into work to get it settled. Paris was hanging in the balance, a hazy daydream promising to be real outside all this chaos. Besides, I couldn't afford to miss the paid days. But there was no way I'd get anything done.

Not after last night.

I'd woken up alone in my bed, the early morning birds chirping away as sun streamed in through my windows. Billy was nowhere to be found. I took a long shower, scrubbing every part of myself and trying to use shampoo to erase the shame. It hadn't been enough because Roxy raised her eyebrows at me when I met them on the peer, her nostrils flaring.

I probably smelled like regret. I certainly felt it strong enough, I wouldn't be surprised if it was oozing out of my pores.

But today was a fresh start—fresh penance through dedication to Will. This was why I had to cut work. I had to find him, had to bring him home so I could stop looking for ways to run away from the good man I knew was buried under his cursed self.

I had to keep trying the way he'd promised he would.

The boat engine slowed and then died as we neared the mouth of the harbor. Kelly descended from the captain's deck.

"Alright everyone," she said, handing out ear plugs. "Remember the briefing from this morning. Keep these in until I give you the signal and no matter what, no one gets in the water."

I nodded, my mouth in a firm line, my stomach fluttering.

"This will work," Kelly said to me in a lower tone as she pressed the neon orange foam into my hands.

"I trust you," I said. And I did.

But I didn't trust my circumstances—or my luck.

Not for the first time, I glanced down at my phone willing Caoimhe to text me that SURPRISE! SHE WAS HOME! I was desperate for her presence, encouragement, and ability to make everything feel okay no matter what we were doing together.

Wilhamena wriggled a hand from her pocket and squeezed my shoulder, mouthing "ready?" as I plugged my ears. I wasn't, but I nodded anyway.

The next few minutes passed in silence.

Kelly stood with her back to us, facing out across the water. I had to trust that she wasn't just standing there doing nothing, that she was letting out her siren song across the water—one for Will specifically to bring him home. She turned and motioned to us all to stay. The next part would happen out of sight. My nerves screamed. My stomach twisted. I felt helpless, useless, drifting in the water, hoping that a lullaby would be enough to bring home a man lost to a monster.

Kelly went down to the lower deck, disappearing from view. Now, she would attempt to send her song out through the waves themselves, singing into the water and hoping that Will would hear it regardless of whether he was above or below the surface.

I let out a shuddering sigh. The earplugs were doing their job but that meant I was trapped in silence with only my own thoughts for company. I stared out across the water, trying not to let flashes of last night rise to the surface.

What would I tell Will?

Would I have to tell Will?

Some ugly part of me reasoned that if we never lifted the curse and he continued being his violent, douchebag shark self then there would never be anything to offer. He would be too dangerous—and too uninterested in me—to return to.

The thought settled in me like a velvet curtain, smothering everything in a silent relief before the panic set in.

I didn't *want* to lose Will. Of all the men in my life, Will had been the first to feel like he would stay—and not just because of his promises. He had been taking care of himself, working on becoming the type of person he wanted me to be with but also who he wanted to be.

"I haven't done the 'devoted and loving boyfriend' thing yet. It'll be hard to say goodbye to Han Solo," he said, quirking that perfect mouth at me in a scared half-smile.

The memory pushed up through my chest, carrying with it a sob I smothered into my palm. I glanced at Wilhamena but she continued staring out across the water. I was grateful for the earplugs as I let out another hiccupped sob into my hand.

I missed Will—*my* Will. I missed the feeling in my gut that this could be real and we could be good, just us against everyone and everything else. I missed the moment in time when things had been simple and perfect even though we both had a lot of problems to work through. We had been together at least.

Another fear appeared, clutching at my heart, and sending a cold pulse through my limbs. What if we never found him and that screaming moment on the edge of the Hudson was our final moment together?

A hand squeezed my shoulder. Wilhamena handed me a tissue and rubbed small circles across my back. I let her, wiping furiously at my eyes and blowing my nose.

Kelly appeared, sprinting across the deck and frantically giving us the signal to remove our earplugs.

"There!" she yelled, pointing to the very front of the boat.

I bolted forward, barely catching myself against the railing. I searched the water, every lapping wave a possible fin.

Then, a familiar face peered up from the water.

There was Will, unmistakable in his mershark form. His long powerful tail was a massive shadow deep in the water, his human half appearing above the waves. His skin was a dusted grey, his eyes a predator's sharp black. I shuddered as he stared up at us with those unfeeling, pupilless eyes, flashing multiple rows of sharp teeth. He pointed with a webbed hand directly at me, baring his teeth.

"You'll have to come get me, big boy," I yelled, baring my own teeth back.

Without warning he ducked down beneath the water.

"Evelyn, watch out!"

Then he leaped through the air, his shark tail cutting an arc behind him. For one glittering, surreal moment, he was suspended against the blue sky, all muscle and efficiency and those dark, dark eyes. Then he was falling. Before I could move, he caught himself on the railing, slamming into the side of the boat hard enough to send a shockwave through it. Somewhere behind me I heard Roxy cry out.

I found myself eye to eye with Will in a way I hadn't been for weeks—lost in his eyes like I had been the first time he showed me who he truly was, that night in the frigid dark water. I couldn't look away, I couldn't move, I couldn't think. Everything in me was distilled down to my prey instinct. To move was to be seen, to be seen was to be hurt.

Will would never hurt me.

I reached a tentative hand out, tracing the side of his face.

"It's me," I whispered. And for a split-second my heart leapt at the possible recognition in his face and then my hand was in his teeth and the bright flash of pain was all my brain could process as we tumbled from the boat.

We slammed into the freezing water, all the breath leaving my lungs with force. Salt tore at my eyes and my lips as Will dragged me down, clamping tighter onto my hand. Blood tinted the water around me and struggling only tore deeper at the gashes in my hand. Panic seized my chest as my lungs burned from lack of oxygen. Whatever little air I had left wasn't enough and it took all my focus not to open my mouth and scream.

I kicked Will with what strength I had, a single incongruous mantra rising in me as each second got blurrier, fuzzier, hazier.

Come back.

There was a violent thrashing in the water next to me and then my hand was free. I watched the sunlight flicker through the water, getting closer and closer before realizing I wasn't swimming forward. I was being pushed.

I broke through the waves and choked on the sudden air rushing into my lungs. The hands I hadn't realized were holding me let go and there was a massive movement in the water. Too busy treading water against the smashing waves, I couldn't get a good look at my savior, but a speckled monstrous tail waved as they dove back down.

"Evelyn!" Kelly threw down a lifesaver from the lower deck. I pushed it over my head and kicked as much as I could, battling exhaustion as Kelly and Wilhamena pulled me to safety.

Wilhamena's strong hands pulled me aboard easily and I fell onto the deck, gasping and choking for air.

"You're alright," Kelly said, kneeling next to me with a first aid kit. "It's gonna be alright."

"Fuck yeah it is," I gasped out. "Leith is back."

"How?" she asked, as if I had any idea how our friendly whale-shark-merman had made it back from Ireland just in time.

Shouts from above mixed with a strange metallic dragging—they were moving something heavy across the deck.

"What is that?" I asked, hissing through my teeth as Kelly put pressure on my bleeding hand. I couldn't look at it without feeling light-headed and I wasn't looking forward to explaining to the ER doctor how I got a shark bite in November in Boston.

"Before you freak out," Kelly started, looking everywhere but my face. "It's totally safe. It just looks scary."

"Kelly…"

"He's a big, mean dude right now, Evelyn," she said, busying herself with the kit in front of her. "I don't like it either but—"

I stood, clutching my hand to my chest and started for the stairs, the rocking of the boat growing rougher and rougher with the thrashing in the water. I slammed into the stairwell, the reverb shuddering through my shoulder and down into my already fluttering stomach.

Once I reached the upper deck, I stopped dead, braced against the railing, horrified by the contraption in Wilhamena and Roxy's hands. A wicked-looking chain mail net covered the entire deck. Beach ball-sized weights were arranged around the edges. I watched the two BUS members struggle with lifting one edge up above the railing before it dawned on me what they were doing.

"No!" I screamed out across the boat.

"Evelyn, look at me." Kelly gripped me by the shoulders before I could go any further. She was breathless from having sprinted up after me and she was still clutching a piece of gauze in one hand.

"You're going to kill him," I shrieked. I couldn't tear my eyes away from the massive weights, sitting in menacing silence around the boat. The image of Will dragged writhing down to the bottom of the harbor flashed over and over in my mind. "You're going to kill him," I said again.

"I won't let that happen," Kelly said, holding firm as I pushed against her hands. "Evelyn, you have to trust us, this isn't what it looks like."

Roxy yelled and my gaze was pulled to the massive forms leaping from the water. First, Will—all grey-skinned muscle and teeth, haloed by the sun, vengeful gaze turned to Leith rising behind him.

"Jesus fucking—"

Leith was *huge.* Unlike Will, his human half was a little less recognizable—more like the suggestion of a man fused to the prehistoric length of his tail. His skin was dappled in a variety of brown and white spots against navy, and where Will had claws, Leith had long delicate fingers reaching forward through the air. His massive eyes took up more of his head than I'd expected, giving him a distinctly fishy look compared to Will's predator gaze.

While I was still taking in the scene above us, frozen in the world's longest split-second, Leith pointed to Wilhamena. And then he flipped mid-air in a feat of giant athleticism, smacking Will in the chest with his dinosaur tail.

"Get down!"

Time caught back up with us as Will came slamming down directly onto the deck, landing in the middle of the chainmail net that Wilhamena and Roxy had been wrestling with. The boat tipped dangerously forward from the sudden weight, rocking back with a sickening tilt as it worked to right itself.

"Now, Wilhamena!"

I barely registered the cascade of water slamming over all of us as Leith descended under the surface. In the same moment, Wilhamena made a commanding motion with both her hands and the weights on the edges rose into the air, snapping together like magnets. They effectively sealed Will within the chainmail he was now thrashing against before settling gently back down on all sides of him.

Will's screams of frustration tore through the air, rising above the sloshing water as he struggled against the metal net. The entire boat rocked with each thrash of his tail. My heart snapped in half. This wasn't fair. This wasn't right. There had to be another way.

I took a step forward, desperate to soothe the pain out of the sounds coming from him, but Kelly wrapped her arms around me and planted her feet.

"You have to wait," she said. "I know it's awful, I'm sorry. We have to let him help himself."

There was so much in her words—a knowing that gnawed at me with something like jealousy, something like rage. We had already watched Will destroy himself only to begin to rise from the ashes. Why were we doing it *again*? When would it stop?

Slowly, the thrashing ceased and with a sickening crunching sound, I watched Will shift into his human form. It happened so quickly the boat shuddered, rocking and tilting to account for the sudden loss of what to be a cool thousand pounds or more.

Wilhamena and Roxy both approached, the dwarf commanding the weights to move again with another set of gestures and Roxy descending on Will before he could react. She tied his hands and feet like a seasoned cowboy at a rodeo before Wilhamena threw a blanket over him—to keep him warm, I imagined, but also to save everyone else having to eyeball his full-frontal.

The muscles in Will's neck stuck out and his face was flush with rage.

"Fuck all of you! Do you know what I am? I will kill you." He struggled against the zip ties Roxy had used. *"I will kill you and leave your flesh to rot at the bottom of the ocean. I am the KING OF THIS WATER LET ME GO NOW."*

"God, he's gross like this," Kelly sighed.

"How're we gonna get him through town?" Roxy said, hands on her hips, breath ragged. "It's gonna look like we kidnapped a crazy man."

"Not too far off," Wilhamena sighed. She reached into her parka pocket and produced a small purple vial. Roxy immediately shook her head.

"I'm not carrying him," the werewolf waved a hand through the air.

"You don't have to," Wilhamena leaned over Will, flipping open the top and hovering above him. "Here, your highness, open up."

Will clamped his mouth shut so immediately and so tightly it was comical. Wilhamena rolled her eyes and leaned down to pinch his nipple. His mouth shot open in surprise, and she dumped the contents of the bottle down, seizing her opportunity. Will thrashed one more time before confusion crossed his face and then his eyes closed, his body stilling. I counted to three before the steady rise and fall of chest told me he wasn't dead.

Kelly finally let me go and I sprinted across the deck, sliding painfully onto my knees on the chainmail net. I pushed the wet hair from Will's face. Sleeping like this, I could almost convince myself that the gentle, goofy soul I'd fallen for was back with us. My heart clenched at the reminder that even though we'd caught him, there was still so much more work to be done—still so much further to go before we could be together again.

That last part rang through every part of me as I looked down at him, placing my hand over his heart and letting it rest with his steady breathing.

It was going to be a longer road than I'd thought to get Will back. At this rate, half our relationship would be rescuing him from a curse. What if Paris came while he was still like this and I was forced to choose between the two? I closed my eyes and tried to match my breath to his.

Could I do this?

Leith's baritone murmuring pulled my focus. I watched him talk to Kelly, shifted back into his human form, and somewhere, deep in my exhausted, worn-out heart, was a flicker of hope.

All of this had worked out with incredible luck—Leith arriving to save me, the boat not capsizing when Will landed on it in his mershark form, Will not hurting anyone else once we caught him.

A luck that shouldn't follow around someone like me. Which could only mean one thing.

My best friend was home.

17

Will

Boston, 10 years ago

There is nothing sadder than the lights coming up after last call. Not just because it means I can't drink anymore—a problem I only discovered after leaving bartending to start Mister Flipper—but because you're forced to look at the sweaty, beady-eyed losers you've been spending the last six hours with. It forces you to take a good look at yourself in comparison—are *you* the beady-eyed loser that everyone else is now re-evaluating?

The only answer for that level of self-loathing is to keep drinking.

The first time I was invited to an after-party I thought it was human magic. It was as if they took all the drunken comradery and low-light liquored conversation and transported it out of the dive bars where it usually lived but without losing any of the much-needed short-term bonding. It was just in some stranger's apartment.

And that stranger always had more booze.

I started going to shows so I could get an afterparty invite, staying up until the sun rose so that I wouldn't have to reconcile who I was truly becoming with who I felt I was while drunk and happy. And my heavy human heart was buoyed so long as there was schwiskey and some sweet-faced thing to distract me.

For a while, I could even do all this and still show up for the morning tour at Mister Flipper with only a mild headache.

The deeper I ingrained myself in Boston's music scene as a regular at every venue and every show, the more I became a sort of legend. I learned quickly if I was going to sleep around and drink every touring bands entire sponsored keg, I needed to blend in a little. A few back-alley fist fights and one awkward run-in with a manager who remembered me from ten years earlier meant it was time to not stand out so much.

I started to replace my Harrison Ford personality with Keanu Reeves—the kind of laid back hot guy that people's eyes would appreciate but ultimately gloss over in a room. I'd nick a shirt or a pair of pants at each party until I matched the crowd I was following, camouflaged in trendy clothing. And if I hooked up with someone, it was in a bathroom, on a stranger's bed, in the backseat of a car. I never took anyone home, relying on the allure of mystery to keep personal details out of the mix.

The result was *fantastic*. I was drinking and fucking every night with abandon, the heavy weights in my heart always on a constant delay. And I could count on Kelly the next day for the kind of stable friendship that kept me upright and sober during the day.

I felt like I couldn't mix Kelly and the after parties. She would've hated everyone in the room and I didn't want her to know how much I was faking my life in my free time—not when our friendship was forged on the truth of who we were.

But after a few years, I started to realize no one *except* Kelly had any idea who I was. A new kind of weight settled into my heart alongside the usual weights, giving me a whole new problem to try and outrun. Drinking, smoking, fucking wouldn't lift this new one either.

That's when I met Leith.

I didn't realize merfolk could recognize each other on land because I'd never seen another one until that party. I'd assumed he was just another groupie until we locked eyes across the room. Something in me jolted like I'd been kicked in the gut and the sudden smell of saltwater slammed into me. A flickering shadow behind Leith—who was wearing a goddamn flannel and a pair of jeans like some New England coffee shop manager—looked enough like a shark tail that I had to rub my eyes to be sure I wasn't seeing things. He gave me a shy smile and I felt my whole face split in half as if my own shark teeth were pushing through my human face.

I pushed through the crowded room to him and introduced myself.

"Leith," he said, taking my hand.

"Keith?"

"With an L."

"For real?"

He nodded. "Super real." Another shy smile.

"Figures." I shrugged and took a sip of my beer. "You can't be like us and not have a weird name."

"Men?" he asked, but the flicker across his face told me he knew exactly what I was getting at. I leaned into him so that he could hear me over the thudding bass but no one else could.

"Yeah, *mer*men."

When I pulled away his eyes were wide and his jaw was slack.

I clapped a hand on his shoulder good naturedly and laughed, flashing all my teeth again. It felt good—actually good—in that moment to laugh with someone I recognized as my own.

"It's alright, dude," I said. "Your secret is my secret, who would I tell?"

Kelly. I was gonna tell Kelly. I knew it immediately. I didn't want Leith to leave. I needed him around. I needed him to stay.

I didn't want to be a secret anymore.

"You leaving tomorrow?" I asked, hoping I sounded nonchalant.

"Look, man," Leith looked a little uneasy, but the kindness never left his eyes. "You're very handsome, but that's not really my—"

"*Dude.*" I glanced around the room. I'd worked so hard to not have a reputation anymore, was it already preceding me? "I'm not trying to fuck you."

"Sorry." That was all he said. We both looked at each other, equally confused, and then burst into simultaneous laughter.

Later, over a couple of beers on the couch of the now empty rockstar suite, I told Leith about Kelly and Mister Flipper. I offered him a spot with us, told him he should consider staying in Boston instead of moving on to the next city with the band.

Incredibly, he agreed.

It was just the three of us for a long time. With Leith in the crew, I could take the later tours, which gave me more time to sleep off my slowly growing hangovers. I even started getting closer to the water with Leith when he went for his swims—although I never got in. I cracked open a fresh six pack while he transformed, waving from the deepest part of the harbor that accommodated his massive mershark form.

He kept trying to get me to swim. I still hadn't told anyone about Mirra's curse—I was still working on getting people to like me enough for it to break. Although all that after party business had sort of been a long hiatus from seeking forgiveness. Fucking tour managers' girlfriends and guitarists' wives was *not* a good way to get humans to like you.

So I kept having to tell Leith that I'd do it next time. Next time turned into the time after that and maybe "another time" until he stopped asking with regularity. But he never gave up on me entirely. Leith's a good guy like that. He sees what you're capable of and nudges you toward it.

But it wasn't enough. I couldn't face the screams I knew waited for me under the waves and not even Leith and Kelly's continuous, patient support was enough to make me feel brave enough to try.

Then I met Evelyn.

18

Evelyn

Boston, Present Day

"Eve, you look rough."

"It's exhaustion chic, C." I rolled my eyes trying to play off the joke, but my voice fell flat. Caoimhe crossed the BUS meeting room at a near sprint and slammed into me, wrapping me up in her arms and squeezing me tight. The girl had the uncanny ability to always smell like a pile of laundry fresh from the dryer. I was so relieved to see her—to not be alone in this anymore—that I closed my eyes and inhaled.

"Are you smelling me?" she whispered, rocking our hug gently back and forth but not letting go.

"Shut up and let me be creepy," I whispered back. We both devolved into giggles and when we finally separated, we said, in unison:

"I have so much to tell you." Which only prompted more giggles.

"You can't ever leave me alone again," I said with mock admonishment.

"Apparently," she said, teasing me back. "I'm gone a week and all hell breaks loose."

God it was so good to have her home. My best friend was about six inches shorter than me with wild blonde curls that cascaded down her back and sparkling hazel eyes. There was something magical and mischievous about her, but if you didn't know you'd just think she had one of those charming Irish faces.

I knew better.

"How was it reconnecting with the leprechaun royalty?" I asked.

Caoimhe rolled her eyes and blew a raspberry.

"That good, huh?"

"It wasn't so bad," Leith said, joining us from upstairs. He was still damp from his swim, his shoulder-length brown hair pushed back from his face, but he changed into one of his usual flannels and a pair of jeans. Leith had eyes like the sea and a smattering of stubble that looked almost too perfect. He was a romcom star who had no idea he was handsome and he was Caoimhe's recent love.

Their love story was why mine had blossomed with Will.

Before it crashed and burned.

I shook the thought off as Leith squeezed my shoulder.

"It'll be okay," he said. I nodded, avoiding his sympathetic gaze. Will had been his best friend for *way* longer than I'd been in the picture. I felt guilty accepting his comfort without offering my own. He turned to Caoimhe. "I'm going to run up to Will's and get him some clean clothes."

"I'll come," I said.

"That's okay," he said, tilting his chin toward the back of the meeting room. The BUS had erected a temporary room behind their dramatic table. There was a simple twin bed, a nightstand with a pitcher, and thick iron bars encircling both. "You should be here when he wakes up. In case—"

"Please," I said, cutting him off. I didn't think I could handle seeing Will be Not Will anymore. Seeing him sleeping, so familiar yet so different from before, was more than my heart could take. I was desperate to be away from the whole situation, even if just for a break.

Leith nodded and I followed him up the stairs, squeezing Caoimhe's hand on the way out.

"Come with us?" I asked. She nodded and followed in silence.

My own hand throbbed dully beneath the bandages Kelly had expertly tied. The bleeding hadn't seeped through and aside from the pain and the exhaustion, I felt fine. I'd fended off four different offers to go to the ER on the way back into the city.

The only thing I could think about was getting back to see Caoimhe. Everything would make sense again with my best friend by my side.

We climbed the stairs, the only sound the creak of the boards beneath our feet, the huffed breaths between the three of us. When we reached the third floor, Leith pulled out a key and casually fit it to Will's door, swinging it open and clicking on the light against the gloomy late afternoon. My phone buzzed in my pocket and I glanced down to see Carrie's picture flickering on the screen.

"Shit," I whispered. "I have to take this. You guys go ahead. I'll be there in a second."

I took a deep breath, steeling myself for both the phone call and the apartment ahead of me, the door wide open to the dark shadows beyond.

"I'm so, *so* sorry I'm doing this," Carrie's gentle voice meshed with the hum of background noise in the office.

"It's okay," I sighed. "Did my text not send?"

"No, I got it but—"

"But you need it now." I rubbed the side of my face where a headache was growing in my temple. "I'm not at home, actually. Are you sure it can't wait?"

"It really can't, Evelyn." Again, she was apologetic, almost to the point of whining. "It was already late to start with and now we're losing out to other pubs running first. If I wasn't so sure your piece would offer something different than everyone else, I wouldn't hold out. But I trust your work."

I bit the end of my pinky to keep the tears from leaking out. I was relieved she couldn't see me as I put resolve into my voice. "I'm so sorry for all the back and forth, Carrie. I promise I have it finished. My inbox or yours must've eaten it."

"I have to have it by five or the story gets killed," she said, voice low. *Shit.*

"Doesn't matter," I said, trying to recover. "Because you'll have it by five. I swear."

"Thanks, Evelyn," Carrie sighed. "I'm really sorry. I know the timing is shit. How are you holding up?"

I didn't want to do the "I'm sad but my coworker offers me sympathy" dance right then.

"It'll be alright," I said. "But I gotta go. Thanks, Carrie." I hung up before she could say anything further.

"God *fucking* damnit," I hissed to the empty landing. I punched the air a few times, enraged there wasn't anything for my fists to connect with.

Had I not just been telling Marie how much I was crushing it at work? Was I not so convinced *hours* earlier that I was a shoo-in for the Paris reporting trip? And now I was fucking up simple deadlines for coverage that had been awarded specifically to me—I had been *requested* by the designers.

I couldn't fail. The piece had to run.

I looked from Will's open door back to the stairwell, my head drifting between the two like some solution would materialize out of the creaking wood floor.

Goals, gold, and Gucci. Those were supposed to be my focus. Those were supposed to be my guiding light.

What goal was I accomplishing by playing the wounded girlfriend to a cursed mershark? What gold was I earning by deferring a career defining assignment? I didn't even have to ask about the Gucci—Will wore the same three black t-shirts and jeans every day.

I looked back at the apartment's open door. I thought about the soft shape of him sleeping downstairs, at peace for the moment before he would be helpless against his curse again. An ache stretched across my heart and I rubbed my chest as if I could ease it.

Will was nowhere in the three Gs, but the longer I sat there, the more I realized I couldn't just leave him. I couldn't just strut back to my apartment and pick up work like the last forty-eight hours hadn't happened—like someone I cared deeply for wasn't in trouble.

Someone I maybe…

I shook my head and let out a loud sigh, running a hand through my hair.

"Let's not drop bombs, Evelyn," I muttered to myself. My heart fluttered against my chest, my gut squeezed, my legs trembled. My whole body was telling me the same thing everyone around me had been echoing, but I wasn't ready to drop the L word.

Not yet.

Rolling my shoulders back, I decided I would help Leith and Caoimhe pick out clothes for Will and then I would go home and handle my shit. That was it. I could always come back after.

Inside the apartment was exactly as I remembered it from before the New York trip. Will didn't have much—a couch, a bed, enough clothing to hang in the closet to keep it from looking bare. He'd told me it was because he was never home, but the longer I looked around, the more I thought about Pete's lux modern apartment downstairs, about Caoimhe's apartment across the hall, filled with mismatched furniture and posters for the artists she'd ushered into the world. I thought of my own studio, filled to the brim with thrifted clothing I treasured and a budding teacup collection. Even Leith's bachelor pad had a potted plant or two.

Will's home, by contrast, suddenly felt painfully empty.

Lonely.

While Leith and Caoimhe checked Will's kitchen, speaking to each other in low tones, I stepped into the bedroom. I flopped down into the bed and nearly broke into sobs at the musky, sharp smell of Will on the pillows. It made my entire heart clench when I remembered the last time we'd been here together.

The image flashed through me chased by the teeth of guilt as I remembered being with Billy the night before.

"Such a fuck up," I whispered, pushing myself out of the bed as if punishing myself. You don't get to smell your boyfriend's sheets if you just cheated on him.

"My non-serious boyfriend," I whispered to myself, standing up and going to the closet. "My non-serious boyfriend of only a month or two who may never recover from a curse that makes him a gigantic jackass."

My heart squeezed in my chest in protest.

Will's closet had the usual sparse t-shirts and jeans, a single extra work jacket for cold days on the water. Downstairs, he was confined to a space with just a bed and a nightstand. He wouldn't need only jeans. Where were his pajamas?

I turned to a rickety dresser on the far wall. I tried to pull the top drawer open, but the whole thing shuddered and *clanked*.

"What?" I asked no one. I pulled again, harder this time, and the drawer flung open, startling me. Inside was wall-to-wall empty whiskey bottles—the brand he sometimes drank from Joe's Corner Store downstairs. I yanked open another drawer to the same sight.

The next three drawers were all the same.

Five drawers stacked full of empty whiskey bottles. How long had he had these?

Frantic, I grabbed the two storage containers from under the simple metal frame of his bed.

More whiskey bottles—these were larger, older, but the same brand.

"Holy shit." Caoimhe's voice came from the doorway. When I looked up, I realized I'd strewn the drawers and containers all over the room, creating a chaotic pile-up of glass bottles as I searched Will's room. And I was smack in the middle.

"I can't do this," I said suddenly. "I cannot fucking do this." I gestured weakly at the bottles before letting myself drop to the floor in tears.

One hundred different thoughts slammed through me in that moment. I hadn't been watching him close enough. I hadn't been with him enough. I hadn't been enough. I should've done something different—I didn't know *what* but I clearly should've done *something*. I should've done anything that would've slowed down the constant onslaught we were facing, that would've kept Will out of the center of the bullseye.

Soft clanking and shuffling steps. Caoimhe's curly hair soft on my shoulder, her arms around me squeezing.

"This isn't your responsibility," she said. "You can't fix this."

"I just—"

"Look at me." I obeyed, finding Caoimhe's face in all the carnage. There was compassion like there always was, but there was something fierce there too. She wiped tears off my cheeks with the pad of her thumb. "You're always carrying other people on your shoulders. This is Will's burden, not yours."

"I do not."

She arched her eyebrows at me. "Oh right, so fake-dating Will to get me and Leith together was...?"

"That's you, it doesn't count," I said, sniffling. And I wasn't being petulant. I would've proposed marriage to the CEO of Walmart if it meant Caoimhe would be happy. "You would've done the same for me."

"Okay, how about my birthday last year?"

I blinked. No one else had planned anything for C, so I had skipped an all-hands meeting to arrange a surprise picnic dinner with two tickets to the outdoor concert series that night (also swiped from work). But again—I'd do anything for Caoimhe.

"Or Harvey's tie collection?" That man needed help. I couldn't be held responsible for the fashion crimes he committed daily so I'd taken him shopping on our lunch.

"Your dad?"

I looked away, staring into the bottom of an empty bottle. Maybe she had a point. I'd tried a thousand different ways, a hundred different times, to find the secret key to keeping my dad in a good mood, to easing whatever made him so angry all the time. I knew underneath his temper was the dad who made us laugh and who loved us more than anything else in this world. I was still constantly trying to bring that dad out, despite how much he continued to fall into himself these days.

"Sometimes love is letting people solve their own problems," Caoimhe said, squeezing me tighter. "I know you hate watching us fail because you're so much smarter than we all are, but you're just gonna have to suffer through this one."

"Did you live through an after school special in Ireland?" I asked, squeezing Caoimhe back.

"I'll tell you later," she said. "But let's go, Will is gonna freeze naked in that basement."

I grabbed the clothes from Will's closet before following Caoimhe out of the bedroom. Leith was waiting in the hall and he touched my shoulder as I passed.

"Will's drinking has gone on a long time," he said. "It's bigger than any of us and he won't let anyone help. It's not your fault."

"That's the longest sentence you've ever said to me," I said, trying to keep my lip from shaking. A tear slid down my face anyway. Goddamn it.

He gave me a weak half-smile as we left the apartment, clicking the door shut behind us.

Downstairs, Will was up and moving, pacing the length of the bars that surrounded him. Given that I was holding his clothing in my arms, I shouldn't have been surprised that he was prowling naked. I had to stop myself from letting my eyes rove hungrily over him—I missed my Will, not this stranger in his athletic, double-dicked body.

Wilhamena and Roxy were leaned over the far end of the table, talking in hushed tones with the vampires who had clearly just been woken up. Patrick's hair was sticking up at all angles and he was routinely rubbing his eyes. Billy's usually flawless exterior was rumpled and rushed, his hair in soft waves around his face. He caught me staring and I looked away immediately, feeling his eyes on me as I crossed the room to Will's enclosure.

"Here," I said, holding up a black t-shirt and a pair of jeans.

"I don't need your cloth, little fish."

"So, you remember me." My heart lurched and I tried to reign it in.

"You are all fish," he said, stopping his prowl in front of me. He ran that predator's gaze over my body and I held in a shudder. I missed him looking at me like he would devour me whole. I missed knowing I was safer than I'd ever been wrapped up in the arms of a dangerous man. "But yes, we have met before." He cocked his head at me as if trying to remember where.

I stepped closer to the bars, words falling from my mouth in a hopeful rush.

"Yes, yes, we have. Will it's me. It's Evelyn."

He stared at me, leaning his forehead onto the bars.

"Come closer," he murmured. "I think…"

I started to step even closer. I would've rubbed my entire body across those bars if it meant he'd remember me. I would've leapt into the cage with him, risking the potential threat to my life if it would bring him home to me.

"Evelyn." Leith stuck an arm between us, and Will immediately thrashed against the bars.

"You traitor!" he screamed, a muscle straining in his neck. "You human-lover!"

Leith silently took the clothing from me and slid it through the bars, leaving it on the ground at Will's bare feet. He looped an arm around me and guided me away.

Will kept shouting.

"Guppy-gilled bottomfeeder!"

I let Leith bring me to the table where the others were talking. Several more ancient-looking leather books were open, spread across the table. Pete was nowhere to be seen but with Kelly present I assumed he'd appear shortly.

"*Vegetarian!*" Will screamed.

"Put some pants on or I'll come in there and dress you myself," Wilhamena yelled back.

Will, incredibly, was cowed, eyeing the dwarf petulantly before picking up his jeans and shoving his arms through them. He scissored them up and down mockingly while pulling a gruesome face.

Wilhamena closed the book she was reading and took one step away from the table.

Will immediately corrected the pants and had them zipped before she could take a second step.

The dwarf returned to her spot at the table, reopening the book and calmly addressing the rest of us. I glanced at Will and watched him flip her off with both hands before slamming himself onto the bed, bare feet dangling off the edge.

"I don't mean to be harsh," she said. "But I could not stomach watching his dicks swing another second."

"Oh, hush, I know you're jealous," I said. Again, my joke sounded sadder than I'd meant. Again, I felt Billy looking at me. I refused to look back.

Wilhamena gave me a sad smile but continued. "It's clear that Will is struggling with an existing curse, but we haven't been able to understand the new layer of enchantment. It's meant to make him forget and somehow that interacts with the rules of the first spell."

"Like chemistry?" I asked. I didn't think magic would be so complicated. I'd assumed it was all finger snaps and wand waving.

Wilhamena nodded. "Unfortunately, this level of spell work is beyond me, and Pete's library hasn't held an answer yet."

"Wait," I leaned forward. "Are you guys not a group of magical people in Boston? Do you not know any witches?"

"There hasn't been a single witch in New England in hundreds of years," Roxy said. "They didn't really mesh with the Puritans."

"So call one?" I snapped. What good was knowing magic was real if you couldn't use it to fix your problems?

Wilhamena gave me a look and I leaned back in my seat.

"Pete is working on it," Kelly said. "In the meantime, we have something else we can try."

"No," Billy said.

Kelly rolled her eyes. "It's not your call or your choice," she said, looking to me. "It's hers."

"Yes," I said ignoring Billy's exasperated sigh. "Whatever it is, I'll do it."

"You can't—"

"You don't get to tell me what I can and cannot do," I said, words slow and calm enough that my threat was clear. I finally looked at him and held his gaze, refusing to look away. When he finally did, I turned back to the group. Caoimhe had a look on her face that said we would be talking about "whatever that was" the minute we had a chance.

"Tell me what to do," I said.

Kelly slid an open book to me. It looked like a recipe, with ingredients and instructions written in spindly ink.

"There is a potion for remembering," she said. "It's basic counter magic and it might not be strong enough to undo Mirra's work. But it gets exponentially stronger if taken willingly *and* if given by someone the person has loved somewhere in their memory."

"That's incredibly specific," I said, arching an eyebrow.

"Magic is all about intent," Caoimhe said, finally breaking her silence. Her arms were crossed and her face was the most serious I'd ever seen it. Leith stood behind her like a shadow. Jealousy ached in my gut at the way he watched her while she spoke, eyes soft, mouth parted slightly like he could swallow the vapor of her words.

"Our connections with Will are what can pull his memory back through the spell. If we fuse that intention with the potion's, we might be able to kickstart his remembering while Pete finds a witch," Wilhamena finished before leaning across the table to me. "He seems to respond best to you currently. But you do not have to do this if you're not up for it."

I jutted my chin forward like a challenge. "I said I'll do it."

Someone the person has loved. What if everyone was wrong? What if he had never loved me and my part of the cure didn't work? I shoved the thought away, gripping back onto the urgency of the current moment.

Wilhamena's eyes searched my face before she nodded. "You'll be first once the potion is brewed. It'll take some time and it will need to be delivered quickly. I'll tell Pete what we've decided, and we'll begin in his apartment."

She turned to the rest of the group. "In the meantime, everyone should take a break. Go for walks, call your jobs, check in with loved ones. This is going to be an intense process."

My deadline. I glanced down at my phone and wasn't surprised to see no signal. I'd have to go all the way back upstairs to call Carrie. And at that point I should just head home and get the article. I glanced back at Will as everyone began to file out.

Just one more try. Then I'd fix my shit.

Caoimhe headed straight for me but I waved her off. "One sec," I mouthed. She nodded and took Leith's hand, pulling him away from where he was staring at the back of Will's prostrate form.

Soon enough it was just me and Billy.

"You have sweet nothings you wanna whisper through the bars?" I asked.

"I have first watch," he said, looking away uncomfortably.

"Oh, so you wanna eavesdrop."

"I'll give you a moment," he said, still avoiding my gaze. I waited until the door closed before turning back around to face Will.

He was already up, pressed against the bars, and watching me.

19

Will

Boston, two months ago

I knew I loved Evelyn the first time she touched my ass.

I was drunker than I'd been in a long time, running from the usual due to the added stress of Leith having thrown a potential Mister Flipper investor into the harbor over something stupid. Caoimhe found me on the corner and led me home with Evelyn. The girls shoved my sorry ass up the stairs but couldn't get past my front door. Evelyn found my keys but not before she skated her hand over my ass and gave it a pinch.

I had to have her after that.

But of course, she played hard to get.

This was new territory for me with humans. Usually my looks were enough alone, but if that failed, I could try whichever celebrity I was impersonating that week—Tom Hiddleston, Idris Elba, Aziz Ansari.

Not with Evelyn.

* * *

"I can't believe you're standing up."

We were on the upper deck of Boat #1. Leith and Caoimhe were on the pier, meeting for the first time. We didn't know what was ahead of us, how we would all collide. I didn't care.

Evelyn had streaks of purple through the front of her hair that she wore cropped short and close to her face, leftover makeup from the club the night before, and was making her t-shirt and bike shorts look sexy as hell that morning. I couldn't stop looking at her—every piece of skin that slipped from beneath her t-shirt, every flex of her ass as she popped a hip and crossed her arms to look at me. She had a look on her face that was somewhere between curiosity and disgust.

It worked for me.

"It's the third leg," I said pointing at my crotch and sticking my tongue out.

Evelyn rolled her eyes. "You were so drunk," she said. "We had to carry you."

"Not so drunk I forgot you said you liked me." I flashed her a grin.

Incredibly, she flashed me one back.

"I like babies when they fall over too," she said. My heart thudded.

"I don't think you play grab ass with babies," I shot back.

She threw her head back and let out a full laugh, the kind that shook her whole body and rang through the air like the best kind of bell. "I sure fucking don't," she said, clamping a hand over her mouth. She was supposed to have left. Caoimhe had already admonished her for not leaving for work—as if she were her mother and not her best friend. "You win that one."

"What do I win?" I asked, pointedly moving closer to her.

She glanced over the edge of the boat, back down at Leith and Caoimhe, distracted.

"What—"

"Shhh." She waved a hand at me before I could repeat myself. "Shut up."

"Rude," I muttered, but I pulled myself up so I could see what she was looking at.

Leith and Caoimhe were facing each other on the pier, not more than a foot apart. I'd begged Caoimhe for her publicist services after Leith threw a man overboard in front of investors, ruining our chances and our reputation at the same time. It was out of character for his normally calm self but he'd been off kilter since his ex left.

Apparently, my begging had worked, because I'd barely begun my shift when Evelyn hopped up onto Boat #1 and cornered me with her big hazel eyes.

And now Leith and Caoimhe were apparently talking business—except they were holding so still the wind seemed to miss even ruffling their hair. There was something about the tension between them, the way Leith looked at her like he'd never seen anything so wondrous—the way she looked at him like finding comfort for the first time.

"Holy shit," I whispered.

"I know, right?" she whispered back. "We have to set them up."

"I don't know if Leith would go for it."

"Caoimhe either."

Then in unison:

"She worries too much about me."

"He worries too much about me."

That's when the fake dating thing started. It was only meant to be a single performance, something to nudge our favorite people together by way of demonstration. But the more time I spent whispering with Eve, giving her a heads up about how I'd be touching her, receiving instructions for what to say next so she would laugh, the deeper in love I fell.

And for the first time in decades, my heart felt a little lighter without my schwiskey dosage.

The night I felt the change, the one that told me I might finally have a chance at breaking my curse, Evelyn was in my room.

She showed up unannounced—we'd just sent Leith and Caoimhe off on their first date, so I'd assumed we'd have the night off. She was carrying Chinese takeout and she flashed me two pairs of chopsticks as she strutted by me into the apartment. It was like she belonged there, and I suddenly felt ashamed that the place wasn't set up to welcome her better.

"I don't spend much time at home," I said, gesturing to the still-full moving boxes I probably wouldn't unpack. I'd developed a habit of getting evicted every few months because none of my Mister Flipper money was going to rent anymore. I told Kelly and Leith I was on a quest to find the perfect spot. There was a look in their eyes like they knew something else was going on, but neither of them questioned me. Although every time I moved, Leith suggested I go for a swim—because of course he did.

I showed Eve the kitchen and let her start unpacking the takeout while I ducked into the bedroom.

My empties were *everywhere*. The pisser about having to buy your own schwiskey doses is the physical evidence. At least in the bars I could throw the bottles out with the rest of the waste from the night. No one ever batted an eye. But if your new neighbor puts twelve empty whiskey pints in the recycling, you notice.

Careful not to let any of the glass clink together, I lined the bottom of a dresser drawer with them. I coughed loudly while I shut the drawer to cover the sound. I threw the blankets back up on the bed, grabbed an unopened bottle from under my bed, and stepped back out into the apartment.

I waved the bottle as Evelyn held up two plates heaped with Chinese food—orange chicken, chow mein, beef and broccoli, and an egg roll balanced carefully on top.

She wrinkled her nose at me. "I don't think gas station whiskey goes with our dinner," she said. I shrugged, taking the plate from her.

"I didn't think we had plans tonight, but I, for one, am capable of trying experiences outside my expectations." I stuck my tongue out while she rolled her eyes.

"I have an ulterior motive," she said, plopping down on the couch with her food.

"You've come to tell me I've won you over with my charm and wit?" I rinsed a shot glass from the sink and measured out an evening dose. I cheered her solo before downing the shot.

"Actually, yeah," she said. I choked, sending the liquor through my nose and burning my lungs.

Evelyn liked me? I groaned, bent over the sink, trying to ride out the burn in my sinuses while frantically thinking of a smooth response. If I wasn't careful, I was going to crawl across the carpet to her on my hands and knees. I was going to worship at her feet and let her use me however she saw fit. I was going to drool in her lap until she banished me to the corner like a dog.

Evelyn liked me.

Finally, I looked back up, rubbing my face, somewhat recovered. She was watching me. Her face was a study in nonchalance, but I could see it in her eyes—a level of guard there that was lower than usual but ready to slam back up.

"You don't have to look so surprised," she said. "You're exactly my type. Hot and fucked up."

"You have no idea," I breathed.

She arched her eyebrows at me and everything in me screamed. I couldn't tell her. I hadn't told anyone but Kelly and that had been a drunk mistake she somehow didn't disown me for.

And she was human—which, at that point, was what she thought *I* was. She'd run from the room screaming if she knew the truth.

"I am so fucking hot," I added in the same tone, hoping the joke relieved the tension pulling between us.

It didn't.

"Look," she said. "We don't have to make a big deal out of this. It's not even exclusive. Just, I think we should try it. For real."

I let the word "exclusive" slide over my brain before disappearing. I didn't need a definition if it meant I got to be closer to Evelyn. She could fuck ten other guys and I wouldn't care—because at some point she'd come back to me and that was all I wanted.

And I would make sure she always came back.

"I like when mommy tells me what to do," I purred.

I ducked as a piece of orange chicken whizzed by my head.

"If you aren't into me, just say it," she said, but I could tell through her joking tone that she meant it.

"Of course, I'm into you, Evelyn, are you insane?" I gestured widely to her. "Look at you. Look at *all of that* and tell me any man wouldn't be tripping all over himself to be with you."

I cleared the distance between us, vaulting myself over the back of the couch and landing with our hips touching. I slid an arm around her shoulders and hauled her into me, sending chow mein slipping off her plate and into my lap.

"You telling me I can smack that ass in public and *mean it* this time?"

"God, no," she said, but a blush crept up from her neck to her ears. I'd revisit that request later.

"I'm serious, Eve," I said, sliding a hand across the soft plushness of her face and tilting her to look at me. I was fed by those eyes, fulfilled in ways that food, alcohol, sex couldn't begin to touch. "I'm with you. Let's try it."

"I don't know what it is about you," she said, eyes half shut, angling her mouth up to mine.

"I was hoping you could tell me," I said before pressing a kiss to that lush, perfect mouth.

Our first.

And it was perfect, even with the takeout food all over my couch.

I took the plate from Evelyn's hands and set it on the floor.

"I was eating that," she protested before sliding both hands up along the base of my scalp.

I pulled her hips to me, angling us both down onto the couch and pressing into the delicious softness of her. "I promised to fill your mouth with something else." And I hadn't been faking that part.

"Like that little thing is gonna fill me up."

Her challenge went straight to my cocks, twitching hard enough against my jeans to make me pause. She was grinning up at me like she'd hit a bullseye and I wanted to swallow that smile, capture some part of it to keep inside me on bad days.

"It's not the size, it's what you do with it."

"Like I haven't heard that before."

I nipped her bottom lip and she lifted her hips to me, gasping.

"Does that feel like disappointment?" I asked, savoring the way her eyes grew wide, how her cheeks flushed.

In answer, she pulled me down to her, claiming my mouth with hers. We kissed each other with a renewed frenzy, each sweep of the tongue rewarded with a soft gasp, each gentle bite on the lip sending a pulse through my body. Heat was coursing through me, touching every piece of pent-up frustration and setting it alight. It had only been a few days of touching each other, grabbing one another, holding one another, making threats and promises. But every single moment had felt like hours and every minute delayed had made this week feel like a lifetime.

Now, Evelyn couldn't dance out of my grasp.

I gripped her hips, pulling her against me and burying my face in her neck when she let out a moan as she ground herself on my jeans.

She gripped me by a fistful of hair and hauled me up to look at her.

Holy shit, I'm gonna marry her.

"Bedroom," she gasped out.

I nodded, practically leaping off the couch and grabbing her hand to lift her up. Our bodies snapped back into each other, unable to weather even a few inches of distance. Evelyn pressed against me, running her hands across my chest and shoulders, and kissing me like she would swallow me whole if she could.

We stumbled tangled steps down the hall and collided with the door frame, breathless, needy, starved for each other.

She slid her hands across the plane of my stomach before reaching for my cocks through my jeans like a woman who owned me.

God, she did.

Evelyn gasped, looking up at me with a startled expression.

"What do you have in there?" she asked. I couldn't focus on the question. Everything was reduced to Evelyn's hand and my cocks and the infuriating layer of denim between them. She squeezed my balls before drifting her hands up to my zipper and although I was seeing everything in a horny mist, an alarm went off in the back of my mind.

Right.

Two cocks.

Human woman.

I gently gripped her hands and shook my head.

"Too much?" she asked, pulling away and lacing her fingers with mine.

"I just have something I should warn you about," I said between heaving breaths. I let go of her hands so I could run my own across my face, trying to clear it of sex fog.

"Yeah, you do," she said, arching an eyebrow and looking meaningfully at my crotch. "You're smuggling a prairie dog in there and I'm not a meadow."

"Yeah, about that…" I looked at her, beautifully flushed, lips plumped, eyes bright and watchful.

Where would I start? How much could I tell her without coming unraveled?

My mind began to race, one thought trampling another before it could complete. Evelyn liked Will the human—whose worst offense was drinking too much and sleeping around. She didn't know Will the mershark who destroyed families and betrayed friends.

I could tell her the same thing I told all the other women—the extra dick is a lucky birth defect.

But I couldn't start this thing between us with a lie.

And Evelyn was so far above "all the other women," I couldn't treat her like that.

"I can't," I whispered, defeat making my shoulders slump.

"Hey, that's okay," she said, voice sympathetic. She reached forward and rubbed my shoulders. "It happens to everyone, it's totally normal."

"No, no." I shrugged her off. "Everything works just fine, I just can't. Not until…"

I turned and let myself settle heavily onto the edge of the bed, trying to hide from the understanding on her face with my hands.

"I want to do this with you, Eve," I said, looking up at her in the doorway. She was watching me like I'd seen Leith watch musicians perform—open, ready, waiting for me to pull her heart through her throat. "But I don't want to fuck us over before we start."

"What do you mean?" she asked.

"I did horrible things before," I said. "Things I can never make right no matter how hard I try. There is so much blood on my hands and it will never come clean."

She was quiet for a moment as my words hung heavy between us.

Finally, she came and sat next to me.

"Would you do it again? Given the chance?" The cheap mattress dipped, slinging us against each other, knee to knee, thigh to thigh.

"I don't know, Eve," I said, tears making my throat thick. "I lose control of myself when I'm—" I stopped, squeezing her hand but avoiding her gaze. "When I'm like how I used to be."

"I don't know a lot about you, Will," she said after another long moment. "But I've been with men way worse than you because they weren't even willing to admit their wrongs."

She leaned over, pulling my gaze up to hers.

"I believe in your ability to make things right," she said. "And you aren't alone in it. Leith is with you, Kelly's with you…" she hesitated, sighed, nodded to herself. "I'm with you."

I searched her face for some sign that she was faking it but found only earnestness.

"There's so much I need you to know," I said, overwhelmed by where to start, drowning in her comfort. "So much I haven't done yet. I thought I'd be in a better place when someone like you came along."

"Someone like me?"

"Someone who could save me."

"Only you can save yourself," she said, brushing hair from my face and letting her fingers linger on my cheek. "And you are worth saving."

In that instant, I felt a sudden lightness in my heart, as if one of the weights always clamped around it had released its grip.

* * *

I woke the next morning to persistent knocking on the front door. Careful not to wake Evelyn, who was curled up in one of my t-shirts, snoring softly, I padded to the front door.

Caoimhe was there, dressed for work and clearly pissed about something.

"Are you a merman?"

Thankfully it was early enough I didn't have to fake looking confused, squinting at her in the morning light.

"Is that what you're into?" I deflected.

"Don't be gross," she said, shoving her way into my apartment. I let her. Although some part of me perked its ears, watchful of Eve sleeping in the next room. "Answer the question."

"If I am?" My nerves were skittering to life, and I found myself reaching up to remove the cigarette that wasn't in my mouth. I usually had a smoke for this kind of bravado. "You gonna have Pete kick me out?"

We all knew Caoimhe wasn't human. She had a fairy tail none of us could account for, a stupid nickname for the magical retinue that followed royal fae. In her case, it was just the single, tiny, bug-like lower fairy but still—it meant not only was she fae of some kind, she was *important* fae.

She shook her head, blonde curls bouncing. "You can be my neighbor, but you cannot prey on my best friend. If you're a merman, you have to break up with Evelyn."

"Then I'm not a merman."

She looked at me accusingly, narrowing her eyes and setting her mouth in a grim line.

"*If* you are a merman," she stepped forward, crossing her arms and pushing her shoulders back. She looked like she was about to throw down a gauntlet and I couldn't help but be a little worried. "And if that hurts Eve in some way, I will make sure you are in pain for the rest of your life."

"You promise?" I deflected again. I hadn't expected the "I will crush you for dating my best friend" routine this early. Caoimhe and Evelyn really had something special together.

"I promise, Will Burleigh," she said, using my full name like a threat. Funny how a name pushed together by chance and a baby name book kept getting wielded like that.

"She can make her own decisions," I said, hoping Evelyn wasn't hearing any of this. She'd already decided to ignore Caoimhe's warning the first time, but how serious would the fear be before she agreed to leave me? How much more prodding would it take to dissolve something that hadn't even gotten started? Especially after last night. "She can make her own decisions, 'dangerous' or not."

"You look like you eat takeout more than human women," she whispered.

"Is that supposed to be an insult?" I mocked.

"Fine! Don't tell me." She dropped her arms, defeated. "Keep your secret."

"It's a not a secret if you've figured it out." The words fled my mouth before I could stop them. All of this holding and keeping and sneaking was beginning to get the best of me. I didn't know if Leith had told her anything yet and now I was maybe endangering *their* possibilities as well as mine and Evelyn's.

"You know," she barely breathed the words.

"I suspect," I said, desperately trying to cover. "Should I know?" Could I flip this back on her?

"I don't know anymore," she said, looking down at her shoes.

I thought back to Evelyn last night, her promise that I wasn't alone. I recognized the crushing weight on Caoimhe's shoulders, the desperate need to talk with *someone* but not knowing if it is safe to do so.

"It's okay to trust people sometimes," I started. "Everyone has secrets, I think you'll find more support than you know."

She snapped her head up, staring at me with a mixture of fear and desperation. Wordlessly, she turned and left, practically sprinting down the stairs.

"You can trust Leith," I called after her.

I closed the door, trying to shut out the interaction.

It looked like me and Caoimhe had more in common than I thought—a massive secret we couldn't bear alone anymore and a practically fatal need to protect Evelyn.

20

Evelyn

"Now you've got me, little fish, what're you gonna do with me?" Will humped the bars and stuck his tongue out. Believe it or not, this made me disgustingly homesick. It was the type of antics Will would pull when we were just goofing off together or trying to make Caoimhe roll her eyes.

But this wasn't my Will and this version of him meant the actions to make me uncomfortable.

It wasn't gonna work.

"Do you know who I am?" I asked, taking a few cautious steps toward the enclosure.

"My next meal," he snapped his teeth with an audible *click*. He was only wearing the unbuckled jeans that Wilhamena had threatened him into. His muscles strained against the bars he held in each fist and there was a light sheen of sweat across his body. His breathing seemed frantic, coming in heavy gusts as if he'd been running, and I thought of tigers at the zoo, pacing back and forth, baring their teeth at the many sets of eyes peering in at their captivity.

I shook my head, maintaining my slow forward pace. He didn't scare me—even like this. He had never scared me. The one thing I was with Will was safe. And I knew, deep down under this curse, he knew who I was.

Why hadn't he killed me already? He'd had several chances and *yes*, I'd been hurt. But he could've destroyed me in the water. He didn't.

My Will was in there, fighting for both of us.

"Careful, little fish," he growled as I got closer. "You are so delicious I won't be able to stop myself once I start."

"You've said that before," I prompted. "Do you remember?"

"I've never seen a little fish so delicious," he said.

"You said, 'I won't just stop at one,' do you remember what we were doing? When you said that?"

"Hunting," Will said. I was close enough to the enclosure now to smell him, sweat and saltwater.

"No, guess again."

"Eating."

"You could call it that," I tilted my head, stopping just beyond his arm's reach outside the bars.

I watched his dark eyes swallow me and I tried not to shiver as they ran the length of my body. His nostrils flared and he took a deep shuddering breath.

"I can smell it on you," he said, voice no more than a gravelly murmur.

"You haven't guessed yet."

He turned his head so that he only glanced at me out of the corner of one pupilless black eye. He was in his human form now, but his eyes and his manners were all shark.

"Fucking, little fish," he said, baring his teeth at me through the bars. He rattled them in his hands and gnashed his teeth. "You love to fuck the monsters. What a naughty guppy."

"So you remember." I tilted my chin up.

"Fucking you?" He shook his head and tutted between closed lips. "I would never. It was a guess, little fish."

"Really?" I stepped within his reach this time, the danger of it trilling down my spine, lighting every nerve on fire. This was still Will, somewhere. I was safe, even if every instinct in my body was screaming to run. "You don't remember how I licked your balls or how you ripped my panties off?"

He stilled as I grew closer, his breathing slowing to a more natural pace. Still, those pupilless eyes took me in.

"Naughty guppy," he growled again. "Such language."

"You really don't remember? The champagne and the sheets that were so nice you stopped fingering me so we could both feel them for a minute?"

His mouth was hanging slightly open as he watched me, and for a split-second I swore I saw Will in his eyes again.

"What about when you stretched me to take both cocks at the same time? And we were finally joined together after being so patient for weeks? Do you remember that?"

My Will was in there. And the same desperate mantra from under the water found me on dry land.

Come back.

We stared at each other for what felt like an eternity, and the longer I looked, the more I started to see a flicker of Will in the predator's gaze.

I was almost directly against the bars now, within touching distance of not-my-Will.

"It was unforgettable," I said. "I know you remember. Come on, baby."

I placed one hand gently over his, clenched around the bar. And *there* for a full second this time, was the Will I knew.

His eyes softened, his jaw relaxed, his teeth slid back behind his soft lips.

"Eve?" he breathed.

"Yes," I sobbed, nodding emphatically.

With a roar, he whipped himself away from the bars, snatching his hand away.

"Nasty guppy," he screamed, turning back to me this time more shark than man. "I am safe when I am fearless, and I am buoyant when I am focused. You are a distraction that makes my heart heavy and then the screams come back through the water. Go away."

"Will—"

"*Go away! Go away! Go away!*" His screams chased me out of the meeting room and back into the stairwell where I slammed straight into Billy's hard chest. He was dressed in a navy blue ensemble, a flash of deep mustard yellow silk peering through the vest. Small diamond studs winked in his ears, reflecting the lowlight. His chiseled face was pointed in concern, red eyes wild as they found mine.

"Evelyn—"

I slammed the meeting room door shut behind me, sending a rumble through the building and a wash of dust over us. Acting purely on instinct as I ran from the shitshow warring in my heart, I reached forward and hauled Billy down to my mouth the way I had the night before.

I needed to work off the tension I'd built up with not-Will. I needed to feel something that wasn't disappointment.

I needed to know sex with me wasn't forgettable.

I needed to know *I* wasn't forgettable.

Billy followed my lead, colliding with my teeth and lips hard enough to bruise—hard enough to send a shudder down my spine where it lit my lower nerves on fire. I wrapped my arms around his neck, lifted a leg up to his waist, relieved to find he was already hard.

"Lift," I said before swiping a commanding tongue into his mouth. His firm hands found my other leg and lifted, supporting me under the ass and pressing me hard into the ancient wood door. I ground my hips against him, desperate for the friction between us.

I pulled away, gasping for air as he scraped his fangs along my neck—not biting, but teasing, sending jolts of lightning to my pussy with each scrape.

"You have to fuck me," I moaned.

"Not here," he said, voice rough with want.

"Yes, here," I said, turning his face to meet mine. "Here and now."

"The others—"

"Won't be down for a while," I said. "They're brewing a potion."

"Answer me something first," Billy said, pulling away but still holding me in place, practically pinned to the wall with his dick.

"It's just a quick—"

"Did he remember you?"

I looked away.

"Evelyn." The way he said my name meant so much more than an admonishment. It was understanding. It was encouragement. It was sympathy.

"I just need a break," I said. "It's all too much."

"Evelyn," he said again, pulling my gaze back to his with just his voice. "That's all this is?"

I nodded. I knew it wasn't fair to him, I could see it flash across his face. But I needed a way out of all of this, no matter how short.

He let out a slow sigh, resting his forehead against mine.

"I can give you that," he said. "But it can't be sex."

I nodded again. That was fair. I couldn't ask for more than he could give.

"And it's not going to be in the stairwell," he continued. "You might get off on nearly getting caught but we need a different crowd to potentially discover us. Kelly will murder us both on sight."

I winced. Deep in my gut I knew screwing around with Billy wasn't only hurting myself. There would be other casualties if everything was righted and back to normal.

If.

I closed my eyes, willing the massive hypothetical away from our goals, willing the world to stop trying to swallow me whole while I hung in limbo.

"Where, then?" I breathed.

Billy set me down, straightening his clothes and gently taking my hand. He led me beneath the stairs, ducking into the darkest shadow in the corner. I listened as a *click* sounded and then a gust of chill air washed over us.

"It's alright," Billy's voice came from the dark as he pulled me forward into what felt like an underground chamber. I glanced back at the wooden door to the BUS meeting room one last time before it was lost from my view and everything became a cold darkness, the only sound our breath in the air.

I don't know how long we descended into that dark, Billy's hand in mine the only anchor, but after only a few moments I lost myself to it. There was no worldly problem that could reach me here, deep underground where neither light nor cell signal could survive. There were no frustrated screams from an enraged, cursed boyfriend. There were no sympathetic glances. There were no missed deadlines. There was no weight of curse breaking on my shoulders.

It was just me and the dark.

And Billy.

Billy stopped suddenly and I collided gently with his back, resting my face against his firm shoulders and quietly inhaling the expensive cologne he wore.

Another *click* and we stepped into a strange but luxurious room. It looked for a moment as if someone had carved a guest room out of bedrock but closer inspection revealed it to be more complex than that. The stone walls were manufactured and even, although the floor was rough dirt. Above us was a series of rusty metal pipelines that ran the length of the room, continuing into the darkness.

Candles were scattered all around the room and I squinted in their lowlight.

In sharp contrast to the surroundings were the furnishings—dark polished wood and iron metal finishes, a deep red Turkish rug spread beneath the four poster bed with a velvet canopy. On the nightstand stood a silver pitcher, polished to a low sheen. Hanging off one drawer pull was a satin sleep mask, which nearly made me burst into giggles.

"No coffin?" I asked, my voice cracking.

"We've evolved," Billy said, guiding me forward into the luxurious underground room in a waltz-like gesture. The image of Will's empty apartment stacked high with empty whiskey bottles flashed across my mind.

Here it was, all my vampire dreams coming true.

And all I had to celebrate was a massive pit in my stomach.

21

Will

Boston, two months ago

ame to believe that a Power greater than ourselves could restore us to sanity.

Something impossible had happened since that moment together in my bedroom—Evelyn's simple act of understanding had loosened some of the guilt that threatened to weigh me down.

I felt brave again.

After Evelyn left my apartment, I went to the edge of the pier and looked down into the water. I promised myself it would be brief—simply testing the waters with an ear for echoes. If it was too much, I'd change back and climb up the back entrance to Kelly's office like Leith was always doing.

I was barely in water deep enough to support my mershark form before my murderous past rose to meet from the ocean floor. But this time I did not flinch when the voices slammed through me. This time

I did not run when the grief pulled me down.

I let it sink me. And when I was at the very bottom, fins throwing up a soft dusting of sand, I let it hold me down as all the pain and sadness I had caused flooded through me.

All the while I thought of Evelyn's hand on the side of my face, the look in her eyes, the shape of her mouth as she said the phrase that unlocked my lonely human heart.

"You are worth saving."

It was rapid fire pacing. It was barreling toward a 50-50 chance of disaster with my eyes closed. It was trust in insanity, faith in chaos.

It was love for the damned—a holy light amid the fires of hell.

It was all I needed.

When I finally pushed myself up from the bottom, rising to meet the flickering sunlight above, the echoes did not silence but they did not grow either.

For the first time since Mirra's curse, I felt like surviving this was possible.

* * *

Later that night, I pulled Evelyn toward me in the water, her human body tiny compared to the bulk of me cutting through the frigid dark. I was all too aware of how easily I could destroy her if I wasn't careful.

To her credit, Eve was shocked but not frightened. If anything, she seemed mostly curious, treading water in her underwear, eyes lit up with the moon.

"W-w-w-what the actual f-f-f-f-uck?" she shivered.

I grinned, aware of how many teeth I was showing her.

"I thought you were in the fucking mob, not a…um…" her words trailed off as she looked me over, rising and re-settling in the water with a swell. Her lips were rapidly turning blue and the shakes looked like they were getting more intense. We could talk more later—when I could respond.

I ducked beneath the water, settling Eve's legs across my back and rising up. I heard her screech in delight as I took off, careful not to let her drop too far below the water. How the shark swims it, the park where we'd left Leith and Caoimhe was only a few short moments away and quickly I was shifting back into my human form. I boosted Evelyn up the ladder before following her.

I'm never going to forget the way she looked at me when I finally reached the grassy patch where we'd ditched our clothes. It's the only time a woman has made me feel shy.

She looked like she was going to eat me whole on the spot—like someone had delivered her a fantasy made real and she wouldn't waste any time indulging.

"That's no prairie dog," she whispered, shimmying back into the short dress she'd worn to meet me. I noticed she'd ditched her wet underwear and was squeezing out her bra cups into the grass.

"It's uh…hard to explain," I said, blushing all the way to my toes. Eve knew the truth now. I felt stripped clean and laid bare in a way I never had before. All my usual bravado went out the window.

"None needed," she said, reaching a hand to me as I struggled to get my jeans on. "But we should go someplace private."

"Yeah?" I wiggled a little extra as I shrugged on my t-shirt. "You like what you see?" I gestured wide with my arms and did a stiff shimmy.

It earned me a cackle and a playful thump on my chest. I barely had time to grab my shoes before Evelyn was dragging me away from the bobbing lights of the harbor and across the street. The pavement was sharp on my bare feet but I kept up the chase, tip-toeing through a back alley where even the streetlights wouldn't reach. I heard Evelyn mutter to herself a moment before gasping in surprise and glee.

"*There it is,*" she whispered. There was the tell-tale sound of a keycard being accepted and a door opened in the dark, sending a golden slant of light across us. Eve turned to me and pressed a finger to her lips.

We were in a hotel hallway with identical white doors flanking each side. Soft piano music trickled through a speaker somewhere and the ivory carpet was plush beneath my feet. Striped, yellow wallpaper made everything feel tighter than it was and I wondered if rich people enjoyed feeling squished in the halls they walked every day.

Eve pressed an ear against one door, shook her head, moved onto another. She repeated this process until we were halfway down the hallway when she finally keyed a door open. She motioned for me to wait and then crept inside, gently closing the door but not letting the latch click shut.

Seconds pressed on for an impossible amount of time and I immediately realized I was wet, barefoot, and underdressed for the weather. What was I going to tell someone if they came by?

A rattling cleaning cart sounded from around the corner and my pulse thrummed. I weighed my options, wondering if I should go in after Evelyn or if I should make a run for the elevator. Right when my instincts couldn't take standing still anymore—I had lifted one foot to step away—I felt Eve's hand clamp around my arm and haul me into the dark room.

"What the fuck are we doing?" It was a sharp question but I found myself laughing through it, adrenaline pumping, human heart finally flying free. I heard the door click shut behind us and relief lifted me higher.

"It's my most famous party trick," she whispered back.

"Here I thought I was special, but you're going around sneaking entire parties into hotels."

She laughed, and I grabbed her waist, pulling her into me, seeking out her mouth with the careful nudging of my nose across the soft curves of her face.

One searing kiss and Eve's hands were everywhere at once, sliding under my shirt to dance along the sensitive skin there, hooking beneath the waistband of my pants and tugging. I groaned into her mouth as she found the zipper and freed my already hard cocks, fisting first one and then the other.

I let her press me against the hotel door with a thud, lifted my hips as she pulled my jeans and boxers down in one push, sliding to the ground with them. She kneeled and looked up at me, barely silhouetted in the dark.

"It's okay if it's too much—" I started but she shushed me.

"It'll be more than a mouthful," she said in a murmur that hit me straight in the gut. "But lucky you, I am *starving*."

She leaned forward and licked across the top of one cock, sending a shuddering wave of heat through me.

"You have to do one thing for me," she said.

"Yes, I will murder the president," I groaned out as she licked across the second cock.

"Not that drastic," she said. "I need you to tell me I'm a good girl."

I paused. "Evelyn—"

"It's not that deep," she cut me off. "It just does it for me. Kinda like you."

"I'm not that deep?" I couldn't help the flinch. I had just bared myself *literally* to this woman. Did she not think we were something?

"No," she sighed, frustrated. "That's not what I meant. I'm not eloquent with two juicy cocks staring me in the face."

I huffed out a laugh and thrust forward, wiggling my hips back and forth so my cocks swung directly under her nose.

"Solve for the Pythagorean theorem now, smarty pants."

She reached around and pinched my ass.

"Can I elaborate after I suck your dicks?"

"You can do anything you want if that's the trade off."

"I thought magic people weren't supposed to make deals like that."

"Evelyn, I would let you kill me right now if it meant you'd let me fuck your mouth…like a *good girl.*"

She hummed a joyous note and then flicked that tortuous teasing tongue across my cock again.

"Careful," she said, licking the second one again. "I will hold you to that."

"I've lived a long life," I said. But I couldn't finish my joke as she gripped the base of one cock and wrapped her lips around the other. I was lost in the warmth of her, the expert way that she never stopped stroking one cock while she sucked on the other, alternating just when I thought one was satisfied and the other would be blue later.

"That's right," I groaned out. "Just like that, good girl."

The praise earned me a hum along the length of one cock that nearly finished me before I was ready. I didn't want this moment to end, didn't want to let go of the care and attention I was receiving at the hands of a woman I was probably going to let stab me later. Or whatever it was she would cash this in for.

I looked down to see her glancing up at me, a self-satisfied glint in her eyes.

I really had lived enough life. It was okay if she killed me.

Right when I wasn't expecting it, she continued stroking me this time with both hands and there was the soft pressure of her sucking on my balls.

"Not a good girl," I rasped out as heat pooled and tightened within me. "The *best* girl."

"Where do you want to finish?" she asked, and the question spun my head.

"You want logistics right now?" I managed through gritted teeth as she palmed my balls calmly—as if they were a fine-motor exercise.

"My tits it is," she said, gleefully flinging off her dress and *fuck me* the sight of her naked and kneeling before me, plunging her mouth down along one cock with a hum sent vibrations snaking up into a very tight coiled part of me desperate to spring free.

Then the sex goddess of my dreams, the only woman I would bow to forever more, the human who had offered me understanding and mercy, stuck her pinky into my asshole and curved it.

Pleasure exploded through every part of me as I found my edge and sprinted over it, freefalling into hazy, loose-limbed bliss. I cried out as I came and I forced myself to open my eyes so I wouldn't miss the sight of those white-hot ropes landing across her perfect sloping tits.

"Marry me," I whispered between gasping breaths. "Right now."

"No," she chirped from the floor before tugging me into the bathroom behind her. She ran a washcloth under warm water and cleaned us both up.

"How'd you do it?" I asked, mesmerized as she wiped the cloth across her tits.

She shrugged. "Men love having their asshole touched."

"No, the hotel room thing."

"Oh. That." She blushed and I was amazed at what embarrassed her. "An ex-boyfriend made me a master key a long time ago."

"Couldn't have been that long if it still works."

She swatted me with the cum towel.

"Jealous?"

"Does a jealous man offer to let you murder him?"

The door beeped and we heard the lock turn.

"Holy shit," Eve breathed. Her dress was still in the hallway.

"Jerry, I told you already, we'll have the brief done before tomorrow. It will all be smoothed over—oh goddamn it."

I pressed against the door to shut it and re-engage the lock as I snatched up Eve's dress and my pants, silently stepping back into the bathroom and turning off the light.

"No, not you, Jerry, I'm having trouble with the hotel room door."

The door beeped again and this time it opened. From where I peeked through the cracked bathroom door, Evelyn pressed against me in the dark, I watched a middle-aged blonde woman in a beige suit-dress stumble through the hall. One hand pressed a cellphone to her ear and the other dragged a tiny black wheely bag.

She continued yelling at poor Jerry about making things right with a wronged investor. Her voice carried from the far end of the room and that's when Evelyn shoved me.

"Now," she whispered, and I sprinted for the door.

My heart was pounding, and my pulse was in my ears. I glanced behind me to see Evelyn carefully shutting the door as silently as she could, before shimmying back into her dress and sprinting after me.

Once back in the alleyway, I grabbed Evelyn and kissed her hard, just once.

"Marry me," I said again.

"You're demanding today," she laughed, wriggling free of my grip. "And no. I'm a floozy but even I don't move that fast. Come on, let's go check on Leith and Caoimhe."

"Why?" I whined.

"Because otherwise we'll be up all night fucking and *they'll* be up all night fucking and two women with simultaneous UTIs is no bueno, mi amigo."

I followed her out of the alley and to a brightly lit corner where she tapped on her phone a few times. "I'll get us a ride back to your place," she said. "It's probably okay if I crash with you since you've proposed twice."

I nodded emphatically. If she never left my sight again, I'd be satisfied.

"Are you really that worried about your friend's vagina?" I asked.

She shook her head, peering up at me through those enticing

eyelashes. Her mouth was plump, and her cheeks were flushed and the streetlight made her eyes bright in an otherworldly way.

"No," she said. "But I *really* want to have sex with you, and I don't think you're ready. So, we need a distraction."

"I'm not ready?" I thumped my own chest in disbelief. She was entirely right, I wasn't. Not for sex with the woman I would let destroy me. That was going to need build up.

"Look," she said, popping a hip at me as she checked her phone screen. "I'll be completely straight with you. I use sex to run from my problems or avoid feelings. But I don't want to do that with you. Something about you feels different but I don't know what yet."

"Is it the double cocks?"

She thumped my shoulder.

"I'm serious," she said. "I know how things went last night, but honestly, if you hadn't stopped us I probably would've. Something about you and me, it works."

"Is that what you meant by 'it just does it for you?'"

She nodded, smiling shyly.

"Aren't you a writer?" I cocked my head and tapped a finger to my chin in thought. "Google, what are synonyms for 'just doing it?'" That earned me another playful thump and I rubbed my chest, laughing.

"I'm serious," she said. "We're on a fast track already, let's not rush the good stuff."

Our car pulled up and I opened the door for her.

"Besides, you know what they say about people who wait," she said, kissing me on the cheek.

"I'm pretty sure they die before they get to the good stuff."

22

Evelyn

Boston, present day

I settled hesitantly onto the edge of Billy's bed. The frantic urges I'd had in the hallway dissipated. In their place was a steady low vibration of anxiety punctuated by spiraling what-ifs.

What if they finish the potion and I'm not there?

What if they make the wrong potion and we accidentally make everything worse?

What if the potion doesn't work?

What if I never get Will back?

That last question bounced through me, echoing louder and louder until the hypothetical grief threatened to overwhelm me.

I felt my old defenses slide into place—the same ones that kicked to life when we had to leave town again, or Dad didn't come home again, or I was left with a mess after a breakup *again*.

If Will never returned, I would be sad for a while (*maybe forever*) and then I would go back to work. I'd meet someone new, someone normal who didn't hide a liquor store's worth of empty bottles under their bed and was well-adjusted. I imagined myself on the arm of some handsome faceless stranger, attending a runway or boutique opening. I imagined myself laughing and content with that life.

My dissociative fantasy felt possible. It always felt possible. I'd imagine the screaming match in the kitchen was coming from a TV, that my parents were watching a drama and soon they'd come in to kiss me goodnight just like everyone else's family. I'd imagine the boxes weren't piled up to leave again, that we were just getting here and we'd start unpacking soon to stay a long time. Each time, the fantasy felt fuller than my real life—safer, better, more comfortable.

But this time it felt empty.

Billy handed me a silver goblet. The candlelight flickered across its surface, wavering in the red liquid.

"Exactly as I would've picture it," I sighed.

"And yet I'm sensing that I've horribly disappointed you," Billy said, settling on the bed next to me.

I took a sip of the wine—tart and bold—before turning to Billy. I was sure I looked like a hopeless mess, dark circles under my eyes, clothes fucked up from practically humping him mid-leap in the stairwell.

"I'm sorry," I said. "This is all such a mess and I'm not very good at staying in messes until they're straightened out."

"No one is," Billy said, cupping my face in his hand. I leaned into his touch. "I've lived longer than I care to admit and I'm still figuring out how to not run from hard things."

"And I've dragged you into all this." I looked down into my wine glass, guilt swirling up to meet me.

"I dragged myself into this, thank you very much. Don't go taking all the credit."

He gave me a teasing half-smile and it nearly broke my heart.

"Why?" I asked, voice barely above a whisper. "Why put yourself in the middle of my mess? Why let me…"

"Let you what," he prompted, tilting his chin up.

"…why let me use you like this?"

"You think you're using me?" His eyebrows shot up nearly into his hairline.

"You're the one saying things like 'I can't let you regret me' while you're fucking me with a vibrator," I said, only a little proud of how good my attempt at his accent was.

He threw his head back and laughed, the sound bouncing off the walls around us and landing back at my feet. It felt so close, so tangible in this space with no natural air, no windows, no other sound but us, I wondered if I could reach down and grab his joy off the dirt floor.

"Evelyn," he said. "I like you. But I know exactly what I'm doing here."

"And what *exactly* are you doing?"

"Enjoying an incredible human woman while she'll let me," he said. "All my time with your kind is short-lived. This is just particularly so."

"So, you don't mind that—"

"I don't mind that as soon as Will returns to his right self that you will leave me—and Evelyn." He brought his other hand up to the side of my face so that I was cocooned within his soft grasp. "He *will* come back to you. There is something powerful between the two of you and we all see it."

The gentle encouragement and reminder of how deep Will was attached to my heart was too much. Heat built behind my eyes, tightened in my chest, threatened to spill out in never-ending sobs.

"I'm a bad person," I said finally, voice choked with tears. Billy pulled me into him, and I immediately regretted how much snot was leaking out onto his silk shirt.

"You are doing the best you can with what you have," he said, rubbing a soothing hand across my back. "And right now, what you have is your friends and me."

"We're not friends?" I was trying to tease him.

"I can't be friends with someone like you," he said, voice lowering as he leaned into me.

"That's rude." I glanced down at his mouth, now much closer than before.

"If we're friends, I'll never be able to move on from you, Evelyn. You are too enrapturing, too all-consuming. There is no in-the-middle friendship with you."

Outside this room, my friends were working tirelessly to rescue Will. Outside this room, Will was suffering a curse that pulled him so deep down within himself he barely remembered me. Outside this room, there were forces greater than us at work, forces that made me forgettable as always.

That was outside.

Here. Now. I was so beguiling, so wonderful, that an endless being wouldn't be able to enter the same room without feeling the pull of it.

In here, I was powerful. I was greater than any outside force.

I was unforgettable.

"Then you should kiss me, so we stop fucking around."

He did, slowly, sensually, as if the moment was meant to be sucked clean of its bone before it could slip from our grasp. I forgot I was holding a wine glass and I heard it clatter dully to the floor as I met his kiss, parting my lips and allowing his questioning tongue to enter. I gripped his shoulders and pulled myself up onto his lap. His hard cock met my center immediately and I groaned, rubbing my hips against him for that delicious friction.

His quick fingers found the edge of my shirt and slid up against the exposed skin, sending a wave of warmth across my nerves before he gripped the fabric and pulled it up over my head. His mouth landed on the swell of my tit above my bra, kissing and nibbling across my chest as he kneaded the flesh through my bra. My nipples were hard through the material, and I pressed into his touch, desperate for more contact.

My bra slipped down over my shoulders as if someone had unhooked it and I paused, glancing first at his hand gripping my hip enough to bruise and the other still working my tit.

"What good are my powers if not for reducing friction?" he asked, glancing up at me and grinning before swirling his tongue around my now exposed nipple. I arched into the sensation, heat sparking and pooling between my legs as he raked his teeth across the sensitive bud. He moved his attention to the other tit and I felt my orgasm building, low and hot along the base of my spine. He said we weren't going to have sex, but I didn't think all we'd do was nipple play.

It was apparently doing it for me, but I was a little disappointed at the singular focus.

"What else can your powers do?" I gasped out, teetering on the edge.

As if reading my mind—which, maybe he was—Billy leaned back against the plush comforter, propping himself up on his elbows. He slid his hands along the plane of my stomach, sending butterflies loose across all my organs, then pushed my skirt and panties down in one swift motion.

"Allow me." He gave me a self-satisfied smirk and before I could decide if I was going to punch him or not, I found myself levitating just a few inches above him. My stomach flip flopped as I glided through the air, the chill making me want to close my legs and cover myself. But then I was dangling, pussy first, directly above Billy's face, and I was *lowering*.

The invisible force suspending me meant I didn't have to support myself in a squat as Billy's tongue licked up through my folds. I relaxed into the hold of his powers, leaning back and letting the pleasure of him feasting below me shudder up my spine and tremble through my legs.

He ate like he couldn't get enough, like I was his last meal before certain destruction. When his mouth found my clit, tongue swirling around it as he clamped down sucking hard, I lost it. My orgasm ripped through me like a gale force wind, and I was left screaming in its wake.

Without thinking, this time, I reached behind and between us, twisting Billy's nipple through his shirt.

He yelled in surprise, and I found myself thrown off him none-to-gently.

"Why do you *do* that?" he gasped out, rubbing his chest, face still glistening with my release.

But I was lost to the joyous endorphins of a supernatural orgasm, limbs heavy, heart hazy. I giggled and stared up at the velvet canopy above us, letting the sweet nothingness wash over me.

For at least another few minutes, nothing else existed.

Nothing else mattered.

* * *

Assured that the potion was nowhere near completed, I headed back to my own apartment. I was relieved as I stepped through my front door, inhaling my own apartment, the familiar city lights through the window warming my heart.

I didn't realize how bad I needed to be home until I was in it. I pulled my laptop out on the kitchen table, pausing to glance at how Billy had arranged my furniture, an echo of our time together I didn't want ringing permanently.

But first—my draft.

I flipped open my laptop, fussing with its charger as the screen came to life. The thing thankfully still had battery—I hadn't opened it in nearly a week—but I didn't need it dying in the time it took me to send a career-determining email.

After typing a quick note to Carrie apologizing for the delay *again*, I clicked through to the article draft sitting ready on my desktop.

My heart plummeted.

I had one line written. That was it. The rest of the document glared bright white and blank at me in the dark, illuminating the horrified look on my face.

"What the fuck was I doing?"

I tried to play my memories like a film reel, rewinding back to the last night Will and I had together—before his disappearance, before the fight on the street, before the fancy dinner.

I'd been writing while Will was in the shower. It had been hard to focus because I was such a horny, obsessed mess. But I couldn't have been *so* obsessed that I literally didn't do my job?

I closed my eyes and leaned my head in my hands.

Will got out of the shower, I cat-called him, he put his dicks on my keyboard and—

"I was blowing my boyfriend instead of working," I said to my ceiling, leaning my head back and slumping in the chair. "You dumb bitch, Evelyn."

How did I get here? This only happened to women in movies with billionaire boyfriends. Because they could afford to forget about the rest of their life. Will made practically nothing at Mister Flipper—a fact I would need to inspect further given how many whiskey bottles were in his house. The chilling possibility that he was drinking all his money while I was footing our takeout bills wasn't doing anything to help my current mood.

My stomach twisted and a chill ran through me. All the helplessness and overwhelm I'd felt sitting in Will's room earlier returned two-fold, as if holding it back resulted in bottled lightning—half the size, twice the intensity.

Was this going to be my life with Will? Constantly so pulled into his orbit my own home planet begins to collapse?

I thought about Kelly's words on the sidewalk.

"I don't want you to have to hold him when he can't hold himself."

Maybe I shouldn't be holding anyone either. If Will got back to himself—I shook my head. *When* Will got back to himself.

When.

We were going to have a lot to talk about. Our relationship was going to need more than the brakes in place at this point. I needed to not go running to him every spare moment I had. I needed to not be swallowing his problems as if they were bubbles out of the air.

I needed to be okay being alone when there was the possibility someone loved me in another room.

And he needed to take out the recycling.

I looked at the clock. It was ten p.m. If I could slam this article out and send it to Carrie before midnight, I'd still be meeting the "tonight" portion of the deadline and maybe she'd forgive me. I knew I was running out of grace.

I went to the fridge and grabbed a canned energy drink from the back where I kept them for emergencies. It tasted like chemicals and stress, the carbonation immediately making me belch.

"Tell me you wouldn't blow off a deadline to suck two cocks on the same man, Carrie, I mean..." I gestured emptily to the air. I definitely could *not* say that to my editor.

Sipping again on the toxic soda I hoped would fuel my next few hours, I sat down at the blank screen and began to write.

23

Evelyn

Boston, Present Day

I'd written, submitted, and rapid-fire corrected my coverage of the mermaid fashion show by 11:59 p.m. And then, when Wilhamena texted to let me know things were still brewing, I had gone back into the office.

Carrie showed me the stats from my article that ran that morning—three times the traffic of any other piece on the site and twice the social media mentions of any of the competition.

"I knew you'd deliver," Carrie said, scooping me into a tight hug. She was a curvy Black woman who refused to let her height keep her from designer heels. I worried the stress oozing out of my face would rub off on her pressed white blouse that she'd paired with a brilliantly patterned pencil skirt. But as usual, nothing ruffled her.

"And you picked the perfect day to come back in," she said, eyes crinkling at the corners. "We're planning the Paris trip and I need you there."

I was going to the one place I'd dreamed of my entire life, doing the only job I'd ever imagined myself doing, and the only thing I could think about was how much I wished Will was there to celebrate with me.

That night in the BUS basement, Wilhamena handed me a small glass vial. It looked like a repurposed fancy mustard jar that had been filled with a sparkling green liquid and then sealed with melted red wax across the top.

"The only thing that matters," she said. "Is that he drinks at least some of it willingly."

"Sure, no problem," I said, bracing myself for re-entering the meeting room. "Just gotta convince the version of my boyfriend who hates me to swallow a strange liquid I hand him with no explanation."

"If anyone can figure it out, it's you," the dwarf said, squeezing my shoulders and giving me an encouraging smile. "You have the hardest job of all of us. The more he begins to remember, the easier it is to convince him to drink the next doses."

"You can do this, Eve," Caoimhe gave me a tight hug, squeezing extra hard at the end. I didn't see Leith anywhere, but I imagined he had gone off alone to figure out his strategy for getting Will the next dose. Kelly would be last.

"We'll be right upstairs if anything happens," Roxy said, flexing her claws like she couldn't wait for a reason.

"Just remember what they say," I said, giving everyone fake finger guns as I pulled the door open. "If the cage is a rockin' don't come a knockin.'"

Various confused noises from the BUS were muffled as I closed the door behind me.

"That was fucking stupid, Evelyn, why did you do that?" I whispered to myself as I turned to face not-my-Will.

He was splayed across the bed, still wearing only his jeans. The obvious chill in the air didn't seem to be bothering him.

"Hey," I called across the room. He lifted just his head gazing at me lazily. "You thirsty?" I dangled the jar in the air in front of me.

"Little fish wants to poison me." He let his head fall back onto the pillow.

"What makes you think that?" I moved closer to the cage, already pulled toward him like before. My feet were practically tripping over themselves to be closer.

"You lock me up, keep me underground, starve me," he sighed up at the ceiling. "You're trying to kill me."

"No," I said, stepping up against the bars now. "I'm trying to help you."

"No point in lying, little fish."

"So you don't want any whiskey?" The lie formed seamlessly across my tongue before I could think about it. Will sat up in bed, propping himself up on his elbows and giving me a full display of his athletic, toned body. I had to blink a few times to remind myself that *yes,* my boyfriend was fucking hot but this version of him was not for drooling over.

"Whiskey?" he asked, eyeing me curiously with those dark eyes.

I nodded. "Special import," I said. "From Paris. I had to smuggle it in my—never mind. You don't need to know that part."

He stood, pushing himself off the bed and clearing the distance between us in a single fluid motion. The vial was barely snatching distance away and I was suddenly terrified that he would smash it out of my hands before I could convince him to drink it. I steeled my face, hoping there was no hint of fear there, that he couldn't smell the stress radiating off me.

I pictured my Will, powerful and sharp in the water, pulling me toward him that first night. How safe I'd felt in the face of all his power. I pushed that memory forward, cradled it in my mind.

"Why is it sparkling?" he asked, squinting at it.

"It's the gold flecks," I said. "It adds to the taste."

"The taste?"

"Yes," I said, breaking the wax seal and lifting the lid. Some liquid dribbled down across my hands and I hoped a few drops gone wouldn't matter. "Try it, see if you can taste the gold."

"This is a trap, little fish." He said it so simply, no growls, no threats. It was as if he were pointing out a bird in the sky.

"It's a gift," I said. "An apology for keeping you here like this."

"You're forgiven," he said, and turned to go back to his bed.

"*Wait,*" I practically screamed, and he turned slowly back around, those black eyes roving all over my body again. This time I let the shudder roll through me, using it as momentum to adjust my body, to pop my hips to the side and let my shoulders drop. I pushed my lips out into a pout and glanced up at him from under my eyelashes. "Please take my gift. It's already opened now and the air will ruin the taste in a few more minutes. Please."

Again, that impossibly fast, fluid movement had him in front of me. I had to hold my breath to keep my composure because he still *smelled* like Will, sharp, salty, musky and the memory of waking up in his arms, safe, comfortable, at home, flashed through my mind.

"You first," he said, watching my face.

"What?" I faltered.

"If it's not poison," he said. "And you just want me to drink your gift before it's spoiled, you have a sip first."

"No, I couldn't. It's—"

"Then goodbye, little fish."

"Okay," I said, before he could turn away a third time. It was just a remembering potion, right? What could a sip hurt? "But it's far too rich for me, so just a tiny sip. Then it's all yours."

I lifted the vial to my lips, trying not to flinch at the overpowering smell of herbs, dirt, and something metallic I didn't want to think about.

It slid down in a single chunk—tasteless and textureless but not entirely liquid.

I let out a satisfied sigh.

"Exactly like an afternoon along the Seine," I sighed, putting what I hoped was a dreamy look on my face. I held the vial out to Will, who pounded it like a cheap shot of tequila. If it actually had been expensive whiskey, I would've been insulted.

He made a face as he swallowed. "The French know nothing about whiskey," he spat. "Are you satisfied, little fish?"

"Not until you stop calling me that," I muttered, watching his face for some sign of the real Will that I'd seen earlier.

He considered me for a second, glancing from me to the vial and back again.

"Little fish likes what she sees," he said, swinging his hips obscenely toward me, a feral look spreading across his face. In a flash he was against the bars again, clamping his hands over where I hadn't realized I was clutching the bars while watching him. "Or little fish is hoping the poison will work fast." A dangerous light flashed through his eyes and for the first time in all of this, I felt fear run a single icy finger down my spine.

"No," I whispered, my voice choked in my throat with nerves. Everything was swallowed by this creature's pupilless dark eyes and flashing teeth.

I was going to die.

Over someone who can't be bothered to go to the recycling.

"Evelyn." Leith's voice cut through the air, breaking the trance between me and Will. I heaved a breath as if I'd been underwater and pulled my hands free.

"Everything alright?" It wasn't a question, more a command that things *be alright* or there would be consequences. I forgot that we'd initially met Leith because of his temper and was thankful, glancing over at his stern face and the tick in his jaw, that we'd never had any reason to encounter it ourselves.

"Eve?" Will's voice came from through the bars. His hands hovered uncertainly just on the other side of the bars from where they'd been clutching mine only a moment ago. "What's going on?"

I wanted to shove my hands through the bars to grab his, to pull him toward me. But I didn't know how long his clarity would last and the bandages on my arm still flexed against my skin.

"Yeah, baby," I said, voice cracking. "You're here now."

His stormy eyes scanned my body quickly, snagging on the bandages. "Did I do that?"

"It doesn't—"

"I did, oh *god* Evelyn." He grabbed the bars in front of me before sagging to his knees. "I'm so sorry. You weren't supposed to get wrapped up in any of this. I thought I could handle it. I thought things would get better if I could just keep trying."

"You did. They are." I knelt to meet him on the ground, reaching through the bars and cupping his face in my hands. "This curse is bigger than either of us. That's why everyone is helping. Leith, Caoimhe, Kelly, Pete, Patrick, Billy…"

"Billy?"

I flinched and watched recognition flash across his face.

"It doesn't matter," he said. "You do whatever you have to while I continue being a total piece of shit."

"Thanks, I will," I tweaked his ear and tried to smile, the usual banter heavy between us. "And you keep fighting this thing. I'll be here on the other side."

"Aren't you already on the other side?" He gestured to the bars and made half-assed finger guns. The giggle died in my throat.

"I hate this," I said.

"I'm sorry," he said.

"If you don't stop apologizing, I'll give you something to be sorry about."

He gave me a lopsided smile and my heart twisted in my chest. I missed him so much, even after just a few days. I wanted our joy back. I wanted our jokes. I wanted our adventures. I wanted all of what we'd had for those few stunning weeks so full of promise.

And I would get it back, even if I had to hunt down Mirra myself.

"We're going to get through this," I said. "Remember when you said you'd keep trying forever? Just keep trying. Promise me."

"I—" He shivered, the vibration rolling through his whole body out through his fingertips. I snatched my hand away just as he glanced back up with those pupilless dark eyes, his teeth gnashing inches away from my skin.

"Careful, little fish."

Leith's strong hands found my shoulders and hauled me up to my feet. I let myself slump into him as he guided me out of the meeting room and up the stairs. We followed a strange earthy smell into Pete's apartment where the rest of the BUS were buzzing in action.

Wilhamena was calling out instructions from one of the massive leather books that Pete had been carrying earlier while Pete and Roxy plucked, chopped, and prepped ingredients. Caoimhe was stirring the source of the strange smell—the potion, I assumed—with a conspicuous hand immobile on one of the stock-pot handles. Kelly flitted around the apartment, refilling wine and water glasses like the world's most nervous waiter.

"What, no one could find a cauldron?" I asked.

"Please, you think we're that old fashioned?" Caoimhe's joke had more heart in it than mine. She waved her free hand to me and I followed the gesture, accepting her vise-like side hug as the other hand stayed fixed on the pot. I wrapped my arms around her and leaned my head on her shoulder. We stayed that way for a few moments and I breathed in her comforting scent. I had never been so relieved to see her.

"You okay?" she whispered.

"Fuck no." I whispered back as she squeezed me again. "What's with the camp counselor hug?"

"I'm imbuing the potion," she said.

I leaned back, catching her gaze and offering a weak smile in return for the wink she threw me. It was easy to forget that Caoimhe was a leprechaun because she spent most of her time looking as human as me. And then she'd say things like "imbuing the potion" and I'd be jolted back into the hybrid magical world we lived in—the world she'd always lived in but that was still so new to me.

"With luck?" I asked. She nodded.

"I've never done it before but Wilhamena says this should help."

"So you're just stuck here for as long as the potion brews like a 1950s housewife?"

Caoimhe laughed.

"Basically, but instead of bringing someone their slippers and a cocktail, I have Kelly to bring *me* a drink."

"What color is it C?" Wilhamena called from across the apartment.

"Like, puce?"

"More fish oil and rosemary then."

Roxy appeared at my side, silently flinging in a fistful of rosemary and then dumping in a pungent oil.

"I still don't know what puce is," she muttered.

"I'll get out of the way," I said. I gave Caoimhe a final squeeze and wandered over to Pete's immaculate white couches, settling across from Wilhamena.

"How are you holding up?" the dwarf asked.

"I don't think I am."

"That sounds right."

"Where's Billy?" I needed to talk to him. I needed to tell him that we wouldn't be doing anything anymore. If I was going to ask Will to keep trying his hardest to come back to me, I needed to do the hard thing and sit still long enough for him to resurface. It wasn't fair to him for me to be flailing around like this.

I could face the hard parts too if I knew Will was going to be with me.

And that meant more than all the levitating sex on private jets in all the world.

As if on cue, Billy stepped from behind the door separating the rest of Pete's apartment, another leather book under his arm. We locked eyes and he either read my mind or my face, but he nodded. Did I imagine the wince? The flash of sadness?

"It's alright," he said.

"Thank you," I said. I would never be able to truly tell him the kind of support he'd given me—a support and comfort I could never return but that I hoped he'd find for himself someday.

"Ignoring whatever *that* is," Wilhamena muttered from behind the book. She held her hand out for the other volume that Billy was holding. She glanced quickly at the title on the front before holding it out to me.

"See if that sparks anything in you," she said.

"Can I look at whatever it is later?" I asked, not taking the book.

"If you'd rather just sit here and wait with your own thoughts, you're welcome to." Wilhamena waggled the book in the air. I took it. A strange tingle ran through my hand—like touching my family's old TV screen after it'd been turned off when I was kid, a sort of electric air that pushed back against my palm.

But I didn't open it. I was too distracted to try and read, whatever force inside the book was compelling me. Instead, I let my gaze wander around the apartment, watching the BUS work hard to bring Will home.

I noticed Pete and Kelly had paused their work. Pete was holding his wine glass out to her with a delicacy that was not misplaced given his taste but that still surprised me given his form. Kelly locked eyes with him for barely a moment before parting her lips and allowing him to pour the gentlest sip of wine into her mouth. Her eyes closed half-way and she seemed to be relishing whatever she was drinking with pleasure. A hungry look formed on Pete's face as he watched her but was gone as soon as she opened her eyes again. Kelly flashed him a smile and nodded, then said something I couldn't hear before reaching over to refill Roxy's rapidly diminishing drink.

I pulled my gaze away to see Wilhamena watching me watching them.

I tilted my head toward the pair silently and she nodded.

"Oh yeah," she mouthed. "They're next."

24

Will

There is a flash in the darkness, Eve's voice, her hand on mine, a spark of her light when I've been down here so long, alone. The taste of something not liquid yet not solid. Something sharp and alluring. The dark turns to grey turns to the earliest morning hours before even the birds wake.

I was suddenly slammed back into my physical self after a lifetime of reminiscence.

Then all too soon, dragged back under.

How to get back?

How to travel the hours lost, the opportunities wasted, the hope destroyed—how to start again when I keep fucking it all up?

Another swallow—sharper, stronger. I was pulled forward again through the light, gasping at the sight of Leith's face as if his presence was the air my lungs were deprived of.

"Easy," he said, gripping my shaking shoulders through the bars.

I didn't know how long I'd been in my underground prison. I didn't know what I did to warrant it—but I'm sure I deserved it.

When I was lost to my shark self before, not knowing was a blessing. Now it was torture. Who had I hurt? Who could ever forgive me?

"You're here now," Leith said. I found his grey eyes, reached out and clasped his shoulder back, reassured by the solidness of his presence.

"Thank you," I rasped out. My throat felt like I'd been screaming for hours. Maybe I had been. Whatever my shark self was doing while I was suspended was out of my control, and really didn't matter so long as I wasn't hurting anybody. But I remembered the bandage on Evelyn's wrist and her hesitancy to approach me when I last resurfaced.

She was my only worry, panic gripping my heart tightly.

"Is...?"

"Yeah," he said, eyes crinkling at the corner even though his smile was worried. "She is." He squeezed my shoulder again before letting go and stepping to the side.

The breath I'd just recaptured was knocked loose at the sight of her. Dark circles stretched beneath her eyes and she danced lightly from one foot to the other, arms crossed across her chest. But most worrying of all was her outfit—she was wearing a pair of jeans with paint stains and a loose t-shirt.

DIY project clothes out in the world?

Something was *very* wrong.

"Eve, listen to me," I said, trying to fight against the pain building in my chest at what I was about to say.

"Will, I did something awful," she said before I could continue. Her voice cracked and she twisted her shoulders inward trying to protect herself. "You weren't here. You weren't yourself you were—"

"I know," I said. "It doesn't matter. None of it matters."

"You don't understand—"

"I do." My shark smelled another on her, sent the alarm floating down through the ether to me. I didn't blame her. I didn't care. "You're right. I wasn't here. I wasn't myself. I may never be myself again—"

"Don't you *dare*—"

"We have to expect the worst—"

"The hell we do." She tilted her chin up at me, striding purposefully toward the bars and reaching through them to grab me by the neck. She hauled me to her and kissed me forcefully. It was sparks filtered through church glass. It was comfort in a raging blaze. "We will get through this. You promised me."

"You deserve the world," I said, finding her gaze and holding it. "And I wanted to be the one to give it to you, but this might take longer than we planned. It's not just the drinking anymore."

"I'll wait," she said. "I know I haven't done a good job of that so far—"

"Stop," I said, reaching up and trace the lines of fingers where her hand still rested along the back of my neck, searing into my skin. "Whatever you had to do to get through this—I forgive you."

"Then let's forgive *each other*," she said.

"I'm unforgivable," I said, fully aware now that a fat tear was running down my cheek. I didn't care. I didn't deserve this—I didn't deserve her.

"Bullshit," she snarled. "You are worth saving, remember?"

"And I'm the only one who can save myself," I snarled back. "And I can't do it. Mirra will always find me. She won't quit chasing us for the rest of our lives."

"Then I'll get better running shoes."

I had thought it a hundred times before over stupid shit like blowjobs and bad puns and sexy outfits. But this time I meant it.

I was going to marry this girl.

"My entire life has been people making promises that they'll change and then doing *nothing*." Evelyn's voice was shaking as she reached her other hand through the bars to wipe away the tears now freely falling down my face. "Except you. You said you'd do anything for me and then you dumped all your alcohol and swam in your shark form and here—here you are fighting a curse just to talk to me."

I grabbed her wrist and traced the soft skin there, hating the bars between us, hating the ticking clock before my shark would pull me under again.

"I don't care how much money someone has, how well-dressed they are, how good the sex is—if they aren't willing to try like you, then they aren't it," she said. "And Will, you're it for me. I know it."

I pushed myself against the bars until they bit into my skin, slipping my hands down to her hips and hauling her as close as I could get her. I devoured her mouth, tasting every piece of her I could, savoring the sound and smell of her.

"I wish we could be closer," I said.

"We will be," she said against my mouth before kissing me again. "And Will, I really am sorry. I was just so scared you'd never come back, that you'd really forgotten me and I just…" Her voice cracked and a piece of me broke with it. "I let that fear make me believe I would just end up a guest appearance in your life. And I told you before I'm so—"

"You're my leading lady," I said, bringing her fingers up to my lips and kissing each tip gently, savoring whatever moments we still had together. "Whatever side plot you explore doesn't change that. We're still meant to end up together. Even if it takes a couple more movies."

And I knew it in my core. If she said I was it for her—that she was choosing me—then I trusted her completely. I believed her. I wasn't threatened by her seeking creature comfort from some other dumbshit.

But I *would* kick his ass later. Just in case.

"Don't let it take that long," she said. "I'm impatient."

I let out a low laugh, fighting against the flash of darkness behind my eyes.

I didn't have much longer.

"You know I hate to make you wait," I said, using every ounce of willpower I had to let her fingers drop. "But I think the other guy is getting antsy."

She nodded, crossing her arms around herself again and stepping away from the bars. She never took her eyes off me.

"Thank you," I said, turning to Leith. He strode quickly up to the bars, clapping me against him in a hug as best he could.

"Keep fighting," he whispered.

"I promise," I said. He leaned his forehead to mine for a moment, and I remembered Mirra under the water that first meeting, the relief at not being alone, the touch of her scaled skin to mine in the same gesture. But this time there was no seductive telepathy, just one friend holding another in a moment of uncertain terror.

I held that comfort as close as I could, even as I felt darkness pulling me back under, swallowing me back into the weightless nothing where I would have to wait until my next chance.

25

Evelyn

I was torturing myself at this point, following Kelly down into the depths of the meeting room, spiraling away from the warmth and comfort of everyone gathered in Pete's kitchen. I hated seeing Will locked up, hated listening to his shark self spew toxic bullshit. I wanted to punch him in the face every time he called me "little fish." But the laughter upstairs was thin and nervous, covering the worry that the last twenty-four hours of potion brewing would be for nothing.

That every stolen moment with Will would be our last.

I would rather have the frightening, torturous truth than feign being okay for another second.

Kelly put her hand against the meeting room door but hesitated, turning to me. The final potion was clutched in her other hand, glimmering in the low lamplight.

"Okay," she sighed. "I'm going to give this to him, and when he comes to, I only need to say two things and then he's all yours."

"You don't have to—"

"He loves you, Evelyn," Kelly said, giving me a soft half smile. "More than he loves himself. He'll come back for you. He'll break the curse for you. Show him you love him back."

"How?" My heart fluttered against my ribs, begging for escape.

"Well, you could start by saying it," she said, arching an eyebrow. "But I'll leave the room if you're more of a show-er than a teller."

I blushed.

"Did you just tell me to fuck him to break the curse?"

"Men've gone to war over sex with a woman, I have no doubt you've got what it takes to knock him free of that curse."

I threw my head back and laughed, like *really* laughed.

"Kelly, that's the nicest thing you've ever said to me."

She looked away, a little shy.

"I haven't been the nicest to you," she said. "I'm sorry. I worry about Will. I always have. And humans aren't usually so…" She gestured to me in my "house painting" outfit.

"Fashionable?" I said.

"Yeah," she said, laughing lightly before heaving a sigh. "That."

"Thank you," I said. And I meant it. Not just for the compliment, but for all her support, for all her help, for the way she loved Will for so long when he couldn't love himself.

She nodded to me, then rolled her shoulders back and closed her eyes for a moment. She let loose a slow breath through her nose and when she opened her eyes, she opened the door to the meeting room.

As soon as we entered, Will leapt up from the bed and began pulling on the bars to his enclosure, screaming at the top of his lungs. Spit flew from his mouth and landed on the dirt floor and I could see bruises growing along his chest from where he'd clearly been flinging himself against the bars. His dark hair was stringy with sweat and clung to the side of his face, standing out against his pale skin.

"That's *enough*," Kelly said, striding purposefully to the bars and standing there, legs hips-width apart, the potion held meaningfully in one outstretched hand. Will snarled at her and raked a clawed hand through the air. He missed her so narrowly that I watched her hair rustle in the breeze of his swing.

Kelly did not flinch.

"I want you to drink this," she said.

"Fuck off, bird bitch."

"I also want you to get more creative with your insults," she said. Will's pupilless eyes found me over Kelly's shoulder and I tried to mimic her confidence, wished I could hold even half as still as she did in the face of this monstrous creature wearing the face of someone we loved.

"Ah, little fish. Back again."

"She doesn't have anything for you," Kelly said, voice staying even and calm. She twisted one hand behind her back and opened it, revealing a pair of ear plugs. I snatched them quickly and what I hoped was silently, but it wasn't fast enough.

"You can't trick me," Will snarled. "I see your plans. I won't be lured, siren. I won't fall for it."

I looked to Kelly, searching her face for some hint of her true plan.

The potion had to be taken *willingly*. If she sang and took control of Will, it would no longer be his free will. She had to know that.

Trusting her to do what she had to, I reached up to push the foam into my ears.

"Wait!" Will cried out. "We can make a deal."

Kelly motioned to me to wait. I clasped a sweating palm around the earplugs.

"I will drink your concoction, as you wish," he said. "If you give me a human. It has been *so long* since I've had a proper meal. I am wasting away." He pulled a sympathetic look, not unlike a large, terrifying, flesh-eating puppy with soulless black eyes.

"Is that all?" Kelly popped a hip, placing one hand on it in disbelief. "Ask me for something hard."

"That's all I want," he said. "All I desire. A few bites of sweet, sweet human flesh before your poison consumes me."

"It's not poison you drama queen," Kelly sighed, pinching the bridge of her nose. "You're even worse when you're like this."

"I want that one," he said, gesturing to me.

"Drink first," she said.

"Kelly, what the—"

"Shut up," she snapped over her shoulder.

"I'm gonna eat you so slowly, little fish," he snarled, voice low and soft. I couldn't help the shudder that rippled through me. "You'll feel every bite and it will make your flesh that much sweeter."

"The longer you take to drink that thing, the longer you have to wait for a proper meal." Kelly waved a dismissive hand. She closed the gap between them, handing him the potion. He twisted off the cap and lifted the bottle to me in cheers before downing it.

I could feel sweat dripping down my spine as my fingers grew numb with fear. Was Kelly really going to shove me in the cage with that monster? What if Will didn't come back fast enough? What if he came to while the monster was—

Will hacked up a cough halfway through the potion and paused, sputtering and wheezing.

"That's much worse than the last one," he growled. "Give me my meal now and then I'll finish your poison."

"No." Kelly was examining her manicure as if it offered clues to a hidden treasure in microscopic hieroglyphics.

"*Now*," Will snarled again. "Or I'll break this vial and your potion will be lost."

"You can finish what I gave you or I can have Pete come down here with the whole pot and spoon feed you," she said before finally glancing up. "Naked. You want a troll cock in your face while you suck on a wooden spoon?"

"Foul witch," Will muttered before resigning himself to the potion bottle and finishing it.

"That's kinda mean," I whispered to Kelly who waved me off.

"Who do you think offered if he didn't cooperate?"

"Naked?" I put a hand over my mouth trying to imagine Pete offering to get naked in front of Kelly.

"Oh god no," she said and I didn't imagine the blush that crept up her neck. "I…embellished a little."

The sound of broken glass made us both turn back to Will. He let out a rancid belch and gestured to the mess in front of him.

"There," he said. "I've finished your task. Give me the little fish."

Kelly said nothing, holding perfectly still. She stared at him, unblinking.

Will returned the stare for a moment before waving a hand at me through the bars.

"Give me the human," he said, flexing his fingers at me as if it would give him more reach. "I drank your thing, now I eat the flesh."

Kelly stayed silent.

"*GIVE ME THE—*"

Will seemed to choke on his own voice for a moment, gripping his head and doubling over as if someone had punched him. When he stood back up, running a hand through his sweat-damp hair, his stormy eyes were back, the quirk of his mouth tilted back up.

"Well," he said, flashing Kelly a full smile. "I know I'm in trouble now."

Kelly took two steps to the cage, cocked her arm back and slapped Will across the face. I flinched at the impact.

"You are *not* hot enough to be this lazy," she hissed, jabbing a finger into his chest.

"I love you too, Kel," he said, swatting her finger away and laughing. The two hugged fiercely through the bars before pressing their foreheads together in same way he had with Leith.

"If you don't come back to us, I'm selling Mister Flipper and running away to Greece," she said.

"You won't make it ten minutes, you hate olives."

Kelly pulled fully away, wiping hastily at her face before reaching through the bars a final time. She traced her flat thumb across Will's forehead and in a booming, dramatic voice yelled, *"REMEMBER WHO YOU ARE."*

Then she flipped Will off before turning on her heel and leaving the room.

"Knock when he's an asshole again," she called before closing the door behind her.

"You should probably just go knock now," he said, sighing and letting his shoulders drop. "I've never stopped being an asshole."

"That's okay," I said, relieved and terrified at his return. That was the final potion in the sequence. Now all we could do was wait to see if the effects stuck. "I'm too much of a bitch to date nice guys anyway."

"Hey, that's my girlfriend you're talking about," he said, giving me a mock stern look.

We stared at each other for a moment, taking each other in. I let my eyes drink in every piece of skin, ever twitching finger, every shifting step he took. I held myself still while he did the same.

"I got Paris," I said, finally, unsure of what else to offer in that moment.

"Of course you did," he said, flashing me a winning smile. "Who else were they gonna send? Fucking Mike?"

"Oh god no," I huffed out a laugh. "But I was thinking…maybe when we're out of here—"

"Evelyn." His voice had a finality in it. "It was always an if. And I hate to say it, but you might need to—"

"Don't," I snapped, stepping up to the bars, hands clenched at my side, breath heaving in and out so fast my throat burned. "Don't you *dare*. Not after all this. This potion will work, and you will break the curse, and I'll have gotten through all this bullshit while *still* working hard enough to go to Paris so when I get there it will all be couture baguettes and sideways hats and you're going to fuck me under the Eiffel Tour."

"Berets," Will said, laughing. "They're called berets."

"I know what they're fucking called." I was so relieved to see him laughing, the light in his eyes, the shape of his cheeks as they lifted up and away from his teeth that were just a little too sharp to be human. I reached through the bars and hauled him to me, kissing him as if he had just returned from war.

Which, in some ways, he had.

He kissed me back, just as hard, just as desperately, and I felt his hands on my hips, digging in with bruising strength. I found the hard bulk of him through his jeans and ground myself against it, earning a soft moan from him that I swallowed as if it were water in the desert.

"Fuck these bars," he groaned, reaching back to knead my ass.

"I've got something else you can fuck," I said, kicking off my slip-on sneakers and pushing down my pants and underwear in one swift movement. I swatted away his trembling hands and undid his jeans, my mouth watering as both cocks sprang loose. But there was no time for tasting, no time for teasing.

Will pushed my t-shirt and sports bra up and over my head before hauling me up against him, scooping me beneath my ass. I was able to slip one leg through the bars and hook it around his waist, the other I wrapped around a bar for support.

I was already wet, but Will dove down and feasted on my nipples anyway, sucking and biting and licking until I was humping his midsection so furiously, I wished one of his cocks was there instead.

"God, I missed these," he breathed, the warm words tickling over the wet flesh and sending goosebumps across my entire body.

"I missed you," I said, running my hands up through his hair and tugging, pulling his head back so I could get a better angle on his mouth. I slanted my mouth over his, accepting his tongue and sucking on it hard. He groaned again, readjusting our position to give him better access to my pussy. I felt the head of one cock nudge in teasingly.

"Both," I growled, tugging his hair harder. "Now. Don't fuck around."

"That's my good girl," he growled back before thrusting up into me. Just as the first cock slid home, I felt the second nudge in along its base, pressing me deliciously wide. I breathed deep, throwing my head back in ecstasy at the fullness I'd been missing this whole time. As the second cock slid deeper, filling me more and more, I found the soft space where Will's neck met his shoulder and held on, wrapping both my arms around his shoulders. I inhaled his saltwater smell and rode both his cocks slowly, adjusting to the stretch of him until I felt my orgasm building slow and sweet along my spine.

I untangled myself from him, keeping my legs clamped tightly in their place but gripped the bars with my hands instead of his shoulders, using their leverage to support myself while I sped up my pace. The additional support meant I could lift up and slam down harder and harder on both cocks as Will thrust up into me. Soon, I was both lost in the heat and the rhythm of us, my pulse thudding through my core, building faster and higher and tighter.

"I love you, Evelyn," he groaned, breathless and heaving. I'd never hated anything more than I hated those bars in that moment.

"Don't leave me," I gasped out, just as I lost myself to chasing the peak of my orgasm, riding both cocks harder and faster over the edge. We cried out together and then I was tumbling into a hazy, blissful abyss.

Slowly, I was able to tell my fingers to let go of the bars. They trembled, red and angry where the iron had cut into them. My shoulders screamed. My legs shook.

I didn't want to let go.

Will reached one hand to where my leg was clenched around the bar like it had been welded there and rubbed my calf and thigh in a lazy, soothing motion. When I finally unclenched, he caught me before I could topple over. He set me down as if I had been freshly sculpted from wet clay and he couldn't bear to see me dent or bend, unhooking my leg in a final kind of way from his waist.

I would've stayed on top of him like some kind of horny conjoined monster forever if he'd let me.

"This is the longest I've made it," he said.

"Don't be too hard on yourself, I had a great time," I teased. He flipped me off and swatted at my nipple as I pulled my t-shirt back on. The meeting room was drafty and cold without Will's heat pressed against me.

"I meant out of the curse," he said. "Maybe we finally did it."

I stepped into my pants and reached for my shoes, glancing down for only a moment before—

"Ah, little fish."

I was able to barely dance away before Will reached for me through the bars. My heart cracked in two then, watching his form, still covered in sweat from our sex, but pupilless and enraged.

"No," I breathed. Sobs choked up through my throat and I shook my head violently. "No, no, no. This isn't fair. *This isn't fair!*"

"This is much more touching than I expected," a feline voice called from across the room.

"You," Will growled out, turning his attention to the intruder.

A familiar scarred red head in yet another striking purple ensemble was holding a power stance on the meeting table. She pointed a dramatic finger at Will and smirked.

"You," Mirra said. Then she leveled that same point at me. "This delicious little morsel has become more of a problem than I anticipated. I hate to involve myself further, but I can't have you ruining my plans *again*."

"I'm not ruining anything," I said, brain racing, broken heart tumbling into my stomach. How long had she been there? How much had she seen? My skin crawled at the thought. "Nothing works against your curse."

"Don't play stupid," she snapped. "If he remembers your love, his punishment gets cut shorter than I'm satisfied with. And I know the smell of a remembrance draught anywhere."

"If it's that easy, it's not much of a punishment. Why don't you just lift it and leave him alone? It has to be more work than he's worth."

A cold blast of air flashed by me and suddenly I was pressed obscenely close to the sea witch, an invisible force clamping me to her side. She was easily a head taller than me—what I wouldn't do for her height—and this close, I could see the way the scar on her neck pulled at her skin beneath a threatening string of shark's teeth. I shivered.

"There is no punishment long or painful enough for what that creature took from me," she sneered down at me. Her nostrils flared and a strange light danced in her eyes. She closed them halfway before leaning down and inhaling deeply from my scalp. I tried to push her away but was frozen in place by that same invisible force. My insides boiled and my skin crawled.

"They have no idea what you are, do they?" she whispered into my hair before pulling away. "It's a shame I'll have to kill you. That would've been interesting to watch develop."

I had no time to guess what the hell she meant. My feet were pulled out from under me, and I had to close my eyes against the sudden gust of wind that swallowed us, hauling us up and up and up. I heard Will's voice scream my name before the only other thing in my ears was the screaming wind and Mirra's triumphant cackle.

225

26

Will

Made direct amends to such people wherever possible, except when to do so would injure them or others.

If I'd known that all this would've happened because of the pain I caused Mirra—that my actions all those years ago were enough to pull her out of the woodwork when my curse began to lift—I would've done anything to make it right.

I would've done anything to seek her forgiveness.

But by her own words, it wasn't her forgiveness the curse needed. It was a human's.

A human just like Evelyn.

In the dark again, I waited, desperate for another flash of light to follow home, for another taste of that strange concoction that brings me back to myself. My heart pounded in my chest, my pulse pushed against my skin.

I had to get back. Those few precious moments weren't enough—I wanted every second with her. I'd wasted too much time caught in this strange space.

But the light didn't come. The darkness grew heavier.

I had to do something.

I tried to push myself into movement but it was like I was caught deep in the bowels of an endless kelp forest and the roots had grown around me. I didn't go anywhere no matter how I waved my arms or kicked my legs.

All I could think about was Evelyn's face, Kelly's laughter, Leith's firm grasp on my shoulder. These things were going to be lost to me forever if I didn't find a way out of this.

There. Like a trick of your eyes when you're overtired, for just a split second, a flash in the dark.

I pulled up the image of Kelly telling me I wasn't hot enough to be this lazy and held onto the comforting joy the old joke welled up in my heavy human heart. Again, a quick flash like lightning before it was gone. I wasn't imagining it.

I could spark my own way out.

Evelyn swimming toward me in the water, shocked but sure.

Leith laughing, eyes crinkled up at the corners.

Clinking beers together with Kelly in the office our first day with Mister Flipper.

The warmth of Evelyn in my arms, the blanket shared with Caoimhe and Leith rustling lightly across our legs as we all adjust on the couch to watch some stupid movie.

The flashing light flickered, wavered, but grew brighter with each memory.

Arnie bringing me into the warm, well-lit bar.

Running with my favorite of his huskies through town as the first rays of sun make the town glow a soft orange.

Laughing at baby names in the bookstore with Kelly while we try to find me a last name.

The light is a steady pulse now, glowing brighter and brighter as if it's getting closer.

Evelyn telling me we should try being together.

Our first kiss in my kitchen, her lips soft, a single sigh in her breath.

The way my heavy human heart grew light when she believed I was worth saving.

The light was on me now, nearly blinding, and the human part of me wanted to fight it, some primal idea about "following the light" and "death" being intertwined.

But I knew better. I knew this was not a path that would kill me—although it definitely wouldn't be painless.

"Okay," I whispered to myself. "For real this time."

I closed my eyes against the burning brightness, letting it wash over me completely until—

I screamed for Evelyn the second I had control of my mouth, slammed myself bodily against the bars of the cage surrounding me.

But all I could do was watch, helpless, as Mirra vanished with Evelyn out the door and up the stairwell, blowing past the rest of the BUS before the shock could even register on their faces.

"Let me out! Now! We have to get her let me out!" I screamed, waving my arms frantically through the bars. Leith and Wilhamena were in action before anyone else, sprinting across the room to me. The dwarf woman had the keys and unlocked it. I ran past her, ignoring the pain from slamming my bare feet on stone, but a strong, cold grip stopped me dead in the stairwell.

Patrick yanked me back, shoving me toward the darkest corner of the underground entrance.

"Billy's gone after them," he said. "But our kind can't enter your domain. You're her best hope." He pressed against the wall in the dark and a door slid open. A waft of stale air assaulted my nostrils.

"Follow this past the guest room and straight on until you hear the ocean. The exit should be a good place to shift and catch up with the witch."

I nodded and took off.

It felt like I moved through the dark forever until I finally found what Patrick called the guest room—a cavern containing a dramatic amount of candles and an ugly four-poster straight out of those shitty movies Evelyn loved so much.

The air was less stale here and I hoped that meant the exit was closer than I originally thought, but something made me pause—another scent in the air.

Was it...?

Let's forgive each other.

Evelyn. I wouldn't mistake her smell anywhere. Mixed in with her signature expensive perfume was an even more exclusive scent. I didn't love that this vampire whore-house smelled like my girlfriend had sex in it. But I'd meant it when I told her I didn't blame her for doing whatever she needed to get through this hell we'd been thrown into.

None of that mattered now and it sure as fuck wouldn't matter if she was dead.

I continued, chasing the freshness that grew salty in the air around me.

Thankfully—luckily, if Caoimhe had set her mind to things at all—it wasn't much longer in another dark tunnel before the sound of the harbor reached me. As Patrick promised, the tunnel opened into a cleverly hidden area built from brick and stone. I stepped out onto the man-made ledge and dove into the water, swimming quickly past the undersides of several larger private sailboats that were anchored just beneath the opening.

I filed that piece of magic away for later. I had a lot of questions about how it worked—how had we never known about that tunnel and its opening on the water?

For now, the only thing driving me forward, the only sound in my heart and in my lungs was Evelyn's name, pounding again and again and again.

When the water grew colder and darker, I knew I'd reached a point where I could shift comfortably, and I let the change tear through me.

With my shark's tale, I could cut through the water like a torpedo, aimed directly at where my instincts told me Mirra would take Evelyn.

"She was supposed to be married next week."

"He was a good man. He didn't deserve this."

"Oh God. Oh God please no!"

I let the echoes chase me, speeding through the water.

I broke the water, thrusting myself up as high as I dared and scanned the air for Mirra and Evelyn. Nothing.

I kept this pace, speeding forward, leaping up to check for what felt like an eternity before there was the sudden and distinct vibration through the water. A disturbance that told me a human form had entered, willingly or not.

There. A flash of purple hair and a smell I'd follow to the ends of the Earth.

Evelyn's suspended form hung deep in the water, limbs askance as if the rays of light slanting down around her were puppet strings for some macabre performance. Bubbles from her impact rose around her and *fuck* they were trailing away from her nose and mouth, leaving her lungs emptier and emptier.

I sped toward her, pushing my mershark form to its brink, leaving a massive footprint in the water behind me that would've enticed even the most amateur whale watcher to investigate.

Just as Evelyn was within my arm's reach, a searing pain tore through my tail fin. I refused to let it stop me despite how hard it tried. I fought against it, reaching my webbed hands forward as far as I could until finally, I wrapped myself around Evelyn's dangerously still body.

My own blood was in the water everywhere, tinting my vision red and sending my senses spiraling in panic.

I gripped Evelyn, holding her against me as I tried to push toward the surface. But the pain in my tailfin was too sharp and no matter how I struggled to move forward, it was as if I were paddling through air instead of the guaranteed pushback of water.

Fear slid down my spine and I turned to see what I already knew.

My tailfin was shredded. I wouldn't be going anywhere.

A true shark would've had their front fins to swim away with, to keep the water pushing through their lungs so they could continue to breathe. But I had humanoid arms wrapped around Evelyn.

We were both going to die.

Just beyond the stomach-churning sight of my tail was the sea glass scaled mersibling that still crept into my nightmares. Mirra's otherworldly glow flashed through the water, the necklace on her neck heavier with more shark teeth than the last time I saw her.

She didn't have to transmit to my brain for me to know her thoughts.

This would end now, with one of us dead.

But not Evelyn.

I gripped her as tightly as I could with one arm, and used the other to try and swim to the surface as best I could. But it was no use. My shark tail was too heavy without the fin attached at the end. My true form was a death sentence.

And shifting back put Mirra at an advantage. She'd be able to destroy me and Evelyn both in a single attack if I was in my human form.

Somewhere, far off in the water, I felt the vibrations of a massive creature heading toward us. There was something familiar in it, but beneath all the panic and blood in the water I couldn't pinpoint what.

Mirra struck then, cutting to us in a single line like a knife through the air. She raked her claws across my face and dug into the back of my scalp, pulling my head back so that she could look down at me with those glowing, green eyes.

She slammed her forehead against mine, sending stars shooting through my vision and loosening my grip on Evelyn. But she didn't rear back for a second attack, leaving our heads together instead.

"This will be the last time, brother," she said inside my mind. *"I will take from you what you took from me, and I will make you feel her die."*

"Please, Mirra," I pleaded. Evelyn grew heavier and heavier in my arms. *"I'll do anything. You can have anything. Just let her go."*

"I already have what I want," Mirra hissed. *"My revenge will be complete in a matter of seconds and—"*

Something slammed into us both, pulling Mirra off me and knocking me off center. A massive, speckled tail cut through the water sending waves pulsing through and past us.

Mirra shot through the water with the force of it, far enough away that I was able to take in Leith's massive mershark form. He gestured for me to swim up with Evelyn.

I pointed to my shredded tailfin and held her out to him.

He looked conflicted and I mouthed, as best I could with my shark mouth, *please*.

Leith nodded once, then took Evelyn carefully in his arms. I watched them every moment I could as Leith shot above the surface. I tried to memorize the shape of her as she got smaller and smaller, tried to hold onto the hope in my chest that my best friend would save the love of my life when I couldn't.

Another echoing scream shot through me and I felt my heart growing heavier and heavier by the second. The voices had been replaced with shrieks of terror, varying in cadence but holding fear in every shrill note. Somewhere to my left, I felt Mirra's vibrations tearing straight toward me.

She wouldn't bother with me. I was already dead in the water. But Evelyn had a chance and she wouldn't stop until that hope was crushed.

I steadied myself as best I could, my lungs tight from minimal oxygen passing through my gills, my thoughts heavy from pain and blood loss.

This was it. God, in whatever form, could have me.

But they would not take Evelyn.

I snapped my arms out like an octopus lying in wait for its dinner as Mirra sped by and I latched on. Her sea glass scales sliced through my skin like I'd seen sharks in horror movies do, but I clung on, pressing the razor sharp edges against my arms as she struggled against me until my shredded flesh was enmeshed with her skin. Blood clouded the water around us, blocked all other smells from entering, made everything hazy and confusing for us both.

In her panic, she pulled us both in a new direction, continuing to thrash against me to break free. But I wouldn't let her go, and with the dead weight of my shark tail, I was a thousand pounds heavier than her.

I felt us begin to sink and I gave myself over to it. I let the weights in my tired, broken human heart finally win out, and I did the one thing a shark should never, *ever* do.

I held still.

Quicker than I expected, there was no more oxygen, just a white hot burning in my lungs, a pain all over that was so excruciating my nerves turned off. I no longer felt anything but the dull thud of Mirra punching the side of my head to break free.

With my last ounce of strength, I pulled her down to me by the ropes of her hair and bit down with everything in me onto the delicate flesh of her neck. I held on as she slowly stilled and darkness slid across my vision. I thought, briefly of the moment when a slide projector changed over, sometimes getting stuck in the dark before the next brilliant image was illuminated.

In that dark in-between, that brief last gasp of consciousness before the next moment could pass, my only thought was, *"Please, forgive me."*

27

Evelyn

Boston, present day

I was laying on something hard. I tried to open my eyes but the lights directly above me were too bright, too glaring. Pain thudded dully in the base of my skull and my chest felt sore, like I'd run for too long without a break.

Why did everything smell like bread?

Voices drifted from the other side of a door somewhere, voices I recognized.

"Which is why, if you'd listened to me the first time, none of this would've happened." Wilhamena sounded *pissed*. "As you can see, no one is entering the bakery against my wishes."

"Oh, building wards can protect against someone's individual curse causing havoc for the rest of us? Do tell." Patrick was the most enraged I'd ever heard him—which meant he sounded, to the untrained ear, mildly irritated.

"You bloodless, ancient prick—"

235

"Two hundred *hardly* counts as ancient—"

"Stop," Caoimhe snapped. She had on her "get shit done" voice and I heard the soft tap of her sneakers coming closer. I smirked despite how shitty I felt. I loved when my best friend made people mind themselves.

"Evelyn?" her voice softened for me, and I felt her hand on my shoulder. "Eve?"

I blinked against the light, lifting a hand up to block it and squinting at Caoimhe's round concerned face.

"She's awake," Caoimhe called over her shoulder and there were more tapping footsteps until the rest of the BUS was surrounding me. But there was one face missing.

"Will." I shot up and the world tilted dangerously around me.

"Evelyn, wait, it's not—"

I let my best friend steady me by my shoulders, took in the pained look on her face and felt a crack begin to split my heart.

"Please no," I whispered.

"Let her see him." Leith. From somewhere behind me.

Carefully, Caoimhe helped me off the massive metal table I had been laying on. Seawater soaked the kitchen floor around us, and I barely glanced at the ceiling-high trays of golden scones and proofing rolls as my eyes landed first on Leith, then who he was standing next to.

Laid out on an identical metal table was Will. There was a sickly green color to his skin and massive shadows under his eyes. A blanket had been wrapped carefully around him, but I couldn't miss the pooling blood at his feet. I was going to throw up. I was going to scream.

I was going to lose my fucking mind.

After all this—all the work he'd been doing, all the care we'd put into finding him and bringing him back. And he'd come back. He'd come back like I knew he would I had heard him in those final moments before Mirra carried me off into the sky above Boston. It had *worked*.

How had it not worked?

I stumbled up to the table and looked down at him. His chest wasn't moving but I didn't need to listen to know he wasn't with us anymore. Even when he was sleeping, my Will had a certain energy to his face, as if that playful grin were just beneath the surface of his skin and would light up his face at any moment.

That light was gone now.

"Please, no," I whispered again. My legs buckled, threatening to give out. I gripped the table for support.

"Eve, I'm so sorry." Leith's voice was thick with grief, tears sliding down his stubbly cheeks. Caoimhe's arms wrapped around me, and I felt her shake with one hard sigh.

"He wanted to save you," Leith said, voice full of apology—as if he wished he didn't have to tell me the truth.

"Get out," I said.

"Eve, I don't—"

"Please, Caoimhe," I said. I turned to my best friend, tried not to let her see the emptiness in my eyes. She nodded, squeezed me again before letting go.

"Let's give her a moment."

I listened as all those feet shuffled back out, waited for the rubber whisper that meant the swinging doors to the kitchen were being held closed.

I heard Roxy and Wilhamena quietly offering people coffee and then there was the smothering sound of the grinder, the sharp smell of fresh beans cutting through the bacterial bread proofing smell all around us.

I looked down at Will—still not-my-Will after all that work, after too brief a time together. My Will was alive in every piece of himself, swallowing life—and me—as if we were all a single bite to be savored before it was over.

Before we were swallowed.

Now I knew why.

"I wish you'd told me sooner," I said, pushing his still wet hair from his cold face. "I would've helped you. And then we could've been in this together—you and me."

I thought about the empty whiskey bottles. About his bare apartment. About the pained look on his face that night in the bedroom, our legs pressed together, our breaths in twinned hesitance.

"There was no reason for us both to be so alone."

Tears burned hot behind my eyes and I blinked them away, tracing the length of his jaw, pressing a single gentle finger to the scar across his eyebrow.

"I'm sorry I fooled around when you were gone," I said. "I lost control and I needed to find it anywhere I could. It's always been like that for me. But we all fuck up. You and I especially have made some pretty huge mistakes."

I glanced back down at the bloody pool at his feet. I couldn't bring myself to look beneath the blanket. Whatever damage was there was done—and had clearly finished the job Mirra had started.

"You really should've told me," I said. I tapped his shoulder where I used to punch him when he was being stupid and for some reason that broke the dam. That was the thing that let the sobs shudder through me. "You really should've told me."

"Especially since it's so obvious now that even though I was fighting it, even though I denied it and will probably continue to deny it if anyone asks me." I heaved a trembling sigh. "That I loved you immediately and completely."

I wiped my face with the back of my hand, then leaned down, closing my eyes and imagining that none of this was happening. I imagined that Will was still alive, that we weren't in a bakery-turned-morgue, that there was still a chance for us.

I imagined that what I said next would save us.

"And I would've loved you anyway, no matter what you did in the past, present, or future. Forever."

I pressed a final kiss to his lips, pretending they weren't cold, pretending this wasn't goodbye.

Without looking, I turned on my heel and started to leave the bakery.

I was going to do what I always did when things ended—the same thing my family always taught me to do.

I was going to walk out. I was going to strut passed the front door and straight through the city until I wasn't in Boston anymore. I'd walk until I found someplace new, and I would try all this again when my heart mended.

If it mended.

But before I could put a hand to the kitchen doors, a whirling warm wind slammed through the room, carrying the late summer sun in its arms and sending it flying across every surface.

I crouched down and covered my face protecting it from the brilliance and flying baked goods.

Through the shield of my fingers, I saw the wind find Will. I watched as he was lifted from the table and wrapped in the light. I watched until I couldn't anymore—until it was like staring at the sun itself.

After a few agonizing moments, the light faded and I was able to peek out from around my fingers.

There, standing upright as if nothing had happened amid a tornado pile-up of uncooked dough and pastries, was a very naked, very alive, Will.

He looked at his own hands and feet, touched his own face, and then aimed that undeniable smile directly at me.

"I told you," he said.

I stared, mouth dropped open. This was impossible.

"I told you you'd wreck me someday," he said, eyes bright, smile wide, skin flush and healthy. So very, very alive.

I vaulted across the room, nearly knocking him over as he caught me and held me.

"Fuck you," I said, grabbing his face in my hands and kissing him as if we were in the part of the movie where the screen dimmed and the title text read "and they lived happily ever after."

Which, ya know what?

We just might.

Epilogue

Boston, Today at One

"Thank you, Will, for that uh…narrative," Gary says. "For future reference, we try to keep our sharing to five minutes and under so there's time for everyone in the group."

The boy sits back down, wiping his sweaty palms on his jeans. The gargoyle claps a hand on his shoulder and the gnome mouths "wow" from across the room. The boy feels important, heard, seen.

When the meeting is over, the boy shakes hands with Gary then quickly excuses himself, practically skipping out into the hall. The girl is waiting, just like she said she would, headphones so loud he can hear the punk rock from three feet away. He watches her for a moment, the light in the hall catching in the purple streaks of her hair, softening the curves of her face.

The girl catches him staring, pulling her headphones out and tucking them away. She sticks her tongue out and he returns the gesture.

"How'd it go?" she asks, standing to loop an arm through his. He shrugs but can't help the wide grin that splits his face.

"Pretty good," he says. "I might have got carried away."

"You? Never," she teases.

They laugh as they leave the church, heading out into the midday sun. The girl's flight isn't until that night, her suitcase meticulously packed and waiting at her own apartment, so there is no rush in their steps. They have nowhere to be as they wander, content just with one another's company and the promise growing stronger between them.

This is not their happy ending. They aren't anywhere near that hallmark yet.

But this is their new beginning.

And they wouldn't turn the page with anyone else.

The End

Thank you endlessly to:

My husband, who loves me when I feel impossible to love. My sisters, Amber and Jac, who taught me I was worth saving but I was the only one who could do it. Britta and Molly, the best writing friends the internet could give. My editor, who pushed me to make this the best story it could be.

You, for reading.

About the Author

Kel Bruem proudly writes kissing books set in fantasy and science-fiction worlds. Her Kindle Vella series SNAPPED and BOLD DAMAGES are available and complete. WHAT'S LUCK GOT TO DO WITH IT is the first in her series THE UNUSUALITIES, and her short story "Painter and Muse" can be found in the debut anthology ONE MONSTROUS SUMMER.

You can connect with me on:

https://www.tiktok.com/@kelbruem

Subscribe to my newsletter:

https://subscribepage.io/Iq43sX

Also by Kel Bruem

What's Luck Got to Do With It: Unusualities #1

Caiomhe Ryan is the luckiest girl in Boston—she has a great job, a cute apartment, and a ride-or-die best friend. All her ancestral luck as a leprechaun doesn't hurt either. When she takes a chance on an urgent client, the mysterious man at the heart of a scandal has her wondering how much longer she can keep herself a secret.

Leith Riordan just wants to drive boats by day and turn back into a merman at night—as simple as that. All his plans are destroyed, however, when a single lost temper lands him in a viral social media storm—and on Caiomhe Ryan's client roster. He knows his life can't go back to being simple. After all, it's not easy to tell a beautiful woman you're actually a merman.

Sparks fly and porridge burns when these two magical beings in the heart of Boston must decide if they can hide themselves from the public while still being true to one another—and themselves.

One Monstrous Summer: Tails, Trysts, and Tentacles

Nine indie authors, nine sweet, and spicy, monster romance reads.

Featuring gargoyles, werewolves, demons, and fae, *One Monstrous Summer* guarantees the heat and the happily-ever-afters. Soak up the final steamy days of summer with some seriously steamy short stories from authors Kel Bruem (*What's Luck Got to Do With It*), B.L. Brown (*Shady Depths*), Alexis L. Carroll (*Things Magical Under the Moon*), and more!

www.ingramcontent.com/pod-product-compliance
Lightning Source LLC
Chambersburg PA
CBHW070657010826
48975CB00014B/2216